MUCH ADO
ABOUT
NAUTICALING

MUCH ADO ABOUT NAUTICALING

GABBY ALLAN

KENSINGTON
PUBLISHING CORP.

www.kensingtonbooks.com

To my little family, who makes my heart sing, and to Esi, for taking a chance on me, again. I hope this is the one!

Acknowledgments

I want to thank my lovely agent, Jill Marsal, for helping me hone and shape Whit and cast and Harper Kincaid for brainstorming. It takes a village, so I'm also and always in debt to my fabulous critique partners for their wonderful input—Vicky, Vicki, and Natalie—you're the best.

MUCH ADO ABOUT NAUTICALING

Chapter 1

Quietly opening my front door to avoid being followed by my cat, Whiskers, or waking up my roommate, Maribel Hernandez, I ran through all the excuses I could give to my brother, Nick, for being late to work—if he was there to ask me why I wasn't on time.

Maybe I had fallen in the shower. I'd actually done that at least twice in my new cramped shower stall, anyway.

Or maybe I had locked myself out of the house. That I had done three times so far since I'd left mainland California for Santa Catalina Island a month ago.

Perhaps I had been visited by a neighbor wanting to borrow some kale. Not that I had any of that healthy stuff, and my neighbors knew it. I, Whitney Dagner, a self-confessed eater of all things not good for you.

Something would come to me while I zoomed down to the harbor in my flashy golf cart—what the locals called an autoette—passing the tightly packed houses on my street. They came in all colors from dust to fire-hydrant red, and the styles were just as varied. Window boxes filled with cactuses and trailing bougainvillea dotted the fronts, sometimes contrasting with the color of the house and sometimes making the dull browns pop as a backdrop. Some were big; some were little, like mine. And they all fit together like canned sardines on the street with the sea scenting the air.

Bouncing along at top speed (of seventeen miles per hour), the breeze raking through my short hair, I waved to people taking walking tours and others just strolling along our narrow streets. I was especially careful not to plow anyone down in my haste. It wasn't driving the 405 in Los Angeles, but it could be quite the maze down to the harbor, especially in the summer.

I parked my little zipster at the pier with a screech of tires and then booked it down the wide wood planks. My brother was nowhere in sight, but that was fine with me since I hadn't come up with anything better than the kale thing. And he wouldn't have believed that anyway.

A sigh of relief escaped me and then another one of pleasure as I took in my beauty at the end of the dock. The *Sea Bounder* was a lovely forty-eight-foot vessel custom-made right here on the island. My glass-bottom boat in all her glory. She'd been in our family for years and had done more tours than even I could count. The brass fittings shone in the sunlight, and being near her felt like coming home.

Stepping from the dock to the white deck, I breathed in the ocean air and smiled. This was the life. I'd let go of the stress of the desk job world in Long Beach and moved twenty-two miles across the Pacific Ocean to embrace the calm and freedom of island living. It wasn't perfect by any means, but I welcomed this second chance to follow my dreams. (Well . . . third, but I wasn't going to think about that now.)

The boat had a rectangular open-air deck before the sliding door to the interior. Time to clean up and then get ready to sail the open waters. But first I just listened to the wavelets lapping against the side of the vessel and breathed in the salty tang of the sea.

The sun rode high in the sky out over the water as I grabbed a cloth and my faithful bottle of glass cleaner. This was not my favorite part of the job, but it was necessary. I swiped the cloth over the glass insert to start the cleaning process, then stepped inside to the cool, dim interior of my family's legacy.

The Dagner family had been running tours for generations now and my brother and I were the next in line. Twelve years ago, I'd thought I'd wanted in on the corporate world and had worked at the rail yard. It was time well spent, nothing was ever wasted, but I was glad to have waved bon voyage to that life and return here to sink back into all the things I'd thought I'd wanted to get away from.

While fluffing seat cushions, checking for life jackets in the hulls, making sure the floor was swept and the glass was clean, I hummed a little sea shanty to myself. Something bawdy and full of drinking and thieving references that I'd learned at my dad's knee over twenty years ago. It made me snicker to think about the words and helped cover the sadness that I hadn't seen the man for just as long. He'd taken off for parts unknown without an explanation shortly after I'd turned six, so I held onto the good times I'd had with him. My mom had stuck around until I graduated high school and then took off, too. It was harder to hold onto good memories with her since they were mixed with growing up with the anger and bitterness of someone who'd been abandoned, but I tried.

Shaking off the memories, I popped onto the website for Nautically Yours, our umbrella company name, to see our reviews and was rewarded with some very glowing five stars and of course a not-so-five-star from a couple I distinctly remembered from last week. They'd wanted a refund because during their tour on the glass-bottomed boat I hadn't managed to take them over a whale. In the shallows of Avalon Bay that wasn't going to happen anyway, and I'd tried to explain that to them as patiently as I explained to Whiskers that sometimes I had to leave the house so my lap was not always open for snuggles and belly rubs.

But apparently these people had taken it upon themselves to blast Nautically Yours. Well, I'd just have to get some people on the island to say nicer things. These tours this afternoon should go a long way toward keeping our reviews positive. I'd make sure the journey was delightful for the two families and all things professional and casual for the Chamber of Commerce people who would be touring in between.

In the meantime, I checked reservations and dreamed of someday. Someday, I was going to get a boat full of people who said nice things and cooed about how awesome the tour was and thanked me for my service in towing them around the island of Catalina.

Someday, people would not let their children run screaming through the boat and jump off the wooden seats I polished every night. I enjoyed children mostly, but the screaming part not so much. But someday would probably not be today. And tomorrow probably wouldn't be either, from the looks of the schedule. More summer camp trips and big vacation groups. People looking to escape from their everyday lives to our little slice of heaven.

And with it being near the Fourth of July, the family groups were out in full force. They came to celebrate the holiday, renting houses and going out to restaurants, bringing their copious amounts of luggage on the huge ferries that ran several times a day from the harbors along the California coast to the harbor of Avalon. Some people jokingly called the boats "cattle boats."

I was just thankful for the tourist dollars and the work. Running glass-bottom boat tours was only part of what I did. The other part was running my gift shop, the Dame of the Sea, on Crescent Avenue, which I absolutely adored. So I called the Catalina Express boats the ability to put food on the table and keep my gift shop running and the glass-bottomed boat up to snuff and in tip-top shape.

"Yoohoo!" I heard from outside and sighed. Goldy and Pops were here. Hopefully she had at least stopped to shower before coming here from the beach. Since retiring, my grandmother had taken to sunbathing at all hours of the day and trailing sand behind her like it was glitter.

"Permission to come aboard?" my grandfather asked, and I peeked out the starboard side to see him grinning and saluting like a true sailor. With his Greek fisherman's hat and pipe, he looked like that guy from the fish-stick boxes in the freezer section, minus the yellow slicker.

"Permission granted," I answered. "My first tour starts in an hour, and I still have things to do to make sure I'm on time. I don't want Nick to yell at me."

Pops lifted a hand to assist Goldy onto the back deck and then was the first one through the door, a frown on his rugged face, crinkling his white and gray beard. "He'd better not be yelling at you. Is he actually doing that?" He stalked down the aisle and sat on one of the benches with his shoulders back. "You just let me know and I'll take care of him before the tide changes."

I sat next to him and patted his knee. "Reel it in, Pops, I'm just kidding. He's been fine. We're super busy this week, and he's been hiring more crew to help out."

"I told you that made sense." He said it gruffly but ran his hand over the seat over and over again.

"You're sure you wanted to retire?" I bumped my shoulder into his and smiled.

"Oh, yes. Or at least that's what Georgiana told me."

"And it was time, Thomas," Goldy piped in, walking down the stairs, thankfully dressed in cropped pants and a light sweater instead of one of her many bathing suits. She had killer heels on, too, ones even I wouldn't have dared to try during my office job days and certainly not on a boat. The woman had decided early on that she was not going to age like everyone else, so we'd never been allowed to call her any of the normal names for grandmother. No Grandma, no Nana, no Grammy or Granny, just Goldy. And Goldy also kept her hair highlighted every six weeks and refused to let go of her high heels.

"Yes, dear," Pops answered.

Brushing a hand down his arm, she smiled. "We can live now instead of being anchored to this business. It's in good hands." She bussed me on the cheek as she walked by, then leaned over the wooden box framing one of the windows in the floor of the boat. "You have a smudge here, dear. You're going to want to take care of that before the people arrive."

I held in my sigh and stopped myself from rolling my eyes. I had a feeling that no matter how long we owned the business, my brother and I would never truly be able to get away from being told how to do our jobs. I understood to some extent— Goldy and Pops had run tours for fifty years before handing the business over, and it made sense that they wouldn't be able to totally let go.

I'd just have to keep that thought forefront in my mind every time she used the white glove treatment on the boat, the semi-submersible, or my gift shop. She meant her advice in the best possible way. I'd have to remind myself of that too. "We have a group tour at three, the private group at five, and then another group tour at eight. I still have thirty minutes."

"It doesn't look like you've gotten much done here if you arrived on time." She raised an eyebrow at me. "I heard something about someone whipping along the road as if her tail was on fire not ten minutes ago."

I had thought I'd gone unnoticed, but in a town this little, where everyone watched out for their own, I had been fooling myself. "I was running a little late, but I'll still get everything spiffed up in time. No worries." I wondered who'd told on me. I also knew better than to ask.

Goldy just smiled and placed a kiss on Pops's forehead. "Then we'll get out of your hair, which looks divine now that you let Abby cut it, by the way. So much more relaxed than that severe style you had when you got here last month."

I put my hand up to the layered bob I'd let the girl at the La Fluencia spa talk me into. I loved it too and the natural wave was so much better than all the product I used to put in when I was shooting for a corner office. "Thanks."

"Of course, dear. I'd never steer you wrong, you know that. Now, Thomas, let's go so the girl can do her job. This isn't ours anymore."

As quick as she came on, she also went off, tiny bits of sand trailing off the bottoms of her sparkly heels. I was going to have to get the broom back out.

"You know you can come back whenever you want," I whispered to Pops when she was out of earshot. "Give a tour just to keep your hand in. I'm sure Nick wouldn't mind. And Goldy's always out on the beach so she'd probably never know."

With that he snorted. "Oh, she'd know all right, and it's okay. I have a trip planned to do some fishing and I'm going camping next weekend. I'll find things to keep myself entertained. Plus, you're keeping me very busy making all those treasure maps for the kids who come in your store."

He rose from the bench and I rose with him. After giving him a hug, I waved him off the boat, got that smudge on the glass, and swept the floor one more time.

My cell phone rang fifteen minutes before my first tour group was due. Since it was Nick, I decided I should probably answer it.

"How's it going?" he asked, not saying hello back after I'd answered.

"Good. We can do this, brother of mine. I promise. I know it's only my fourth voyage since moving back but I'm not new at this."

"I know, I know. But I just want it to be perfect. What if something goes wrong and Goldy and Pops feel like they have to come back out of retirement to straighten things out? Those big-wigs who are coming in could make or break us."

Staring out at the beach through the open window, I brought out the big guns. "You know, 'bigwigs' is a literal term that originated in the 1700s. Back then, many European noblemen wore big wigs to showcase their wealth or significance in society. The bigger the wig, the more money they had. Do you think they had to duck under doorways if they had too much money? Did men topple over in their vanity because their center of gravity was all askew?" I secretly smiled to myself as I wiped down the railing. If he was going to be a nervous nelly, then I was going to have to irritate him to get his mind off what could go wrong. It was as simple as that.

Nick sighed and it crackled over the line. Good enough.

My smile grew. "Beyond that beautiful tidbit of the English language, which you did not appreciate nearly enough, I am very much capable of showing some corporate rowdies a good time. So why don't you run along? Go do what you need to do in Murrieta. As always, it'll all be well under control when you get back."

"I hope so. This is important, Whit."

Reminding myself that this was his livelihood too, I took a discreet breath before answering. "Seriously, Nick. I was doing this for years before I left and whenever I came back for vacation, so I know what I'm doing, just as much as you do. You're worrying too much over nothing." It always helped to remind him that I was not a guppy at this whole sailing/touring thing. "And I'll be fully prepared for the Chamber of Commerce people and their celebratory cruise for the person of the year once I get this three o'clock tour done." I wasn't exactly impressed with the person the chamber had chosen, but then no one had asked me.

"You'll be nice?"

"I'm always nice, oh Great Commander of the Fleet, and I know the benefits of doing a good job when it comes to people who actually recommend us instead of posting online that the tour was not exactly up to snuff." Like the one-star review I'd found earlier. That information would not help Nick's state of mind, so I'd keep it to myself. I was a good sister that way.

After a moment, I got a snort from Nick at my comments about being nice. Even better. Soon he'd hang up like I wanted him to.

A light breeze off the ocean ruffled my hair, and I lifted a hand to pat it back down, then decided to leave it. I said I'd be nice, not that I'd be perfect. I didn't have to be perfect anymore.

"Fine, I trust you," he finally conceded.

"You'd better. I know this harbor like the back of my hand. I've got it covered. I wish you'd believe that. Goldy and Pops do or they wouldn't have left the business to us to run while she tans all day and he drives around like a maniac on his golf cart." Only so many full-sized cars were allowed on the island so pretty much everyone else had a golf cart. The waiting list for a real car was rumored to be thirty-five years long. My golf cart—I had to remember to start calling it an autoette again to fit back in—was my pride and joy. It was covered in all manner of bumper stickers from the ridiculous to the profound, and the hood was a watercolor of our logo for Nautically Yours.

Even Nick had to admit it was eye-catching and brought in business.

"I do believe it, it's just that so much rides on this kind of event. I don't want it to go wrong. It's not you I don't trust, it's everyone else."

Well, that was something at least. "Understood, and I'll head off anyone who is trying to cause trouble. Now, seriously, go fly into the sky like the bird you are and let's get this show on the road. I have a few more things to set up, then I'm out on the water."

And with it being near the Fourth of July, the family groups were out in full force so we could definitely do more walk-on tours instead of waiting for reservations. Because of our beautiful weather, the island never went completely off-season. But summer was definitely busier than any other time of year, and it was when we made the money that might have to carry us over the leaner months.

After a few more quickly exchanged warnings, Nick signed off and was gone. Finally. It wasn't for me to worry about his anxiety over our business, though, because the first of the three o'clock tourists were running up from the beach and they had a plethora of kids in tow. Awesome.

Chapter 2

Two hours later, I had made it through the first cruise of the day without a hitch. Even with all the kids and grandmas and parents in attendance, they were a pretty well-behaved crowd—except for the one grandma who kept trying to climb over the ledge and into the box. According to her, she'd been a professional tap dancer in her early years and thought it would be a good idea to try out her skills on the glass at the bottom of the boat.

Wrestling her away from the edge had taken more strength than I would have assumed, but I'd finally managed it with little fuss. And then she'd laughed and smacked my arm hard enough to rock me back a step and told me she was just playing. I'd kept an eye on her for the rest of the trip, just in case. Still, it wasn't that difficult to handle, so my hope grew for the next two cruises.

After checking over the cabin again, I lowered the gangplank for the bigwigs and stood on deck with my best smile, preparing myself for lots of handshakes and chatting before they'd all ignore me like I was a barnacle on a whale.

I greeted those I knew by name and smiled and nodded at

those I didn't. There were far more of the latter than I had been told, and I was a little concerned about reaching capacity when Jules Tisdale, Person of the Year, and his wife, Tracy, finally came aboard.

"Where's Nick?" Jules demanded when I pulled the latched door closed behind him and started making my way toward the captain's seat.

"He had some errands to run." Keeping it short and pleasant normally worked best with Jules, the self-proclaimed Master of the Island.

The frown on the man's face was fierce, so I answered it as best I could with a smile.

"The ride will be wonderful. You're in good hands." When he continued to frown, I tried another tack. "I promise I know what I'm doing."

"You'd better," he said in a threatening tone.

No matter how hard it was, I kept my smile in place and walked away from him. Only then did I let myself grumble and only under my breath. "I do know what I'm doing, Mr. High and Mighty, and I'm going to make this the best cruise you've ever been on in your life!"

It wasn't going to be a long tour, more of a cocktail hour. I wasn't sure why Nick had been so concerned about it going well. All I had to do was make sure the boat didn't sink or lose anyone on the short journey. Hopefully, I wouldn't run into either of those scenarios.

The ride was smooth and people were talking amongst themselves, so I didn't say much, just smiled and nodded, then contorted myself into small spaces when people decided to walk right up against me instead of walking around.

It was funny to watch so many people on their phones instead of taking in the beauty of the sea beneath them. It wasn't my place to judge, obviously, but I found it interesting that Tracy Tisdale, the Person of the Year's wife, seemed to have her eyes glued to her device, completely ignoring anyone who came near her—including the Person of the Year.

They were all missing out on the vibrant life inches away from their feet and the beauty of the lowering sun as it sank into the ocean to our starboard side. I probably enjoyed it enough for all of us, though, as I let the wheel move slightly under my hand and kept a steady eye on both the shoreline and the inhabitants of the cabin.

And then finally it was almost over. I pulled back into port and smiled in thanks as my dock helper hooked the line to a cleat. The VIPs moved toward the exit and I was there to thank them for allowing us to entertain them.

"Whitney, thanks so much for your hospitality." Annie Yeager, one of the members of the city council, was an okay bigwig. I liked her a lot. She tried to do all kinds of things to keep the tourist trade up while also keeping the islanders' needs and wants in mind.

"It was my pleasure, Annie."

She shook my hand and pulled me in a little closer. "We really needed this to go smoothly, and you handled it expertly. With the burglaries that have been happening on the island, it was so important to make this event shine, and you came through for us. I won't forget that."

I wasn't sure what to say. I'd heard about the burglaries, but I hadn't realized things had gotten to the point where it was affecting more than a handful of residents on the island.

"Yeah, Whitney, much appreciated." This from the Person of the Year's wife, Tracy Tisdale. We'd hung out some as kids; it was what you did when you were only here for a short time. And yet, once we'd become teenagers, we didn't have much to talk about. She was nice enough, but I didn't quite understand how she had ended up with Jules of all people. He was about thirty years older than she was and she seemed completely out of her element with the Master of the Island.

And now that they spent most of their time in L.A., I didn't see them often. Actually, this was the first time since I'd moved here. Which was fine with me as I was not a big Jules fan, no matter how much he did for the island.

Being watchful of karma, even if only in my mind, I took that thought back and just smiled at her and nodded. "Congratulations on the award for your husband."

She smiled back, but there was a vagueness to the smile that I couldn't quite comprehend. Not that it was any of my business. I had done my part in taking them, their friends, and our locals around while they hobnobbed around the wooden boxes protecting the glass bottom of the boat. And I had made sure no one slipped in the puddle of champagne someone had spilled, then promptly stepped over like it hadn't happened. Only water was allowed on the boat normally and, as far as I knew, the rules had *not* been bent for this evening, but I wasn't going to make waves just in case my brother had forgotten to tell me about a change in the policies.

At least it was over now.

"Have a great night," I said into the awkward silence. "Enjoy the dinner." They were doing something down at the harbor. Since I wasn't going, I hadn't paid too much attention to the details.

"Sorry you won't be there," Tracy said in her chirpy voice. "You could network and stuff. Jules says that's going to be really important now that you own a business. I try to listen to what he says because I'd like to own a business someday too. I asked Jules if he'd let me buy your shop, but he doesn't want to owe you money. He said it would muddy the waters."

Now I was the one just smiling, strained though it was. I had no idea what she meant about muddying waters, and I knew for certain my shop was not for sale. Fortunately, her husband reached back for her hand and pulled her through the doorway.

"Come along, Tracy, we have to show the island chamber

what a power couple looks like." He smoothed his diamond-patterned tie over his firm stomach and then slicked back his full head of dark hair.

I rolled my eyes at his comment about the power couple. This was Catalina, average permanent population way below power-couple status. Of course, it was an honor to be chosen as Person of the Year regardless of the size of the town, but his ego was so big, I was surprised it fit through the door.

"I have to run by the house." Tracy held up her phone. "I forgot something."

"Fine, but don't be long." He walked away without a backward glance at her. To me, he didn't even nod. No problem. I had another tour in thirty minutes and things to do before the next group boarded the *Sea Bounder*.

"Thanks, Whit," a soft voice said from my left side.

I turned to find Rebecca Tisdale at my elbow, my former babysitter and Jules's cousin. When did she sneak on? I would have known her anywhere, and I didn't remember seeing her or saying hello to her.

With her light-brown hair, designer glasses, and angular face, she hadn't changed much. She had been a quiet teenager, even when I had been running around like a hellion and trying to drag her with me to yet another adventure. Adventures that were usually put together by my Pops over the summers Rebecca had spent here with her family. (Those escapades had often revolved around anything to keep me moving and active so I'd fall into a dead sleep when I got back to my grandparents' house.)

I had loved my grandfather's maps and the treasure he'd hide without my knowing. Pops had been in the habit of making treasure maps and putting them in glass bottles to wash up on shore for me. Or he'd bury treasure boxes in the backyard for me to find. Anything to keep a very precocious and antsy kid involved.

It had taken years for me to understand that the maps weren't actually real. He had made them from vellum and taken a lighter to the edges to age them along with smearing them with tar. And now I had him making them for my gift shop to entertain a whole new generation of adventurous kids.

But no matter how many treasures I set out to unearth, Rebecca had stayed to herself and let me play alone or with Nick.

So Rebecca had been stoic even then and wasn't much different now. I remembered her often letting us run wild while she read a book and looked up at me over her sunglasses every once in a while.

"Hey, Rebecca. It was my pleasure. Are you back for a little while?" She lived in Northern California from what I had heard last and had some big-shot job as a corporate lawyer. We hadn't kept up with each other after she'd stopped coming out to the island for the summer. Plus, she'd been older than me by a few years. In fact, she'd graduated from college while I was still in middle school.

"Just a little while. I thought it was important to show my support for Jules." She straightened the waistline on her beautiful sand-colored dress. It was a sharp contrast from the flashy red sequins her cousin's wife had been wearing, but it fit her and her quiet personality while making her look stunning.

"Well, you're a better cousin than I am a sister. Nick knows he'd have to bribe me with some serious paper-store supplies to make me do something like this if I wasn't working the party."

A little chuckle was all I got, but she did smile. "I'm sure you're a great sister. I'd better go catch up. Don't want to be late or Jules might get angry."

"Of course." And my forced smile was back. Rebecca had been a nice babysitter and was a nice woman. She shouldn't have to run at the beck and call of her relative.

But to each his or her own. She walked along the pier, looking from side to side but keeping precisely in the middle as if she might fall in if she strayed too close to the edge.

Finally alone, I leaned against the railing and watched the reflection of the setting sun on the water and took a second to breathe. It wasn't always peaceful on the island, but it was moments like these that made me so thankful I'd moved back.

As I turned to head back into the cabin and do some straightening up, I caught sight of a pod of dolphins breaking the surface of the sea. Cleaning could wait. A smile broke out across my face watching them play, their slick gray skins a beautiful contrast to the dark ocean.

I spent so long out there that I had to make quick work of prepping for my next group. Mere minutes before they were due to board, I checked the glass in the bottom of the boat. Part of the beauty of going on a glass-bottom boat tour was that you could watch everything below you—from kelp forests to fish, crustaceans, and other sea life—going about their business without disturbing them.

And the not-disturbing-them part was important to me. I was capable of scuba diving, and many people got their certificates here; I'd even been certified to hand them out. And it was beautiful to swim with the creatures, but on any given day I preferred to leave them alone and just watch through the glass.

Satisfied that all was as it should be, I emerged from the boat to greet my next set of visitors. They were right on time, thank goodness, because I really wanted to get things done and get home to my cat and my puzzle making and the quiet of my house.

This time I didn't have to plaster on a smile. I knew some of the people and could tell that the others were relatives.

"Family in for summer vacation?" I asked Jenna Carmichael.

"Oh yeah." She ruffled one of the older kids' hair, then held him tight for a hug as the scent of salt and sea wafted over us. "We only get to see them about once a year, but I make them come to me because I am not built for Los Angeles."

I laughed with her. She didn't have to tell me twice. "Well, hopefully we'll see some awesome things tonight. Is this everyone?" I looked out over the crowd on the dock, doing a quick headcount. It matched what I had logged into the computer.

"It is!" And she started in with introductions. "This is Marcy and Dan, Penny and Clyde, Jacqueline and Doug, Sissy and Juan, and their two kids Jason and Megan . . ."

I knew she said more names, but my brain just couldn't take them all in. If there was a test on the way out, I was totally going to fail. Finally, she finished naming everyone, and I waited a beat to make sure she didn't have more to say.

"Okay, if we're ready to go, I'll get started." I scooted along the dock, herding people in front of me. The faster we got on, the faster we'd be done.

Fourteen adults and seven kids over the age of ten wandered around the boxed-in glass as I put the engine into gear, steered us away from the dock, and then out into the open water. Once we got away from the shore, I turned on the lights framing the glass in the bottom of the boat and the whole undersea world lit up like a dream. Nick had installed tiny cameras in each window that transmitted to monitors on the dash, showing me what the travelers were seeing. It had helped immensely when doing the tours.

There were oohs and aahs as I began my spiel. "Welcome to Santa Catalina Island, home to some of the most beautiful fish in the world. If you look closely, you can see them flitting around the amber seaweed. We also have turtles, and every once in a while, a seal might show up just to wave at you. They're friendly little buggers, but they can also tag along for a while and keep you from looking at everything else because they're attention hogs."

Laughter ensued and then chatter. This was going to be one of those tours where I would probably only answer questions instead of breaking out the whole monologue I knew by heart, but that was a good thing. Jenna and her husband had been on the cruise over the years and were also scuba divers. They knew this place well.

Sure enough, there wasn't much time for me to say anything over the excited whispers and pointing. We circled the bay, coasting over an octopus and a school of garibaldi, our state fish. The orange scales seemed to glow in the dark depths of the water under the lighting. We did indeed pass over a seal that stayed with us, flapping and waving as it rolled over like a dog.

Glancing at my watch and noting the position of the stars in the velvety black sky, I knew it was time to turn around to get the boat back to shore. And then I could call it a night and report in to Nick that not only had I done my duty, but three people had already come up to ask if I could give them a tour during the day tomorrow. Not bad for a night's work.

We slowly puttered back toward the pier, everyone staring intently through the looking glass as if into another world. And it *was* another world. We only knew about a third of what actually lived in the sea. So many places to explore, so many places humans couldn't go. I'd been fascinated by it from the first time my grandparents had taken us out on a boat.

I loved the sounds of wonder coming from behind me as I steered the familiar path. Pulling up to the dock, I threw the line and Nick was there to catch it and tie it to the iron cleat. I waved to him and he smiled. Good. It must have been a productive trip to the mainland.

A few seconds later, the noise level increased. At first it didn't register that it was screams of horror now instead of squeals of delight.

I turned to find out what had happened and determine if I was going to have to use my CPR certification, when I spotted what had turned the tide of the voyage.

A shark swam under the boat and another followed it. They were just small leopard sharks, but you'd think it was a reenactment of *Jaws* given the screams.

"I promise they won't hurt you, and they can't get to you anyway," I said patiently.

There was stifled and nervous laughter, but eventually everyone got off the boat with the help of Nick reaching in.

One of the ladies I didn't know stopped and turned back. "That was very exciting. Do the sharks often come around here?"

I shrugged. "Not always and even when they do, they rarely go near people."

"Interesting," she said, before heading off with Jenna's brother, Doug.

Must be his new flavor of the month.

I returned inside the boat, listening to the group talk excitedly as Nick walked them to the strand. He came back after he'd dropped them off, trooping over the deck and looking mighty pleased with himself.

"They want a day tour tomorrow," he announced.

"I know, they'd already asked about it. I hope you have time tomorrow because I have the gift shop to run and not a lot of wiggle room since you won't help me with my puzzles."

He frowned and I smiled, content with the job I'd done *and* the jobs I'd just thrown down at his feet.

I looked around one last time to make sure no one had forgotten anything in their shark-sighting excitement. It was amazing what people accidentally left behind on the boat. I'd found everything from phones to jackets to jewelry, and even a set of false teeth once, though I tried not to think about how that had happened.

We had a collection box up front that I transferred to the gift shop every week, just in case someone realized they'd misplaced their things. All part of the service—but no one had ever picked up those teeth.

Nick handed me a glove and an earring he'd found on his circuit through the boat. "You're sure you couldn't take a few tours tomorrow? I'd like to run the semi-submersible in the morning. Eric said there were some strange noises coming from the engine."

I eyed my brother over my shoulder. "I could probably do the first run, but I'm expecting a drop-off of merchandise from Lacey Cavanaugh, that woman who makes the psychedelic pottery. I don't want to miss it. As much as I love the boat rides, I also enjoy being able to share the local artistry with the tourists."

He leaned against the interior wall, crossing his feet at the ankles. "I'll work it out, then. But if you could be here at nine tomorrow for the first booking, I'd appreciate it."

"You'll owe me." I smiled at him.

"I seem to always owe you," he answered with his own smile. "Take the tour on this big tub tomorrow morning, and I'll take you out to dinner."

"Sounds good to me." I brushed off a seat and checked the glass one more time for any streaks or smudges Goldy might find if she decided to come by again.

It was a marvel that these boats had ever come to be, but enterprising fishermen back in the day couldn't always make a living just by catching fish. When they'd realized how much people enjoyed looking at the underwater sea life, they had decided to cut holes in the bottoms of their rowboats and installed glass.

They'd rowed hundreds of people out to look at the ocean beneath them, and a business was born. My great-great-grandfather happened to be one of those smart men and now over a hundred years later we were still making money the same way.

I leaned over the glass to use a rag to wipe it, when a shadow caught my eye. The shadow quickly turned into something entirely different, and I jumped back, careening into Nick.

Still, I couldn't resist taking another peek. Designer shoes and well-cut trousers slipped under the boat, followed by a tie done in a subtle diamond pattern. A bald head gleamed in the lights around the windows. The eyes were blank and the mouth open in a silent scream. Who was this? And how did they get into the water? Had they drowned? I was reaching for my phone when the eyes registered, squinty and hard even when blank.

Somehow Jules Tisdale had not only lost his full head of hair, but he was also under my boat. And he was now very much dead when he'd been alive and smiling sharkily less than two hours ago.

Nick and I gasped at the same time.

Holy barnacles.

Chapter 3

At least once a week I called my roommate, Maribel Hernandez, to see if she had time to grab dinner out. We were on opposite shifts, which worked wonderfully in regards to living with each other, but not so much for hanging out. I'd work around her schedule since my hours were far looser than hers as the dispatcher for our small police department, the Avalon sheriff's station.

However, tonight which bar to pop into for a burger was not on my mind. I was far more concerned with how fast she could get someone out to the harbor, and how I could keep Jules from floating away while I waited for them to arrive.

As I placed the call, Nick went out onto the deck to see if there was a way to prevent the body from moving out into the ocean. I heard wood smack against wood and wondered if he was using the oars that were stored up there for decoration.

When she finally answered I blurted out the first thing that came to mind. "Maribel, oh man, I need someone down at the pier right now. There's a body . . ."

"A what?" she said, disbelief lacing her voice.

"A body."

"A . . . where?" She was verging on yelling.

My hand shook and so did my voice. "In the harbor at *Sea Bounder*. Nick is trying to keep it from going farther out with the tide."

"Oh wow." No yelling this time, but that disbelief was even more evident than it had been before. "Uh. Okay, stay on the line, and tell Nick that we appreciate his efforts."

I yelled the appreciation to Nick, who grunted, and then I stuck around as I heard Maribel giving the lowdown to someone.

"Do you know who it is?" she came back to me to ask.

"Jules."

There was a beat of pure, unadulterated silence. "Oh *man*. Okay, hang tight. They'll be right there."

Fortunately, it didn't take long for the sheriff's department to show up, and I was very happily relieved of my post. I stepped off the boat only to be confronted by a series of flashing lights and spotlights. Divers jumped off the pier to do their recovery, and I was left standing with my brother, who had indeed used the oar.

One of Avalon's finest came up to us. Nick took the lead. Deputy Ryan Franklin had efficiency down to a science, but tended to take men more seriously, so I let him and my brother talk. There wasn't much I knew that Nick didn't. I decided to wait to see if there was anything I could add.

"And you saw the deceased's feet first?" Franklin asked.

"Yes, he, um, floated in feet first." Nick cleared his throat.

"No movement?"

"No, other than the current moving the fabric of the clothes. I'm sure he was already dead." My brother gulped, mirroring what I had been doing for the past five minutes until my throat was almost raw. I had never seen a dead body before. I would have been happy to avoid this one too.

"We might have more questions. We'll let you know." Franklin tipped his hat and walked away. I guessed Nick spoke for both of us, then.

"So weird." I hugged my arms around me. Even in summer the Channel Islands were mild weather-wise, but I was freezing in the balmy breeze.

"Yeah." Nick watched the deputy walk away. "I wonder what happened?"

"Do you think he fell in the water and they just couldn't get to him in time? And what happened to his hair? I always wondered if he wore a toupee or if he'd gotten hair plugs. I guess my question is now answered."

"I'm not sure, Whit. I guess we'll just have to see what happens. At least the last passengers were gone before he showed up. Can you imagine?" He gripped the railing behind him and leaned back with his shoulders slumped.

I felt the same tension. "I'd rather not. I'm going to have a hard time sleeping with that vision in my head myself."

He shoved off the railing to hook an arm around my shoulders. "It's going to be okay. Just go home to Whiskers. I'll get the rest of this cleaned up. It's going to be okay."

Did he really believe that or was he just telling me what he thought I needed to hear?

Either way, I wasn't going to argue. I wanted to go back to the comfort of my home. "Right. Okay. Thanks." I averted my eyes when the divers emerged from the water. Could this night get any worse?

One diver split off from the others at the shoreline and was making his way down the beach.

Apparently, it could get worse.

His build, golden skin, height, and the way his hair was slicked back all told me exactly who it was—the very last person I wanted to see. Felix Ramirez.

"You don't mind?" I asked Nick, already inching toward the wooden planks, fully prepared to bolt to shore and run right past the diver. Heck, I was almost willing to dive off the end of the pier and take my chances. "I, uh, have to feed Whiskers dinner and sit down."

"It really is going to be okay," Nick said, patting my shoulder.

I wasn't sure how he thought it was going to be okay when a dead body had recently been floating under our boat, but I needed to get away to process everything that had happened. And that would be so much harder to do if I got caught up in a conversation with the man I'd gone on a few dates with before he'd decided that long distance was not his style. Or maybe it had been me who was not his style. He'd stopped calling with no explanation and no reason, so I could only guess at what went on. I'd moved and gotten over him. Maybe I hadn't done the full job that I thought I had because I wanted to get away as fast as possible.

Quickly, I spotted my waiting golf cart at the curb and made a beeline for it. One of my favorite phrases. And like a bee leading his hive mates to the nearest nectar, I flew in a straight line right for my destination.

I walked fast, not at the run I had originally wanted to, since Felix hadn't seen me. I just strolled at a higher speed than normal, as if I had all the time in the world but didn't want to waste it. Or that *was* what I did until I got to my golf cart.

Then all bets were off, and it was pedal to the plastic. I was off at a bracing fifteen miles an hour up the hill to my small house. That was as fast as the poor little engine could go while straining to conquer the incline.

I had a lot to think about and needed time and space to do it. Once I entered the house, I grabbed Whiskers up and held her close, called Maribel back to thank her, then sat in a chair for a minute to catch my breath.

I'd seen a dead person. Even though I was completely shaken, it was all a little intriguing. How had he gotten into the water? Was it an accident? Had he somehow fallen in and then no one had seen him? Or, if they had, they couldn't get to him?

Whiskers kneaded my lap, yearning for treats, which she very vocally told me about when I wasn't fast enough on the trigger.

Trigger . . . had he been shot?! I hadn't seen any bullet holes, not that I was an expert. But how had he died?

Of course, Jules could have drowned, and there was no way to tell from the glimpse I got of him whether he had any scrapes or bruises. Could he have gotten into a scuffle with someone?

The coroner would be able to tell if he went into the water before or after death. Not that I'd be privy to that information, since it would happen off-island. But it was something to think about while I waited for Whiskers to finish her treat and then circle my ankles in the kitchen as I made myself some dinner.

I stuck to a simple can of soup, not sure I could stomach much more with all the thoughts swirling through my head.

Crime television fascinated me just as much as the next person. In fact, I sorely missed the investigation channels. But I'd cut my cable last year when I realized I almost never watched it and now relied on podcasts and downloadable videos to entertain me. I often found myself intrigued by bank heists and killers, but having it actually here on the island was a whole other thing.

I couldn't recall the last time we'd had a murder. It very well might have been never. Accidental deaths? Absolutely. People doing harm to themselves? Unfortunately. Being such a small town, we still had drug problems and some gang activity, but for the most part we were a quiet community even with the tourist trade.

And now, if it hadn't been an accident, there had possibly been a murder . . .

Would they shut the island down? I hadn't even thought of that. If someone had killed Jules, then it could be he or she had gotten out into the harbor and left on a boat. A lot of people bought slips out in the harbor and used dinghies to get back and forth to shore.

The big ferries had stopped running for the night, but it could have been someone who had anchored out from the shore, brought a dinghy in, did their nasty business, and then shot right back across the stretch of ocean. They could be having dinner right now on the *Queen Mary* in Long Beach, happy as a clam.

I stopped myself right there. First of all, I didn't even know if it *had* been a murder. Second of all, I needed to think about the fact that it could have been an accident and someone could already be explaining that to the police. And third, if it was murder, it didn't necessarily have to be someone who snuck in and then snuck out. It could have been someone I saw day in and day out in our little slice of paradise.

Well. That didn't exactly make me feel better.

I'd follow up with Maribel tomorrow to see what the gossip around the office was. She didn't normally tell me about cases, but I knew all about the other goings-on in our sheriff's department—who was chasing after whom, who had dropped whom, who was leaving, who yearned to leave, and who would be here until they died.

She might have to change her policy on not telling me anything about cases, though, because as I gave Whiskers her stuffed mouse to pounce on, I realized how much I wanted to know what had happened. I would be the first to admit that I had not been a big Jules Tisdale fan, but he'd had a whole life ahead of him and for some reason it had been cut short. Why?

I pondered that question while I got ready for bed, and then pondered it some more as I made a series of logic puzzles for my shop. They appealed to kids and adults alike for their brain-teasing qualities and the sense of accomplishment when you used the clues to figure out who owned which fish or which landmark on Catalina was known for what.

Whiskers sprawled herself out over my paper and meowed

at me. She had no concept of personal space. None at all. But I forgave her because she was so darn adorable.

And I already had a series of the puzzles at the shop, so these were just bonus ones for when I ran out. I sold more than I could make sometimes. In coming up with clues and working out the grid, I was able to forget for a second about Jules without any hair.

It all came rushing back, though, when Maribel called at a little after midnight.

"Oh, Whitney, are you okay? I'm so sorry you had to see that."

"It's fine. I'm fine. I've just been trying to keep myself busy. Any word on what happened?"

"I probably can't do lunch tomorrow," she said loudly, then her voice dropped to a whisper. "Word around the office is that they're almost positive it was murder. They want to pull in your brother for questioning. They're on their way to get him now."

While Maribel's whispered message sank into my poor brain, I took the phone away from my ear and stared at it. Then I had to bat Whiskers away because she thought we were playing, which we definitely were not. The police thought it was *Nick*? They were going to pick him up for questioning *right now*?

Whiskers went for the phone again as I tried to figure out what to do first. I threw her stuffed mouse onto the floor and then encouraged her, gently of course, to go get it by pushing on her bottom to get her off the couch.

Putting the phone back up to my ear—because Maribel was talking again but I wasn't catching the words—I righted my brain and dove back into the conversation.

"Are you serious?" I whispered, though, of course, no one but Whiskers could hear me, and she was preoccupied with her toy.

"There you are!" Maribel said loudly. I had no idea if she was talking to me or someone who was in the room with her, so I repeated my question.

"Thanks for the coffee! It's going to be a late night, from what I hear!" She was still loud, but it was muffled, like she'd put the phone down on the desk she sat at in the front of the sheriff's station.

"Pick up, Maribel! I need you to pick up! Pick up the phone! Come on!" I was definitely yelling here. And with good cause. I needed more information to make a decision as to what to do next. I didn't want to jump the gun, but I also didn't want to sit idle when I could be warning my brother. Knowing what I needed to warn him about was paramount. Other than that they were coming for him to question him further about the death of Jules Tisdale, what else did they think he'd done? Maybe they simply needed clarification on his statement.

Then again . . . maybe not. Oh my stars.

"Pick—"

"Yeesh, Whitney, the entire station can hear you. Stop or you're going to get me into trouble for talking with you in the first place. Do you want me to lose my job?"

"—up . . ." I finished. "Sorry, I just, well, I mean, of course I don't want you to lose your job, but you totally dropped a bomb on me and then put the phone down. What was I supposed to do?"

She blew out a breath that radiated irritation. "Wait? Know I was going to come back? That I'd never leave you without all the information? How long have we been friends now? You've got to know I'm not going to tell you something like that and then just leave you flapping out in the wind like a flag at full mast."

I frowned. "Well, I felt a little more like the sails on a ship in a maelstrom, if you want to start making analogies."

She snorted. "You and your nautical references. Did you do that when you worked with trains too? Was everything about making tracks and blowing the whistle, shoveling the coal? Keeping the steam running?"

"Uh." Was it? I'd have to think about that, but in the meantime, there were far more important things going on. "Look, Maribel, I have to know what they're pulling Nick in for. Is it just because he found the body, or do they think he had something to do with the death itself?"

Her voice dropped back to the whisper. "I'm not sure, to be honest, but I wanted to let you know. Just tell him to go along peacefully, if you can. It could be either of those scenarios, but refusing to talk is not going to help his case either way."

Now I could have sworn I was that sail, flapping in the buffeting wind. But I used a breathing technique I'd learned during one of those notoriously long and tedious team-building exercises human resources had loved to do and calmed myself sufficiently to thank her and get off the phone. Then I sat with the phone in my hands for a few seconds, preparing myself to call my brother.

Whiskers flicked her tail against my wrist and nudged her mouse to me. Sometimes I thought she considered herself a dog. I threw the toy and she pounced after it, rolled around on top of it, and then brought it back to me again.

I threw it one more time, and then hit the key on the screen to call Nick. He'd better pick up.

It rang seven times while I waited, using the time to think of how to warn him to be ready for the visit. Or did I want to tell him to hide? I really wanted to tell him to hide, but he didn't have to do that because he had an alibi. He'd been flying.

So I'd tell Nick to make sure he talked to the police and that he was nice. Not that he didn't know he should be nice, but I felt anxiety crawling all over my body about all this. They hadn't pulled me in for questioning, yet I had been the one driving the boat. Maybe that was what was bothering me.

On the ninth ring, I hung up and tried again. His phone hadn't gone to voice mail, and it should have way before nine rings.

I hit the button again, then waited. Again. He had to answer.

But he didn't. So I texted him in all caps to call me ASAP. What was he doing at midnight that made it so he couldn't answer his phone?

Glancing at the clock, I realized it was actually after one now, and I had to call my grandparents first thing in the morning. What if the police needed to confiscate the boat as a possible crime scene?

And, as it was after one, Nick could realistically be sleeping and have no idea what was coming his way.

I calmed myself some more with deep breaths and ran through the facts. No one was going to think that the boat had been used to kill him, and if they had they would have yanked it out of the water by now.

Everything would be okay. It would all work out for the best and Nick would be cleared of any wrongdoing as a potential suspect. Then our tiny police department could concentrate on the actual culprit.

I hadn't yet put the phone down, so I jumped when it both rang and buzzed in my hand. Whiskers leaped on the thing, probably thinking playtime had moved from a mouse to the phone, and in the process, she declined the call. Yikes, especially when I saw it was the sheriff's department.

Could it be Maribel again? Perhaps she was calling me in for my own questioning when I jinxed myself by wondering why I hadn't been pulled in yet? It was a toss-up, but I wouldn't know the actual answer until I just picked up the phone and returned the call.

I did just that and the call was answered on the first ring.

"Oh, thank heavens," Maribel said, sounding breathless.

"Why are we thanking the heavens? And why do you sound like you've been running? We don't run."

She gulped and my nerves started ratcheting up, filling my stomach and making my fingertips tingle.

"Maribel?"

"Oh, Whit, they went to find your brother and he ran. He fell out of his golf cart when he hit a retainer wall and he looks a little roughed up. I just thought I should let you know before you see him."

Chapter 4

"I'm coming down there. I'll be there in a few minutes. Will they let me see him?"

She sighed, but I wasn't sure what to make of the sound. Was she irritated with me, or just overtired from all the activity tonight when normally our town was pretty laidback?

"I don't know if they'll let you see him. They might want to talk to you too, and it would be good if you just showed up voluntarily. Don't cause a commotion, though, okay?"

"I don't cause commotions." Well, except for maybe a time or two when I was much, much younger. But that was it.

Maribel wasn't going to let me get away with that BS. "Yeah, that's not how I remember it from high school, so please just be on your best behavior when you get here. Flash that pretty smile of yours that lights up a room, use those listening ears that make everyone tell you their life history in two minutes, even on an elevator, and then try to help all you can to figure this out. Everyone here is really shaken up about this, and the captain is demanding it not go over twenty-four hours without a solid suspect and an arrest."

"Wow, does he really think it's going to be that simple?" I, of course, would *love* for it to be solved that fast, but unless some-one just came in and confessed, it seemed unlikely.

"He wants it to be, and he usually gets what he wants. Not to mention I don't think anyone here has ever investigated a murder," she whispered.

"Oh, that's not encouraging."

"Yeah, you're telling me. They're running around here like the place is on fire. So come on down and let's see what we can do to get Nick out of here without further insult or injury."

Not exactly how I thought I'd spend my late-night hours, but it had to be done, and I was not against doing whatever it took to save Nick's rear end. He was my little brother, after all.

I was pretty sure fluffy pants covered in prints of cat paws and a shirt with the word MEOWSERS on it were probably not the most appropriate of attire, so I did a quick change. Whiskers fol-lowed me around like I was the pied piper and then she howled when I left again. There was nothing for it, though, she couldn't come with me. Sometimes I'd take her out for walks or let her stroll around the neighborhood on her leash, but this was not one of those times.

Jumping into my golf cart, I tucked my purse into the little basket on the floor and crushed the pedal all the way down to the floor. The way I was driving lately, I might have to replace my tiny engine sooner than was recommended.

Fortunately, the streets were almost empty this late at night. Regardless, I was still cautious. We didn't need an accident to di-vert the attention of the police.

The station wasn't close, but on an island this small it wasn't exactly far away either. It only felt like it took forever because my worries increased with every turn of my tiny wheels.

Why were they talking to Nick? Why had he run? Where was he when they'd caught him? Had he actually tried to run, or had his golf cart just hit a bump? Had the police actually hurt him and were trying to hide it by blaming any injuries on the golf cart accident? Now that I wasn't talking with Maribel, it was perfectly legitimate to let my thoughts run wherever they wanted to as long as they didn't come out of my mouth.

But what could the police have that would make them think it was Nick? What kind of reception was I going to get when I finally got there? Would the captain do whatever it took to blame someone and fast?

Too many questions, not enough answers. And I wasn't going to get any until I talked to someone besides Maribel.

The soft lights of the sand-colored stucco building came into view after a few more minutes of worry. Pulling up in a parking spot out front, I sat in my golf cart, taking several deep breaths to make sure I was not going to be a mess when I got in the station. After I felt at least in control of myself and my worry, I hopped out of my open-sided vehicle and slowly walked up to the front door. There was no need to make a fool of myself before I even stepped inside. And if they had cameras running out here, I did not want to be caught being a klutz. I had a habit of being clumsy when I was thinking about too many things to consider what I was actually doing.

Putting my hand on the doorknob, I took one more deep breath, held it for seven counts, then blew it out for eight. And then I opened the door to far more calm than I would have expected.

Instead, this was a quiet place, a low hum of computers and the air-conditioning kicking on.

I spotted Maribel around the corner, sitting with her back ramrod straight, her eyes trained directly on me, and her smile a little too forced. That smile looked like it might crack at any moment now. "Good evening, Whitney. What brings you down to the station?" Maribel asked in the voice I'd heard her use on occasion with Deputy Mannon (who always seemed to think she needed to have a drink with him).

But in our many years of friendship, I'd never heard her use that tone with me. It made my nerves tick up another notch. I told those nerves to quit it until I had actual confirmation that something was wrong, but they didn't listen very well.

I measured my steps to her desk, twelve to be exact, and stopped at the counter with a smile. "Good evening," I said back, not sure how long the farce was going to go on.

"How may I assist you?" Maribel folded her hands on the desk in front of her and kept the fake smile going.

"Really?" I whispered out of the corner of my mouth. "Are we going to do this like we don't know each other? No one's going to believe that, you know. We're roommates, for heaven's sake."

"They might not make that connection," she whispered back.

"Ah, best friends telling secrets?" A deputy came in from the back and slapped a file onto Maribel's counter.

I raised my eyebrows at her, and she frowned at me.

"No secrets, Howie. Whitney just came in to see if her brother needed any help, or if any of you had some questions for her. She was the one who found the body in the first place."

I used that big smile that Maribel had mentioned earlier once she was done talking. It wasn't a lie that it opened a lot of doors for me and had for years. A handy weapon to have right now.

The smile didn't fail me this time either. Howie smiled back at me from under his graying moustache. He reminded me of Magnum, P.I.—the original, not the reboot. My grandmother used to be half in love with Tom Selleck, so we'd watched the television show endlessly. I preferred Higgins's dry humor and straight face, but that was just me.

I wasn't sure where to start with Howie, so I went with the safe topic before jumping into the bigger ones. "How are the kids? Did they find the treasure?" I asked into the silence. They had bought a map from my shop last week and Pops had watched them follow the clues. Their squeals of delight when they'd opened the small wooden chest he'd hidden at the end of the trail, to find a doll and a race car, had lit his face up for days afterward.

Taking me in from head to toe, he harrumphed, the smile gone. "I'm assuming they're in bed like most sane people, but I wouldn't know since I have a dead body on my hands and am here filling out paperwork. And I'll probably still be here filling out paperwork tomorrow instead of at their swim lessons. I am going to hear it from Pam for this."

He crossed his arms over his chest, jingling the handcuffs on his belt buckle.

"Well, if Pops can make a map that tells us what bridge to cross and how many paces in the sand it is to find the culprit, then I'll be sure to share that with you at the earliest possible opportunity."

He snorted, then cracked a smile and uncrossed his arms to tuck his fingers into his utility belt.

Giving me the once-over, he rocked back a step. "Interesting that you're here, Whitney. I was going to give you a call in the morning to clarify some of the things on your statement, but since you're here we might as well do it now."

What statement? I hadn't given anyone a statement yet. Franklin obviously hadn't thought I'd had anything to add, so how did Howie have a statement?

I'd address that question soon enough. I had other, more important things to ask first.

"I was hoping to see Nick real quick, if that's okay?" I twisted my fingers together until they hurt. "I just want to let him know I didn't tell Goldy and Pops where he is yet. I thought I'd leave that up to him."

"Oh, I'm sure he'll be thrilled." Howie chuckled. "All right, let's go pop our heads into the room and then I'll take you into the one next door to finish up some paperwork. Maybe I can make it to swim practice tomorrow after all."

"That should make your wife happy."

He snorted but led the way down the hall without saying another word. Fine by me. I'd be able to gauge the situation better once I laid eyes on Nick and made sure the injuries weren't something he should have been seen by a professional for.

The station was small compared to other Los Angeles County stations, but it was the perfect size for us.

It was a short walk to the interview room where my brother sat. I could see the top of his bowed head through the window, but when I waved, he didn't look up.

"He can't see you," Howie said. His arms were crossed again. I wasn't sure if that was just how he liked to stand, or if I should be concerned with the closed-off body language.

Uncrossing his arms, he knocked on the door and the deputy seated at the table with Nick waved his hand to come in without turning around.

After using a set of keys to open the door, Howie peeked his head in. "His sister's here."

I almost thanked him with his first name, then realized we were in his work place and that might not be appropriate, so I rearranged my thinking before opening my mouth. "Thanks so much, Officer. I appreciate you showing me in."

Cutting his gaze to me, he grunted. "I'm not showing you in, Whitney, make no mistake. I'm just showing you your brother and then you and I are going next door. Don't get comfortable."

Okay then! That was clear enough and brooked no arguments.

"You okay, Nick?" I asked.

He hadn't looked at me yet. I was only able to see the right side of his face and the injuries didn't seem that bad. But when he turned to face me full on, I gasped. The whole left side of his mug was scraped and scratched and his eye was swollen.

I ran into the room. "Holy cow!" I said before I was caught by my arm from behind and pulled up short.

It wasn't a hard yank and it didn't hurt, but it did stop me three feet from my brother. Up close his face looked even worse.

"What the heck happened?" I didn't try to step forward again and Howie let me go after a minute.

"Something was wrong with the brakes on the golf cart. I'm going to have to get them fixed. Stop worrying, Whit, it looks worse than it really is." He tried to smile at me, but he winced instead.

"Shouldn't he be at the emergency room?" I demanded.

"Sister mine, just go answer whatever questions they want you to. I don't need you to stand up for me. You might be the older one, but I've got this. I'm sure it will all be sorted out without your help."

The deputy across from Nick shrugged as he turned to me too. I knew Nick could be difficult and bullheaded, but this was also dumb, which he couldn't afford to be when faced with murder charges.

"Why do they think you did it?" I asked, still standing feet away but wishing I could yank him out of the chair and take him home.

"Who knows? We didn't get to that part before you barged in here like a Valkyrie intent on saving me from myself."

The deputy at the table snickered and then straightened his face and his tie at the same time while clearing his throat.

"Go away, Whit." Nick flicked a hand at me like he was trying to whisk away a pesky fly.

"I'm not just going to go away because you decreed it, you idiot." I put my hands on my hips and stared at him long enough that he looked up again. I swallowed at the damage to his face. What could I do here if he wasn't going to leave? I did the best I could with the little to nothing I had. "I hope you're telling them you didn't do this and there's no way you could have. You barely even know Jules. What possible motive would you have for killing him?"

All I got for my trouble was a grunt from Nick and then Howie cleared his throat. "We need to finish up with your statement. Let's head next door so your brother can answer some questions."

My question-and-answer session went without incident. Howie admitted he'd assumed there was a statement and was surprised to find there actually wasn't one. So I gave him the rundown. He was nice enough with his questions and patient with my constantly wandering mind as I tried unsuccessfully to hear what was going on next door. It was all pretty basic from what I could tell. Where had I been when I found the body? What state was the body in? When was the last time I had seen the victim? What had I been doing between the time I saw him alive and then found him dead?

I answered everything with as much accuracy as I could possibly pull out at almost two in the morning, when I'd been awake since five the previous morning. *And* I had to get up in five hours. Dwelling on that wouldn't help me, so I put it aside. It would only make sleep that much harder to achieve when I finally got home.

After I was released, I came out of the interview room to find Maribel's desk empty and my brother sitting on one of the two waiting-room chairs.

"You're free to go?" I asked the question hesitantly, afraid the answer might be in the negative.

"As free as you can be when you're still under suspicion." He kept his head down and mumbled the words. "They didn't exactly tell me not to leave the island, but it was implied. They have no other suspects that I know of."

My gut clenched. Okay, not exactly what I had been hoping for, but still doable. "We'll just have to hand them some other suspects, then," I said. I was sure I could find someone who had wanted to kill the Person of the Year. Or if not kill, then at least maybe had a grudge? Was mad? Owed him money that he or she didn't want to pay back? Anything to get my brother off the hook. "Heck, his wife could be top on my list if I look at it right, and don't those police programs always say that it was the spouse who usually did it? She might look like a meek, mild thing, but she could be a tigress under that soft shell."

He straightened in his chair and glared at me. I was on a roll, though, and ignored him.

"And she said she had to go to their house before going to the dinner, and she brushed him off when he said they needed to show the world their power-couple status. All reasons to look at the spouse."

The more I thought about it the more it made sense. And I knew plenty of people who knew her, even if I didn't. That was task one on my mental list for saving Nick's hide. We'd figure this out.

"Whit, there's no way Tracy killed him. And you're missing the point, anyway. They think I killed him, and they're not going to stop until they prove it." He leaned forward in his sitting position and put his head in his hands.

I patted his back. "But you didn't. So just tell them you were up at the airport, or in the air, and that'll clear it all up."

He shook his head like it just wasn't going to be that easy, but refused to talk about it anymore, no matter how many times I prodded him. Because of my newly blooming headache and the lateness of the hour, I decided to let it go for the moment. I was exhausted and had to get up way too early to take this on right now. The cops had let him out so they couldn't truly believe he'd done it. We'd prove it was someone else before they pulled him back in. I'd channel one of those TV detectives if I had to and find out who had actually killed Jules.

After I got some sleep.

I sighed when I didn't get a further response. "Look, just let me take you home since your autoette is out of service. I'm sure it'll be better in the morning."

He sat back abruptly and then slouched in the chair. "I'm lucky they're letting me leave at all. I never took the plane off the island. I don't have an alibi."

Oh. My heart stopped in my chest and then started beating like the wings of a hummingbird. "What were you doing instead?"

"I don't want to talk about it. Let's just go home. You're right, it'll probably look better in the morning."

He rose from the chair and walked out the door without checking to see if I was following. If I had been, I would have been hit by the door he slammed closed behind him.

After pushing the door open for myself, I ran out on his heels. "You can't just walk away like that without telling me where you were or what you were doing."

"I sure can, and I just did. Let's call a moratorium on conversation until tomorrow, okay?"

"It's already tomorrow," I said.

Nick rolled his eyes at me. "You're right, but I'm tired. I'm accused of being a killer. It's the middle of the night, and I have a headache. At least I'm free for the next little while, so I'd like to sleep in my bed one last time before they decide to arrest me and stick me in a cell with a cot, if you don't mind." He plopped into the back seat of my golf cart, cutting off all further conversation.

I should have taken the hint, I knew I should have, but I just couldn't in good conscience leave him without hope, or myself without answers. "I'm not starting this thing until you tell me where you were instead. If you're in trouble, or need help, you know you can tell me."

"I'm aware of that, and I'll get it cleared up. I don't need you to save me, Whit. I can take care of things alone."

That was not how family worked. I turned in the front seat to tell him so and he completely avoided eye contact, instead looking out over the parking lot as if something there absolutely fascinated him.

Following his gaze, I saw Felix getting out of a truck in that same parking lot and decided it was definitely time to go.

Fine, I would let Nick sleep and then we'd talk about it later today.

I used the time it took to get to his house three streets over from mine to come to terms with this decision. Especially since when I turned around to talk to him again at a stop sign his eyes had been closed. I could take the hint this time. I'd let it slide for now but not forever.

And if I pressed on the brakes a little harder than I should and jerked to a halt at the front door instead of coasting to a gentle stop, then that was for me to know and him to be irritated about.

"Come to the dock in the morning after the first cruise because you and I will be talking." I didn't get out of my autoette, but I did watch him open the front door of his house and then close it behind him without looking at me. There was nothing more for us to talk about in the middle of the night, but I fully expected him to start talking later.

Talking a lot.

Chapter 5

Sunlight shot through the curtains I'd forgotten to close the night before when I'd literally dropped into bed with my clam-diggers and blouse still stuck to my body. My mouth tasted like dirt, my hair felt like a seagull had gotten stuck in it, and the little makeup I'd put on yesterday before this whole disaster started had come off on my pillow.

Whiskers took one look at me and jumped off the edge of the bed, scrambling back to the wall a foot away. Her orange fur stuck straight up like she was being mortally threatened by bad breath and some funky hair.

"Okay, I'm sure it's not good, but it can't be that bad," I grumbled as I made my way to the bathroom in the next room. I flipped on the light and even I took a step back. Okay, I needed some emergency repairs and quickly.

I slammed my elbow into the wall in the shower, then nearly took my own eye out with the mascara wand, but at least my hair was short enough to be able to go without much fuss.

With only thirty minutes to get down to the harbor before the first cruise today, I rolled on some deodorant and shoved my hair into a messy ponytail and my feet into a pair of sneakers.

Tiptoeing around the house, I tried to be as quiet as possible so as not to wake Maribel. Her shift had ended an hour or so ago and I did not want to interrupt her sleep. She wasn't the nicest of people without lots of sleep and at least a quart of coffee, the latter preferably intravenously.

After I threw some kibble into a bowl for Whiskers, I ran out the door despite her meowing for me to come back.

I probably could have biked down to the harbor faster with the crush of golf carts on the road, but I got there just in time.

Thankfully, the police hadn't seized the boat as evidence last night. After everyone had left, Nick had cleaned the boat, so there wasn't much to get ready as the passengers came down the gangway five minutes later.

As I walked up to the small gathering, I kept my smile firmly on my face, but in my head, it was like a riptide. What had Nick been doing in the six hours between his call to me and his showing up at the dock just as Jules floated by? Why didn't he have an alibi?

I forced myself to put that aside. There were a lot of people on the dock waiting for me, Jenna and her family among them, and I didn't want to disappoint them. Walking past the crowd, I got on the boat and then opened for business.

"Welcome, welcome, welcome." I greeted each one, took their money, and kept a head count for the party size I was expecting, but then more showed up, tourists and islanders alike. I had room and this hadn't been booked as a private cruise, so really the more the merrier.

Until a line started forming, and I had to really work to keep an accurate head count. Where was everyone coming from, and what were they here for? I sent a quick text to Nick and prayed he'd get it before I got mobbed.

Then I remembered he'd be walking without his golf cart and texted a second time to tell him to get on his bike as soon as humanly possible.

Three more people and I was at full capacity and still had a line on the dock.

"I'm sorry, folks. Legally, I can only take so many guests and we've reached capacity. The guided tour takes about forty-five minutes. Hopefully, Nick will be here soon to figure things out for you, but we'll be back." I closed the door to the deck and motored away into the bay just as Goldy and Pops came steaming up the dock.

Turning the boat around was not an option because of the arc I'd have to make in the water to get back to the dock, so I checked that everyone was occupied and called Pops then.

"Hey, I'm taking the first crowd. Help me out with everyone still on the dock. We'll talk when I get back." I turned my cell phone off because more conversation could be bad for business.

I figured if nothing else, they could take the overflow on the semi-submersible if they wanted to.

"Welcome aboard the *Sea Bounder*," I said into the microphone. I didn't usually have to take advantage of the speakers mounted in the corners of the boat. Rarely were the crowds so big that they couldn't be managed with just raising my voice. This time, however, no one would hear me over the din, no matter how loud I yelled.

There was about a half a beat of silence and then the chatter started back up. I heard a few mentions of death and "this boat" and "which window?" People started pushing toward the window in the floor at the back of the boat where I'd witnessed Jules float by last night, and the whole thing made sense. I wouldn't actually have to do a whole cruise then, and I could make sure the people who had booked last night got a better ride later on in the day once the fever for CSI died down.

I flagged Jenna over to the wheel. "Hey, I'm really sorry about this."

"Oh, Whit, there's no need to apologize. This is very interesting, and even the animals are getting into it; they must feel the energy sinking down from the boat. We saw a whole pod of dolphins not two minutes ago and those little sharks are back. The kids are having a blast."

"Still. I promise I'll make it up to you with a quieter cruise after, if you're still interested. I don't feel like this is getting the value for the money you put down."

Patting my arm, she smiled. "I'm certainly not going to turn down the opportunity to come back out to sea, but you really don't have to do that."

I smiled when she gave my elbow a brief squeeze. "Just don't tell Nick I'm comping you, and we'll all be fine. Now, let's see what's under us this time, and if we can get an eel or two, then bonus."

As I gave the spiel, this time without worrying too much if it was right or not, I kept an ear out for any information that might help me make sure the real culprit was caught. Other than some speculation and a few rowdy comments about Davy Jones taking the not-so-nice guy to the locker at the depths of the sea, not much came out of the ride. But there were a lot of smiles, and after people had seen all they wanted to see of the now-famous window, they actually had paid attention to the undersea life.

It was a success, even though it had started out a little rocky, and should make my brother happy.

My brother, who was not standing on the dock when I got back. He should have been standing there, waiting to take the next set of cruisers out, and instead all I saw were our grandparents. And the cops currently walking up the dock. I had a feeling they were not looking for a ferry around the harbor to see if they could catch a glimpse of a fish or two.

I threw the line to Pops, who caught it in his strong grip. He tied the boat off with an expertise that I still hadn't mastered. His look of concentration cleared when he looked up at me and winked.

Okay then, things couldn't be that bad if Pops was winking.

Maybe the bruising on Nick's face had gotten worse after he'd slept and he was resting. Maybe he didn't want to scare off the customers by showing up a mess.

I was going with that last one.

"Nick Dagner, please get off that boat," one deputy called from a hundred feet away.

Or maybe not. The police were looking for him and for some reason couldn't find him? That couldn't be good.

"Uh, Nick isn't on the boat," I yelled back as the passengers began filing off. "Just little old me." I raised my hands and shrugged, then sent pleading eyes to Pops.

Staring straight ahead at me, Pops blinked slowly. I would have preferred if he'd winked again.

Pops turned to the deputies who were almost at the end of the dock. The cops picked up their pace. Did they think I was lying and Nick was actually on the boat and would jump off and swim out into the harbor? Run again? Had he done that last night too? Or had the brakes really been out on his golf cart? I still wasn't sure the police hadn't roughed him up just a little bit, maybe manhandled him into their car. And they did have real cars and trucks on the island. They didn't have to wait the thirty-five years to bring a new car onto the island.

They also had golf carts and bikes to patrol with, but I highly doubted they had chased Nick down with a golf cart or a beach cruiser last night. And now they were on foot, although I could see a Jeep on the sand up from the water's edge.

"What is it you need, Jeffrey?" Goldy asked the deputy with a swish of her sun-kissed blond hair and the tap of her impossibly high-heel-shod foot.

She wasn't being over-the-top belligerent, but she certainly wasn't smiling either. I wasn't sure about her use of his first name, since this was an official kind of inquiry, but she had always been bolder than me.

"As you can see, we have quite the crowd ready to go out on

our tour today," she continued, not waiting for them to answer her question. "Unless you have something you need, or you want to take the tour yourself for our normal serviceperson discount, I suggest you step back and let our grandchildren run their business."

The two cops looked at each other and then back at Goldy. Yeah, she baffled me sometimes too.

Pops stepped between my grandmother and her prey. "Deputies, as I'm sure Nick told the gentlemen last night, he is recovering from the cart crash." He emphasized that last word with a frown. "From what I was told, he was given leave to go back to his ordinary life until further notice, and that does include taking the boat out to sea. He is taking today off, though."

I couldn't tell if Pops was telling the truth or not. Maybe that meant the cops couldn't either. Hopefully. Where was Nick? He hadn't called me. He must have called Goldy and Pops at some point if they knew he was taking the day off. Why hadn't he called me?

"I'll let him know you're looking for him," Pops continued. "As you can see, we will be loaded with guests today, but we'll check in often if that helps. As far as I know, Nick is up at his home, resting. There's no danger of him running away. I promise. Do you have new information that has you looking for him again?" He cleared his throat after those last words, and I could practically see the nerves vibrating along the base of his neck.

He was wired, and when Pops was wired things didn't always go according to plan, much like Nick. Which was why I hadn't had much trouble believing my brother had run when the cops had come after him, probably thinking he could outdistance a truck with his little putt-putt.

"Pops, I can run the next ride if you need to stay here." I mentally rearranged my schedule for the day as I stepped onto the dock. It wouldn't be the end of the world if I missed the breakfast I'd planned on before opening my gift shop. Plus, there was far more business out here than there probably was in the town right now.

Lots of business and lots of people standing and whispering to each other as we exchanged words with the police. How had life gotten this out of control?

Right, Jules dead under our boat, and Nick nowhere to be found.

"No, there's nothing else they could have found to point the finger at your brother, so I don't think I'm going anywhere." Pops widened his stance and stuck his pipe in the corner of his mouth.

"And there you'd be wrong." The deputy on the left stuck her hands on her hips and stared down Pops.

Oh, this was not going to be good.

"Pops, please. Just let these officers do their job, and we'll do ours." I stood in front of Pops, who was still standing in front of Goldy. It was like a line of decreasing anger, and I was going to have to be the barrier. It wasn't a new role for me, but not exactly one I relished having to perform here on the island when I had hoped to put that kind of drama behind me forever.

"No." Just that from Pops and nothing else.

I knew I had to talk fast to simmer things down. "Look, I'll go with the officers to see what they have and what we can do to clear Nick's name. You stay here to do the tours and Goldy can organize those who will have to wait." I pleaded with him with my gaze, again, and this time it seemed to get through.

"I'm not happy about this," he said gruffly.

"And you're not alone in that," Goldy chimed in.

I rolled my eyes, swallowing the words I wanted to say. "I get it, but if they have enough evidence that they're jangling the handcuffs, then we have to treat this as a real issue. You do what you do best, and I'll go fumble around in brand-new territory. We'll all be fine. I promise." That promise wasn't one I thought I'd really be able to keep, but I made it anyway.

And it worked. In the end, they gave in. I left Pops to take the next ride out, while Goldy took the money and divided people up into groups that would fit on the boat. She let those who had to wait go about their business and come back at their designated time.

I followed along behind the cops in my flashy golf mobile and hoped that they were fishing for clues and motives instead of having anything concrete.

My stomach dropped to my toes a few times when I thought about what they could have that made them want to publicly arrest Nick this time instead of just asking him to come in for questioning.

Did it have anything to do with the fact that Nick had several unaccounted-for hours? He'd said he didn't have an alibi when we'd talked last night, and that had gnawed at me every second I was awake.

I'd run over and over our conversation in my head this morning when I'd brushed my teeth, and had put it on my list of things to ask Nick. Now I had a new one to add to the growing list: Where the heck was he?

I couldn't come up with any good information with what little I had to work with, which just made the tension and the trek to the sheriff's station that much worse.

Finally, we pulled up to the building, and I hopped out right behind the deputies.

"Do we have to do it this way?" I asked. "Are you going to book him when you find him? Are you charging him this time, or is it just more questions?"

I was largely ignored by both officers and then they left me at the front reception desk when they went to the back and very deliberately closed the door behind them instead of waiting for me.

I sank into the waiting room chair Nick had been in last

night and put my head in my hands, much like he had last night. Man, I wished Maribel were here. Maybe she could tell me something.

Taking my phone out of my pocket while I cooled my heels, I texted Nick to let him know the police were looking for him and to get back to me immediately. Then I texted Maribel before realizing what time it was. With her shift ending just hours ago, they were not going to expect her in this early in the morning.

So I sat there with my head cradled in my hands, and then leaned back against the wall. This could take hours, and I needed to see if I could help Goldy and Pops. And find my brother. I called his number three times and left three messages just to cover all the bases.

Conveniently, there was a bell on the front desk. I rang it a few times and was ignored. Since that wasn't working, I called the number for the department, then waited for someone to pick up. I could hear the phone ringing back behind the counter as I paced out in the waiting room. I gnawed on the edge of my fingernails, then quickly took my hand out of my mouth; I hadn't bitten my nails in months. I wasn't going to start back up now.

Finally, someone picked up. "Dispatch."

"Um, yes." I'd been so focused on someone answering that I hadn't taken the time to think about what I was going to say.

"Yes? Do you have an emergency?"

Just that my life was falling apart and so was Nick's, and I wasn't sure what to do. "Um, well, yes and no. I'm here at the station. Is it possible for someone to come out and talk with me in the waiting room? I just have a few questions and then I promise to get out of your hair. Swear."

The lady cop with the handcuffs came out of a hallway to the right. I wasn't sure if it was in response to my call, or if she was just going to get the rubber hose, but I flagged her down anyway.

"Excuse me, yes, excuse me?"

She glanced my way, and I had a feeling she was rolling her eyes, even if I couldn't see it.

"Whitney, right? Whitney Dagner? Sister of the suspect."

Oh, I did not like that term. Not *sister*, the other one. "Yes, that's me. I was wondering if you could tell me about how long you think you'll be before we can talk? I wanted to be able to tell my grandparents how long they have to stand in for me."

She eyed me up and down in my khaki shorts and my bright-white tennis shoes, a marked contrast to her dark blue uniform with what looked like a bulletproof vest under the button-down shirt.

"I like the patches on your sleeve," I said, trying to make conversation while she looked me over. "They did a great job of incorporating the logo. I wonder if that's something I could sell down at the store, very nice." Oh man, could I have been any more ridiculous? I was sure there was a way I could have been, but I wasn't coming up with anything to top that stupidity.

"Thanks, and to answer your question, I'm not sure. We have some new information about where he might be, and we're following up on that before we talk to you. We have questions for him and that could take a short while if he's willing to answer them, or a long time if he decides to withhold information or lie."

"He told you everything when he was in here, though." Not that he'd told *me* everything, including his whereabouts during the evening before he'd come to the *Sea Bounder*. "What more do you need, and what else did you find out that makes you think it was him?"

"He's barely told us anything, Ms. Dagner. And now that we have confirmation of the method of death, as well as information regarding an incident this last week, we're even more interested in your brother and his whereabouts now and during the fatal incident."

"Couldn't it have been an accident? Jules fell in the water and no one realized it? He tripped and hit his head and then got caught in the current?" Although now that I thought of it, if Jules had been at the scheduled dinner and fallen in the water, he wouldn't have come in under the boat due to the currents unless he'd first gone all the way around the island. I bit my lip. And Nick had been at the *Sea Bounder* for only a few minutes when Jules had come into view. Long enough to have killed him and then run down the dock before Jules appeared?

No, Nick would never have killed him. Right? But then why wouldn't he tell me where he was instead of flying into Murrieta as he'd planned?

How far was I willing to go for someone who was hiding things? Heck, hiding in general.

Chapter 6

Biting my lip didn't help me come up with the right words after her announcement, but I tried anyway. "How did Jules die?"

I'd meant to have a little more finesse with that question but failed.

She squinted at me, then clasped her hands behind her back. Those cuffs stood out for anyone to see and I was looking as I gulped.

"He was strangled with his tie and then rolled into the water down a cliff."

"Oh." Not the most intelligible thing I could have said, but I wasn't sure what else to come up with, but I rallied nonetheless. "Nick never would have done that."

"How are you so certain? We have cause to believe he and Jules were not on the best of terms and Nick is certainly strong enough."

"But they barely know each other."

Cocking her head to the side, she stared me down. "I'm not at liberty to discuss anything further."

That was not good, but I was willing to wade in one more time before leaving. "So is it possible for me to sit in with him when you do find him? If he's being difficult maybe he'd talk in front of me instead of just in an interrogation room. You know what I mean?"

She put her hands on her hips and stuck her elbows out to the sides, a look of disbelief on her face. "You're not going to go away." Her sigh was gusty before she spoke again. "Yeah, I do know what you mean, but the answer is no. He's on the hot seat. If I were you, I'd just walk away and let him fend for himself."

Yeah, there was no way that was ever going to happen, no matter what she thought. Even if it wasn't Nick, I had a feeling I'd be looking into this. Something wiggled in the back of my brain. It felt weird to call it something as innocuous as curiosity, but that was what it was. I wanted to know who had done this, and because of Nick's involvement, I had to know, not just wanted to know.

And I would find out.

I took a "Tell Us How We're Doing" paper from the holder on the counter and wrote on the back. "Here." I handed the paper to her. "It's the number to the gift shop. I don't always answer my cell phone when I have customers at the shop, and that's where I'll be. If there are any follow-up questions after you find him, you can reach me there."

"You're betting the house that he didn't do this, no matter what we have on him?" she asked.

"I'm that certain, and yes, I'm betting the house. I know he didn't do this, and if you all don't find out who did it, I can guarantee you that I will."

With that I walked out, the sound of her chuckling following me out the door and to my autoette. Fine, she could chuckle all she wanted, but I knew I could do this, and I knew exactly where to start.

Heading back to my cart, I kept my head down and tried hard to think of where to begin with questioning. And who to even start with. I wanted to find Nick and tie him to a chair until he answered all my questions like I used to do when we were kids and playing detective.

Heck, at this point, I'd take tickling him until he spit out the answer. Even though the tactic had never worked when we were younger, I was willing to try.

But I had no idea where he was and he wasn't answering his phone. I didn't know where to go next.

I talked a big game back in the station, but as I dragged my feet to my autoette, doubt set in. What was I doing?

I could ask around the island. I could use the grapevine. I could dig into any number of closets for skeletons and motives. And I could also still come up empty-handed.

I considered talking with Jules's cousin Rebecca, but didn't want to intrude on her grief.

I dropped into the autoette and put my head back just to rest. I was so tired from the little sleep I'd gotten and the big chaos I was enduring. So very tired, and I was just at the beginning of things. If only I could take a nap. But I had no time for that right now.

I felt a presence near my left elbow and almost dreaded opening my eyes. It could be a concerned citizen. It could be a tourist looking for directions. Then again, it could be a killer who had just started picking people off the island for an as-yet-unknown reason.

Instead of torturing myself with the possibilities, I opened my eyes and then wanted to close them right away. I fought hard against the urge because I knew this person was not going to be a figment of my imagination. And he might be asking for directions, but I would be sorely tempted to just tell him to put it into his phone and figure it out for himself.

"Felix."

He waited a beat and kept his gaze on me. "So, just a first name? No greeting? I noticed the way you ran away from me last night and thought you were just upset about finding a dead guy. Guess I was wrong, huh?"

There was so much to sort through there, and so many things I both did and did not want to say, that I didn't even know where to start. I cleared my throat and looked him square in his beautiful brown eyes. They were flecked with gold and had shimmered with laughter when we'd dated on the mainland, especially in candlelight when we joked over a table absolutely strewn with seafood.

I shook my head at myself. I had important things to do, things that had nothing to do with meeting up with an ex. Most importantly, a missing brother who was the prime suspect on an island that hadn't seen a murder in years and years.

After a deep breath, I put my best smile on my face and my foot on the gas, ready to push down as soon as I possibly could. "I didn't run from you, and quite honestly I have an appointment in ten minutes, so I'd better get going. Nice seeing you. When are you leaving?"

The chuckle that had drawn me to him at a miniature golf tournament where he'd asked to putt past me came out of his strong throat. "So ready to get rid of me, even if you don't mind that I'm here?"

"I didn't say anything about how I feel about you being here, just want to know when you're leaving." I cocked my head to the side. "A week or less would be a great answer."

"Sorry to disappoint you." He flashed those white teeth at me in a smile that had made me melt when he'd thrown it out to me while leaning on his small golf club. Back then, as he'd stood there in plaid shorts and a T-shirt emblazoned with a now-popular comic book hero, I would have sworn the look came with a spell, but not now. Or if there was one, I was now immune.

"Again," I mumbled under my breath in response to his comment about disappointing me, but maybe not softly enough when his smile fell into a frown. I bulldozed over that simply because I had no time and wished I could take that one word back. "No disappointment here. Ten days works for me too. Isn't that about how long you have for vacation?"

He crossed his arms over his chest and widened his stance. "I'm not even going to ask if you're that ready to get rid of me. But I am going to put you on notice that I'm here to stay, and no matter how resistant you are, I think I should warn you that I'm not going anywhere. You're here, and I'd like a second chance if you can get over your anger enough to at least think about it."

"I wasn't angry then, and I'm not angry now." I almost checked to see if my pants were on fire, but wouldn't give in to the urge. "You do whatever you want. It's a free country, and you're more than welcome to live in any part of it that you want." But why now? I'd jokingly thrown out the idea of him potentially moving to Avalon when we'd discussed my move and then he'd never called me again. So what had changed? I stopped myself right there and decided it didn't matter. Right now, I had to find a killer and keep my brother out of jail. Flirting and fuming were not on my list of things that took precedence.

He shoved his hands into the pockets on his shorts. "Your knuckles are white on that poor steering wheel and it looks like you're about to rip the thing right off the flimsy column." He raised an eyebrow at me.

Relaxing my grip, I hooked an arm over the back of my seat and put on an air of nonchalance. "I'm just in a hurry. Like I said, I have a meeting and have to get going. Welcome to the island." I nearly choked on that last part.

"Wow, I'm impressed you got that out."

"Don't press your luck, Felix. You're here, I'm here, it's a small town, but there's plenty of room for us to not cross paths. I have things to do, and you're in the way of me doing them." I tapped the gas pedal and moved forward just enough to bump into his shoe.

"No chance you'd want any help doing them? Turns out they had a part-time position available here at the sheriff's department for a diver. So I took it. Thought it might be worth seeing what was so wonderful over here that you'd leave pretty much without a word."

This time I did choke. I wasn't sure which words to say first since they were all crowded on my tongue.

"I don't know that I've ever seen you tongue-tied, Whit. It's an interesting look on you."

"I told you I was leaving. I asked you to come with me." There. Apparently that was the most important thing to get out first. "You know what? I have no time for this. My brother is a top suspect for a murder he didn't commit. An old flame"— who's less than a spark of fire under water—"is not on my list of things to handle today."

With that I zipped out of the parking lot and left him behind. I almost missed my turn watching him in my rearview mirror instead of concentrating on driving.

Why did he have to be here, and why now?

I had no time to worry about it, though, as I made my stop sign at the last second with a chirp of my tires that put a smile on his face when I glanced back at him again.

I was more careful as I made my way to the pier to talk over things with Goldy and Pops. And then I'd talk with Maribel when she got up, which should be in a few hours.

Glancing down at my watch, I wondered how it was possible that I'd only been up for three hours so far. Way too much was happening.

It occurred to me that I might need that help Felix was offering. I might be nosy, and I might have a smile that could open doors, but if I was looking for a murderer, I might need more ammunition than that.

Back at the dock, I parked my golf cart and just sat there. What was I going to tell Pops and Goldy? A more important question was, what did they already know? Had they talked with Nick again today?

I'd deal with each issue as it came up. I was schooled in that from an early age, and my skills wouldn't fail me now.

Slowly, I got out of the cart and took in the view of the nearly empty dock. There had been a line of people still waiting to get on the *Sea Bounder* to see the now-famous window when I'd left, but Pops and Goldy must have been running tours back-to-back to have cleared things out. Maybe I should put a sticker on the boat and call it something sassy to get more people to come back. It was a valid proposition, but then I thought better of it. I would, however, take whatever money we could make over the next little while and put it aside until another scandal hit town, just in case we had to come up with money for Nick's trial.

No, I would not think like that. No one had mentioned attorneys yet and I wasn't going to be the first one to jinx things with that conversation. It was better left for later, if necessary.

I would find out who had really done this to Jules, and I would hand them over to the police and be done with it.

Taking a step toward the pier, I ran up against a body that hadn't been there a moment ago.

Felix. Felix was standing in front of me, his dark eyebrows pulled down over those dark eyes. His intensity, his presence, was something I just didn't think I could handle right now.

"Would it make any difference if I told you I could help you, and I believe that your brother didn't do it either?"

Another tongue-tied episode, and those were so rare that I was surprised I didn't fall over from two in less than an hour.

"Are you playing me?" There, I'd found my voice and used it to ask the best question I could think of, other than how the heck he got here before me.

The frown was back, but this was too important to not put the question out there. I couldn't afford to get myself into something that wouldn't help my brother's case.

"Were we not in the same relationship, Whit? I've never played you, and I never would."

"But . . ."

"No buts. I don't know what story you've been telling yourself, since I can't get into that head of yours—no matter how many times I've tried—but let me tell you the one from my side and then we'll get things done and go from there. I would've figured something out. No, a long-distance relationship wasn't my first choice, but it was far from over to me. You didn't give me a chance to tell you that before you cut me off at the knees. So, now I'm here, we're going to solve this murder, and then you and I are going to do some serious talking. Maybe at your house instead of the boat I have anchored out in the harbor, but there *will* be talking. And it's not only going to be you saying all the words."

I stared at him for a long time. When I heard clapping from behind me, I closed my eyes.

"I like you already, young man." Goldy brushed up against me, and I opened my eyes in time to see her reach for Felix's hand. No matter how tan she got she was never going to be the beautiful color of Felix's skin. Both of his parents were from Mexico and he was the first generation to grow up in the States. His mom had been so proud of him the one time I'd met her. And now that Goldy was fawning over him, I had a feeling that she and Mrs. Ramirez would have been best friends.

"Welcome aboard, son." Pops stuck out his hand too, not to be left out. "I like your attitude, but you and I are going to have to talk a little more if you think you're going to date my granddaughter. I'd like to know your intentions."

The word *blush* was not strong enough to describe what was happening to my face. I felt my cheeks flame with fire-engine red and wished a board would break in the pier, or maybe a real shark would jump the dock and swallow me whole. "Pops, we have things going on."

"Yes, I can see that, though I'm wondering why I haven't heard of this young fellow in all the time you've been here."

The flames turned to supernovas as all three of them looked pointedly at me. "I was not going to talk about the breakup. This was going to be a new start, and I left all that on the mainland when I moved."

"Apparently a few things still needed some attention, eh, Felix?" Pops had the gall to nudge Felix with his elbow and wink at him.

"Excuse me," I cut in. "But you might be interested to know that your grandson still cannot be found, and the police are certain they have enough to make a case stick. And he has no alibi, or at least not one he'll tell me."

Well, that finally got their attention off my love life, or lack thereof, and on to the important things.

"What do you mean he doesn't have an alibi?" Goldy splayed her hand over her chest as if to hold her heart in where it was supposed to be.

"That's ludicrous," Pops said. "He was over the ocean in that plane of his. He told me he was taking off in the afternoon for Murrieta and wouldn't be back until the evening. That's why you took the last three tours of the day."

I shook my head. We'd all been told the same lie. That was not good. Nick had a lot to answer for. As soon as he actually talked to anyone. "He told me that also, but now he's saying he never even took the plane into the air. He never left the island but won't tell me where he was instead."

"I'm going to go have a word with that boy." Goldy stalked off in her high heels, clicking along the wooden pier like a fast metronome.

"And how are you going to find him?" Felix called after her.

"You'd be surprised what I can do when I put my mind to it," she returned without looking back.

Pops used a handkerchief to wipe the sweat from his top lip. "I'd better go follow along after her and make sure she doesn't get into any trouble. You know how she can be."

"Yeah, let's not make this worse, if possible." I shielded my eyes with the flat of my hand. "I don't see a ton of people on the dock. Did the furor to see the death window die down?"

"It did. I don't think we've run that many tours in that short of a time in years. I was charging half price because we just went out, did a little turnaround, and then came back. People were more interested in the window than in the sea today. Felt good to be back behind the wheel, though. I won't lie."

I smiled at him. "You know you're welcome any time. I'm telling you in lieu of Nick here, since he's not exactly available at the present time." Why wouldn't my brother tell anyone where he was? The question kept revolving around in my head, and I couldn't get it to stop. Even more because I had no way of getting an actual answer. Maybe Goldy would have better luck than I had. After she found him, of course.

"It looks like I might be coming out of retirement, anyway. Just for a bit, I guess." There was no smile at the prospect, but I could tell Pops wasn't totally bummed at the idea of working again.

"I can help too," Felix said, and I barely stopped myself from snorting. It wasn't like you could just jump into a glass-bottom boat if you'd never steered one before. What did he think this was?

Pops beat me to it, though. "You got experience, boy?"

"I live on a boat, sir." Felix pointed out to the harbor. "That twenty-footer out there is mine."

"The wooden one? The cutter?" Pops looked far too interested for my peace of mind. He loved wooden boats and had tried to pull for the *Sea Bounder* to be built from wood. But it made more sense to go with fiberglass. He did still have his own skipjack out in the harbor, though.

"Yeah, I can't seem to let go of the old beauty. I bought her when I was fourteen. My parents wanted me to live in a boat next to theirs instead of onboard with them. Quarters were way too cramped for the three of us. So, she's been mine ever since then, and she's never caused me trouble."

Now the look on my Pops's face said that he wanted to spend some more time talking about this. I hadn't known about Felix living on his own boat when he'd been a mere teenager. How had we not talked about that?

I had to cut off both of our lines of thought before we lost sight of what was paramount at this point.

"Goldy's at the end of the pier, Pops. If you're going to stop her from causing trouble, you might want to do that now instead of later."

He snapped his gaze back to mine. "Right. I'm on it. But don't you go anywhere, young man. I think we have some tales to tell each other."

"I'm not going anywhere, sir." When Felix answered Pops, he looked right at me.

I did not need this on top of everything else, but I decided to ignore it for now. I didn't have enough energy to fight on more than one front. I had important things to do and my love life was not in the top ten.

I had a killer to find and a brother to save, even if he wasn't willing to grab the freaking lifesaver I was trying to throw out into the water, hoping it would smack him on the head.

Chapter 7

Once Pops took off down the dock in a trot, Felix and I stared at each other for a long time. I wasn't kidding when I said that I didn't have time for this on top of everything else.

"Felix," I started.

"Whitney," he said back to me.

I shook my head again. Maybe I was trying to rattle my brain back to the place where it thought correctly and was happy with my life, not where it wondered when it had all gone wonky and why I couldn't figure out how to fix it.

"I can't do this." I clasped my hands in front of my stomach, hoping that it would settle.

"If you're talking about us, then don't worry about it. I wasn't lying to your grandfather when I said I wasn't going anywhere. We have time. We need to concentrate on figuring out what your brother did or didn't do first."

I took a step back, rocked by how he had phrased that. "We're not going to be able to work together at all if that's your attitude. My brother did not do this. I don't care where he was or what else he was doing, he would not have killed anyone." The words came out forcefully, but my gut clenched. I honestly wanted to believe that he hadn't killed Jules, but if he wouldn't talk, and now was in hiding, then it was possible I was running up against something that was not as true as I wanted it to be.

Felix shook his head and reached out a hand to me that I ignored. He left it there for a few seconds and then let it drop to his side. "I'm sorry. I said it wrong, Whit. I'm sure your brother didn't kill Jules. But now we need to give the police another suspect, or they might not look for one. Especially if they can't find your brother. And if he refuses to talk about what he was doing when they do find him, it will be worse. The people in the department have been great so far, but they also don't have any experience with this stuff. Nick's going to have to be his own best advocate, and the only way to do that is to show up and talk. He didn't give any indication of where he was?"

"He hasn't answered any of my texts, and my calls go straight to voice mail." The sense of defeat I'd been staving off for over twelve hours finally hit me right in the brain. I'd been avoiding it like the plague, but I couldn't hold out much longer now that I was nearly alone and didn't know where to start. If Nick wasn't going to talk, then what was I going to do?

"Then we'll have to find out if anyone saw him anywhere on the island and go from there. Word around the station is that Tisdale's cousin is out for blood on this one, so we need to act fast and should stay out of her way, if possible."

Felix reached out a hand again like he wanted to brush it down my arm, then brought it back to his face instead and rubbed his chin.

"This is going to be awkward, isn't it?" I asked, wishing it wasn't, but knowing enough about awkwardness to know it when it was literally staring me in the face.

I got the shrug again, but he didn't reach for me. "Not if you don't want it to be. Let's just get things done, and we'll go from there when it's all taken care of." He paused, cocking his head to the side. He opened his mouth a couple of times and closed it just as many. Then he finally said what he'd been hesitating over.

"One last thing, and then I promise to leave it all alone for now. I'm not going to say I would've followed you right away, but I knew a good thing when I had it, and knowing you left without giving me a chance to even think it over wasn't the best day of my life." He gripped the back of his neck and then looked over at me with those dark eyes. "Now what should we do first? We need a battle plan."

And suddenly I was in cahoots with my ex-boyfriend, who I had apparently hurt, so that he could help me with my brother. Life sure was beachy.

Standing on the dock for the next ten minutes, Felix and I made a plan. It wasn't as awkward as I had thought it would be, and I was supremely grateful for that. I told him not to worry about the tour-guide spiel, to just wing it when they were over the water if a fish came by.

I didn't know what would happen after, and that was okay, because I had enough to think about now. After would only be an issue once we had Nick, and his story along with him.

So Felix was running the last tour for the few people who had wandered over, and then he would put a sign up that we were closed for the day. I, on the other hand, was on a reconnaissance mission. I went by Nick's house and found nothing, and no one in the vicinity had talked to him or seen him, so I went back to the strand and got down to feeling out the gossip.

As soon as I entered Eternal Flame, the candle store next to the Dame of the Sea, all talking ceased. I knew what they'd been talking about and I wanted them to continue, not clam up around any pieces of sand they might have that could turn into pearls of clues that could save my brother. Felix and I had decided it was best to get the local gossip first. It would serve a twofold purpose—letting him keep his job, since he wasn't doing an official inquiry, while also allowing me to have the freedom to ask whatever I wanted without getting in trouble for sticking my nose in where it didn't belong, according to some people.

Since he was technically a cop, even if it was as a part-time diver, and newly transplanted to the island, we'd decided he had less of a chance of people talking to him. I was a transplant too, but at least I had my summers to fall back on and most people knew who I was. If not, then I'd name-drop Goldy and Pops, who had been here for their entire lives.

I wasn't much for demanding people tell me what they knew, and I didn't want to start trying my false bravado out now. Instead, I walked to the cash register in the candle shop and waited for someone to separate from the crowd to come over and speak to me.

"Whitney, oh Whitney, what is going on? How can we help?" I wasn't sure if those questions were from one person or a few different ones since they all came from the same direction. Trying to separate the gaggle of women from one another would be hard on a good day. On a day where I was seriously doing everything I could to hold myself together, it wasn't even worth trying.

But I hadn't counted on all the women moving in one mass like a school of garibaldi. I felt surrounded but wasn't able to figure out right away if it was with support or just waiting for that spot to get me best between the shoulder blades.

"I'm not sure, Jeannie." I picked the one woman I knew a little better, the owner of the shop. We'd had coffee once, we'd talked shop a couple of times, she'd brought me cookies when I'd rented the storefront for the gift shop. Good cookies, too, so I felt confident I could trust her.

She put her hands over mine and shot a look to the school of fish hovering with gaping mouths. "Ladies, why don't you find something to perhaps scent your houses pleasantly? I'll be with you soon."

After a slight hesitation, they took the hint and wandered away, but not very far. That was fine with me. What I had to say I didn't care if they overheard. In fact, I wanted them listening so they could give me any chatter, or rumor, or gossip they'd heard recently.

"They want to take Nick in for questioning for a second time. I know he didn't do this, but I need to find out who did so they don't charge the wrong guy by accident." I could hear the desperation in my voice even though I had been trying so hard to keep it together and not fall into the trap of feeling like all was lost.

Jeannie put her arm around my shoulder and pulled me in close. "I have some info that might be useful to you," she whispered into my ear, "but it has to stay between us unless you can find a different source to confirm. Let's do lunch at the Cozy Diner, and I'll tell you all about what I heard this morning." Much louder she said, "I'm so sorry, hon. I'm not sure what we can all do to help, but I'm sure no one truly believes it was your brother."

A sea of nods followed her words, and I wasn't sure if they really meant it, or if they were just playing along so they could get the gossip and be the one to be able to tell everyone what they'd heard first.

I did not need a gossip-fest, unless it was going to be one that helped me. I knew Nick had been a hooligan sometimes when he was younger. His shenanigans ranged from spray painting on businesses to drag-racing autoettes and playing chicken on a cliff road. But now that he'd established himself as a solid business-man on the island under Goldy and Pop for years before he'd taken over the business, I had hoped it wouldn't count against him as he was older and hopefully a lot wiser.

"I appreciate that." I turned to the crowd. "If anyone knows anything, I am open to any and all info."

More nodding, but no one came forward to actually say

anything. Well, I hadn't exactly been expecting someone to jump into my arms and tell me they had done it just to save my brother.

Although I wouldn't have said no to that scenario.

Instead, I was going to have to put on my thinking cap and my nosy-busybody hat to dig a little deeper. I'd turn over every grain of sand to find out what had happened. I'd empty every closet of every skeleton if I had to in order to get to the bottom of who had wanted Jules Tisdale dead. And more importantly, who was willing to sacrifice my brother to get away with it.

I just hoped I would survive the fallout if I angered anyone in our small community by the sea. I did still have a shop to run, a brother who had a business that depended on tourists, and grandparents who had lived here their entire lives. Our livelihood depended on this, which just added another brick of weight to my already burdened load of questions and concerns.

After about three more minutes, I caved to the fact that I wasn't going to get anything more at the candle shop, so I left. The chatter started almost immediately. I couldn't hear it, but when I lifted my phone to supposedly check for any messages, I actually turned the camera on selfie mode. And so I watched all the women flock back together, and the moving mouths were hard to miss, even from behind my back and over my shoulder. I had never wished so much to be a fly.

Glancing at the time on my phone, I found I had about thirty minutes until my lunch with Jeannie at the diner and not much idea what to do in the meantime. Opening the store for such a short time would be a waste. Even though manning my own cash register had been high on my priority list this morning, it wasn't now.

I had a list of shops I wanted to go in to see if they had any info, but I didn't want to be late in meeting my source of hopefully some good places to look.

I considered wandering back down to the dock to see if there were any clues that had drifted up to shore.

Instead I decided to call the local airport to find out if the owner knew anything about Nick.

"Hey, Buckey," I said when it was answered by the owner of the hangar Nick used at the island's only airfield, Airport in the Sky, and not the actual owner of the airport. I'd probably get better information out of this guy anyway, so I was glad he had answered.

"Hey, Whit." His gruff voice came over the line a little muffled. He was probably up to his ears in some engine, fiddling with things I would never understand. "I hear there's some trouble brewing down there. What the heck is going on? Is it true that Jules is gone?"

I guess I shouldn't have been so surprised that not everyone knew the details about the death yet. For a small town, we all had our own cliques that people belonged to, and the local newspaper wasn't exactly one that ran on a daily basis. Add to that not everyone used social media, and I highly doubted a death on Catalina Island would have made national news, especially since at this point it only looked suspicious and would most likely be listed as a drowning until the police knew otherwise for certain. Drownings happened, just not after being strangled with a designer tie.

"Yes, he's gone. I'm trying to save my brother's rear end from jail but he's not being cooperative. He doesn't happen to be there, does he? He's not home and not answering his phone."

"Nope, sorry. Haven't seen him since yesterday when he was ready to take off for Murrieta, but then he stopped in the middle of the flight check after a phone call."

"A phone call? Do you know who called him?" Maybe it was why he was unaccounted for and why he hadn't left even though he had the whole trip set up weeks in advance.

"No, again, sorry. But he did look livid when he left, like someone had stolen his favorite wrench."

"Dang. Well, if you see him, can you tell him I'm looking for him? And please don't let him leave in his plane if he tries to fly out."

There was a beat of silence and then Buckey cleared his throat. "Uh, why is that?"

He hadn't agreed to stop Nick. That could be an issue. I tried to convey the importance to him without demanding his compliance. "Because the police think he was the one who killed Jules, and he doesn't have an alibi that he'll tell me about." I said it matter-of-factly, but it made me want to spit nails. Especially when Nick knew he was potentially in trouble and yet wasn't doing anything to help himself.

Buckey threw the brakes on my runaway thinking train. "Well, then, Whit, I can't make any promises. If the man thinks he's going to be taken in for something he didn't do and wants to run, I'm the last person to stop him."

"What? Why do you say that?"

He laughed derisively. Or at least that was how it sounded as it became more muffled. "Gotta go, but I promise to let him know you want to talk with him if I see him. It's the best I can do."

And then he hung up and I was left to stare at the phone in my hand. Was no one without their secrets?

I was going to have to go back out into the shops and see what I could get from the ones on my list. And now I might add the question of who knew what Buckey had done to make him more likely to help someone escape instead of turning him in.

I thunked my head against a wall. This was going to be harder than I thought. And I still had to have lunch with Jeannie, who wanted me to find another person to blame her information on.

Time to get my food on and my amateur sleuth hat out. I could do this!

Quite frankly, I had to.

Pulling up a chair at the Cozy Diner's outdoor table, I waited for Jeannie to show. I had no idea what I expected to hear from her, nor what I'd say if she had information that pointed to Nick having done the deed.

I wished my brother would call, or check in, or something. Not knowing where he was or if he was safe was driving me crazy.

Sophia came by the tall table where I was trying to find the right place for my feet on the barstool. Too low and my legs felt like they were dangling. Too high and I felt like my knees were in my armpits. The trials of a short girl.

"What are you drinking today, Whit? Do you want a Buffalo Milk? Mark's making them with a little extra jump today, apparently."

When she smiled at me, I found myself wondering if there was something behind that smile. Was she thinking Nick did it and felt sorry for me? Was she wondering how soon she could tell all her friends that the sister of the chief suspect was sitting at her table right now, and that if I didn't give a big enough tip she'd tell everyone that the bad seeds ran in the family?

I was being ridiculous. She wasn't thinking any of those things. This thing was making me crazy and it had barely begun.

"It's a little early for a Buffalo Milk." The drink was an islander's twist on your normal Mudslide. In the 1920s, a film had been produced here with bison supposedly and they'd been left behind when the movie had ended. People often mistook buffalo for bison and vice versa but they were definitely different animals. However, the name of the drink had stuck and no one did much more than smirk if they knew it wasn't technically right. No one knew for sure, but the herd was over a century old and the population was monitored but never completely removed. They were fun to watch and we had a ton of things on the island related to them, including the drink. But if Mark was pouring it out today, then that meant I might be too wobbly to even ask the right questions after a few sips. "How about a seltzer with lemon?"

"I'd think you'd want something a little stronger with all the trouble going on." She put a coaster down on the table in front of me before taking out her order pad.

I worked hard not to read anything more into her words than sympathy. "So you heard about Nick?"

"Uh, no." She backed up and stared at me. "I heard about Goldy. She's in a jail cell down at the station for throwing a stapler at one of our illustrious deputies."

My stars, when was it going to end? I jumped up from the table just as Jeannie was making her way across the patio.

"Forget the seltzer, and please let Jeannie know I'll pay for whatever she's having. I need to go." I ran along the concrete in front of the many shops in the harbor and made quick work of finding my autoette. Except I was boxed in by three bikes and a stroller.

Tennis shoes, don't fail me now.

Despite having told Maribel that we didn't run, I was capable of doing short distances in an emergency. I just didn't like emergencies. And I certainly wasn't on board with my grandmother being in jail. I stopped myself short on thinking about what else could happen to make this day worse. Just in time for my shoelace to snap, causing me to stumble on the paving stones and head face-first to the sand.

Chapter 8

A strong set of hands caught me just before I made impact. I looked up once I caught my breath, and sure enough it was Felix.

"Are you stalking me?" I halfheartedly accused.

Of course, he just laughed. "I can still let you drop the rest of the way if that would make you feel better. At least it won't be quite as far as you were aiming for when you started to fall."

I closed my eyes on his grin, and he lifted me into a standing position. "You don't happen to have a spare shoelace, do you?"

After patting his pockets and checking the bottom of his shoes, he shook his head. "Sorry, not one of the standard-issue items that comes with being a sworn police diver. I can put in a request for the future, though, in case I run across another situation."

I groaned in mock disgust but was trying really hard to keep the laughter from bubbling up from my throat and out of my mouth. Maybe I was finally at my breaking point and any second now I'd laugh like a loon as they carted me off.

Instead, I bent over to see if I could salvage my shoelace. I wasn't down for two seconds when Felix crouched down, lifted my foot, and put it on his bent knee. "If you just tie these two ends together, then it should be serviceable until you can get another."

Argh. I did not need him to fix everything, and be this nice, and try to help so much, no matter if my brother was under suspicion or my shoelace broke. I just didn't need the complications. But I had been taught to be grateful for everything, and so I said thank you quickly and turned to start walking instead of running, as had been my intention.

It was one thing for me to go after Goldy. If he didn't know about her being stuck in a jail cell, I'd rather not drag him into this portion of things. At least I was pretty sure I could handle this on my own.

"Want company?" he asked as I started walking away.

I walked backward to keep him in my sights and to make sure he didn't follow. "I think I can handle a walk on my own."

He grinned.

I cut him off before he could start in on my obvious inability to do much of anything without tripping over myself. "Despite the catastrophe you just helped me with, I really can handle this one on my own. Just going to get something to eat, and I need some time to think and have to get back to my store, so I have to be quick. If you find any clues let me know." And I left him in my proverbial dust as I turned around, hoping against hope he wouldn't follow.

And he didn't. When I turned the next corner, I chanced a glance over my shoulder, and he was still standing there. That was good enough for me.

I did pick up my speed a little but didn't actually try to run again, afraid I might take another tumble and find myself in trouble without Felix there to catch me. Not that I wanted him to catch me the first time, but it had been nice to not hit the ground.

I sighed because I knew where this was going to lead me. I hadn't wanted to give up on Felix. I really hadn't. But inside, there had just been something that made me very aware I shouldn't ask someone to pick up their whole life and follow me without knowing if it was forever.

It was one thing to dangle dreamy guys and a slower, laid-back pace to Maribel to get her to uproot her whole life. She and I had been friends for years, since I'd moved to Murrieta in high school and met her in the choir room. We had even planned on opening a dance club together when we were out of high school and naming it something outrageous. But even though we didn't get to that point, we'd lived together on and off since college. Her coming with me had kind of been something I'd counted on. Felix not so much, and now I didn't know what to do with him here.

I reminded myself there would be time to shoo him home once this was all over. Right now, I needed him, no matter how much that rubbed me the wrong way.

Entering the police station for the third time in a twenty-four-hour period felt weird, but at least this time Maribel should be here and maybe she could tell me something helpful.

Except she wasn't at her desk when I walked into the air-conditioned station. In fact, no one was at the desk. Since calling the emergency line hadn't worked in my favor last time, I decided to sit and wait in the lobby until someone noticed me. I grabbed a cup of water from the dispenser and then took a seat.

At this point I had spent more time hanging out in the lobby of the police station than I had at my own home in the last two days. I briefly thought of Whiskers as I sat there, turning a cup of water around and around in my hands.

It wasn't two minutes later that Pops joined me out front. He didn't say much for the first few minutes, just sat next to me with his hands gripped between his knees.

"Heck of a day," I finally said, leaning my shoulder into his.

"You could say that." He chuckled. "You know, you don't have to be here. I'm sure they're going to let Goldy out any time now, and it's not hurting her to cool those heels of hers in an office in the back."

I sat up straighter, almost spilling my cup of water. After bobbling the thing until Pops calmly took it from my hands, I stared at him. "Wait. What? I thought she was in a cell."

Shaking his head, he patted my knee. "No, not a cell. Who told you that? They just asked her to sit in the lounge at the back to calm herself down. They didn't even put her in an interrogation room. She'll be fine. And you have things to do."

I blew out a breath. "Yeah, like find the real killer, and my brother, and make up for skipping out on lunch with Jeannie from the candle store. She thinks she's got some information that might help."

Pops patted my knee again. "See, look at you doing all the hard work. Go ahead and go. I promise not to let them beat your grandmother with a surfboard. She'll be fine, and I don't have anything else going on today until you sell more of those maps." He nudged me. "Go ahead."

I really did not want to leave him here alone. Just in case something else untoward happened. It seemed to be the week for untoward things. "But I don't think I should go."

"Honey, I'll be fine."

Just as I rose to go find Jeannie, Goldy came sauntering out of the back with a bottle of lemonade in her hand and a smile as wide as the ocean. "Look at my welcoming committee. Who knew I'd need to be escorted out of the police station one fine day? I can mark that off my bucket list, at least."

Heaven help me, she looked proud of herself. Pops didn't help matters by chuckling at her. "Whit was worried they might have locked you up."

"Oh, the stapler didn't even come close to anyone. I winged it near the floor like I was skipping a rock on the water's surface." Her smile widened, though I wasn't sure that would have been possible a few seconds ago. "It did get their attention, though, and some answers. Let's go before they decide to take me up on my offer to show them how to do their jobs." And she literally skipped out the front door. In heels. Smiling all the way.

What had I ever done to deserve all this?

Ten minutes later, we walked along the shoreline with Goldy hooking one arm around Pops's elbow and her other around mine. We sidestepped the beach volleyball, then praised a small girl's sandcastle before we broached the figurative whale on the beach of her bad behavior.

She, of course, preempted us, per usual.

"So, should I allow you two to get the scolding out of the way before we get down to the information we now have, or should we just concede that I know you want to scold me and move right along?"

When she put it like that, how was I supposed to stay mad at her?

"I'm willing to concede if Pops is," I said, shuffling along through the sand in my bare feet with my shoes dangling from my fingers.

"After I say one thing." Pops pulled us to a halt. "You were magnificent in there, my girl." And he kissed her on the nose.

One was bad enough, but two who were going against the very law I was trying to protect my brother from was not helping my case.

"You both are incorrigible. How am I supposed to stay in the good graces of the sheriff's department long enough to get Nick off the hook if I'm also trying to keep the two of you under control?"

"Loosen up, my darling." Goldy tipped my chin up and kissed me on the cheek. "Nothing bad is going to happen. We'll figure this out, and it will all be fine. You worry too much."

"Yeah, well, you don't worry enough," I grumbled.

"Oh, believe me, we worry plenty, and we both know this is nowhere near over, but in the meantime, we have to keep on our toes." Pops started up walking again, and I was left to be dragged behind along the sand when I didn't pick up my feet fast enough.

"Now," Goldy said. "It appears there was an altercation with Jules earlier in the week, and your brother was involved. They haven't gotten along well in recent months, ever since Nick took over the business to be exact, but I doubt it had anything to do with that. It's possible I'm wrong, though. It's something to look into, anyway." She held Pops's hand and waved to one of her roasting buddies on the shoreline. "I really need to get some rays in today. Whit, you'll take over from here, right? I have the utmost faith that you'll be able to make sure everything gets sorted out."

I wasn't sure what to say since I didn't have any confidence in anything right now, but they left before I could formulate words.

Okay then, on my own. Maybe I could still catch Jeannie at lunch.

I didn't find Jeannie, but I was left with a big bill. She must have decided to go all out when she realized she wasn't going to have to pay for her food. I ordered the cheapest thing for takeout and finally entered my gift shop around four, for the first time that day. I loved every inch of the Dame of the Sea. From the shelves filled with local goods to the beachy-themed displays, I had set each piece exactly where I thought it showed the best to sell. I had blankets and pottery and knickknacks and pirate stuff, as well as shells and paintings. And it all sparkled in my eyes because it was something I'd built.

Waking up my computer, I surfed the web to see what, if anything, was being said about the murder. We didn't exactly make headlines here on the island, but we did have a small private group on social media to talk about things happening on-island.

Seeing so many people asking where Nick was, and how he could do this to them, was not the way to make my day go any better. I never should have looked. I wished we could go back to talking about the series of burglaries that had been happening in the hills, but when I tried to ask for an update there, I was questioned on why I wasn't out looking for Nick. So I did just that after putting a CLOSED sign up at the shop. No one had come in anyway and my full grand opening wasn't for another month, so it wasn't that huge of a loss.

Forty minutes later, I'd covered most of the town and back-streets and still found nothing.

Finally, I moved forward in my quest to hit up the shop owners around me for gossip. Stopping at Jeannie's shop yielded me a CLOSED sign, forcing me to move on.

The next two shops, a clothing store for island wear and another for sundries, didn't yield any more information than the first several, though I did get a lot of head nodding and promises that if the owners came across anything, they'd be happy to pass it on.

Wandering back to my gift shop, I used my key to enter through the front door. I found a note from Lacey Cavanaugh that she'd stopped by with her pottery and she'd be back later since I hadn't been here. Dang it! I'd missed her and that was bad for business. As much as I wanted to find Nick, and the real murderer, I had to remember I didn't want to have to rebuild everything once I did find both.

I called Lacey and left a message as I watched people walk by my shop but not stop in.

I would have sworn there would be people who wanted to get the gossip from the one who found the dead body, but I guess all the focus was on the one the police thought had killed him.

The one I still couldn't find. I checked in with Goldy and Pops, but they hadn't heard from him either. Even though we lived on a small island, so much of it was undeveloped, to the point where Nick could be anywhere, including off island if he'd hopped a boat.

As I went around the shelves and checked for stock, I scribbled a note to call Carol Bledmont—who made tiny house scenes in half shells—and another to myself to make sure I had more logic puzzles on hand. I was almost out, which was awesome, but I should have planned that better because they weren't exactly easy to make.

I watched traffic out front for a bit as I stood in my store, trying to go over any and all information I had. Unfortunately, the more I thought about it, the less I could say for certain what had happened.

I had no proof it wasn't Nick. I just knew it in my gut, and I trusted my gut. After things had gone topsy-turvy on the mainland, it had led me to walk away from my lucrative career and use the money I'd saved for my master's degree to open this shop. It would steer me true now.

But then I came back to the fact that while I didn't have proof Nick hadn't done Jules in, I also didn't have proof it was him either. But since he wouldn't tell me why he hadn't flown to Murrieta and where he was at the time instead, I was left wondering. And wondering could get me into some serious trouble.

At last a pair of tourists came in with their sun hats and their shopping bags. I wanted to add to those shopping bags on their arms. I had all manner of things from handcrafted pottery to hand-sewn clothes and hand-knitted afghans and shawls. I also carried doodads and knickknacks for those looking for less-expensive souvenirs to take home from the trip to the island. And books—don't forget the books people loved to buy to read on the beach. And the maps that kids enjoyed so much. I should be flourishing, and I would be just as soon as Nick checked in and we found the real murderer.

"How are you ladies today?" I asked after they had browsed for a few minutes. I wasn't a big believer in coming in like a shark for the sale; I much preferred the more subtle approach.

"Oh, wonderful, your shop is so pretty. Do you make all of this?" The woman who answered had red hair and fair skin that had gone lobster on her shoulders and arms. So obviously her wide-brimmed hat was maybe her only concession to protection against the blazing sun.

"I don't make it all, but it's all made here on the island." I pointed out the necklaces that Patty Moran made up on the hill from shells she found on the beach, and to the blankets old Mrs. Yoder spent hours making. Mrs. Yoder only asked me for the cost of the yarn back. I had been adamant it wasn't enough. She'd been just as adamant that she wouldn't sell for more. I'd finally convinced her not to undersell herself at some point and she let me sell them for what they were worth.

The other woman, a blonde with a bronze glow to her skin that looked more like pre-beach tanning bed than real sun exposure, picked up a hand-thrown bowl and turned it over in her hands. "J.S.?"

"Jerralyn Schmidt. She sells on the mainland too, in San Pedro and an art gallery in Los Angeles. She gives us her not-so-perfect pieces and a portion of the sales goes to charity."

"Hmm." She put the bowl back on the shelf and moved on.

"We're looking for more gimmicky pieces," the redhead said. "I have to send something to the nieces and nephews and wanted more than just a reusable shopping bag or something like that."

"How about a postcard?" Those I had made especially for the store from a man who took thousands of pictures a day. You rarely saw Dennis Decatur without that camera up to his eye, an old, vintage-model Nikon. He'd even take shots of people when he was talking to them. No one seemed to mind and he was amazing at what he did, so most people let him do his thing.

"Oh, postcards work!" They both came to the counter as I brought out the shoebox of various cards in plastic sleeves. Dennis did work that really should hang in a gallery too, but he had no desire for fame and rarely even let me tell people who he was. He much preferred to remain nameless and faceless behind that camera of his.

I left them to pick out what they wanted and looked at messages on my phone. I was glad I had when I saw the text from Goldy. She and Pops needed to talk to me as soon as possible.

Just as I finished reading the message, she came streaming up with her high heels and her trailing chiffon see-through shawl. No matter how old she got, she would always outshine and outdress me, but I'd made my peace with that years ago.

She wooshed in the front door. "Sweetheart, how's it going here? Have you managed to find out anything to clear your brother's name from this horrible murder?"

My eyes widened until I thought they might fall out of my head. "Goldy! Maybe not in front of the customers." The two women looked like tourists, and it was possible they had not yet heard of the fiasco.

Sure enough, they both put down the postcards they were holding and turned toward my grandmother. "Murder?" the redhead asked.

"Oh, yes, terrible stuff, although they haven't completely

ruled out suicide, from what I've heard. Although I can't imagine that Jules Tisdale would have taken off his toupee before he took his own life. The man had way too much vanity to be caught without that hairpiece. If you want my opinion, I bet he'd rather have been caught with his pants down than have people know he was actually bald as a baby's bottom."

"Wait, did you say Jules is dead?" the blonde said.

And then she fainted dead away.

Chapter 9

Goldy might have had skyscraper heels on, but she could also maneuver in them like a pro. Much like Felix had done for me, Goldy caught the woman about ten inches from the floor and lowered her gently the rest of the way to the wide-planked wood. I grabbed a blanket from the shelf, promising myself I'd pay for it out of my own money if something happened to it.

The redhead looked baffled and fell to her knees next to her friend. "Sheila? Sheila! What's wrong with you?" She slapped her on the face, but I didn't think that was actually going to work.

Or at least I would have thought as much if Sheila hadn't come up off the floor, sputtering and swinging.

"What is wrong with you, Jasmine? No one slaps someone who fainted anymore. You're a nurse, for pity's sake. Do you slap your patients when they fall?"

Gone was the pleasant demeanor and the soft voice, the smile along with it. But then she seemed to remember they were not alone and buried her face in her hands. "I'm sorry for snapping, so sorry, I just felt scared when I woke on the hard floor."

Goldy and I looked at each other, puzzled by what the heck had just happened. To be honest, at what was still happening as

Sheila rose from the floor with the afghan in her hand. "This is lovely and so soft. I think I'm going to get this as my own souvenir. What do you think, Jasmine? I bet it would look wonderful on that new couch Dave got me for our wedding."

From what I could tell Jasmine wasn't any more in the know than we were, but she played along better.

"Sure thing. I'm thinking it will look wonderful with the sand-colored couch." She looked into her friend's eyes. "Are you sure you're okay? You really took a tumble, and even though this lovely woman saved you from hitting the floor, maybe you hurt yourself?"

"Oh, that fainting? No, no, it's fine. I think my blood sugar is just low." She laughed, a breezy sound that was probably supposed to whisk everything away in a gush of warmth and care-free frivolity. She turned to me with the blanket in hand. "Do you have a delivery service? We're staying on the island and my hands are so full with bags, but I'd love to have this blanket. Would it be possible to have it delivered to the hotel?"

I didn't have delivery service, but she was already handing over her credit card without even checking the price tag, so I wasn't going to fight her. I could run the thing up to whatever hotel they were in myself.

"If I could get your signature and the hotel you're staying in?" I said.

"Fine, fine. It's the Waterman Mansion and we'll be there through Monday."

"We'll have it there by tonight. So, did you know Jules?" I asked.

"We should get something to eat and then head over to the spa, Jasmine." She acted as if she hadn't even heard me. "We have a lot to do before the wedding!"

Wedding, spa, the mansion? Well, at least I could find them again if I wanted to know why this Sheila had fainted at the mention of Jules's death. And why she was actively avoiding my question about how she knew him.

Maybe I'd just found my first real suspect and one the police could look at instead of my brother. I wasn't ruling out Jules's wife, Tracy, just yet, but this woman might be more viable.

Goldy and I watched the two women walk out of the gift shop. For ten seconds, we didn't move, and we didn't speak to each other about what had just happened on the floor at our feet.

"Okay, so is it just me, or does that bear looking into?" I asked as the door swung shut behind the ladies. Sheila appeared to be scurrying while Jasmine did everything she could to keep up with her friend.

"I think the police should look into it, but I don't know if they will." Goldy shrugged her elegantly clad shoulders. "I mean, what are you going to say, 'Some woman fainted in my shop when she heard there was a murder on the island and then she bought a blanket. I think you should look into her alibi'?"

I couldn't help myself, I laughed. At least I tried to muffle it with my hand. Once I got myself under control, I took Goldy in from head to toe. "Good save, there. I really thought she was about to hit the floor. Our insurance surely didn't need that kind of noise."

"I haven't always been arm candy, I'll have you know." And she laughed a full-gut laugh that made her teeter on her heels.

I hooked arms with her and laughed too. "I am fully aware of that, Goldy." But then I sobered up. "This is going to be rough. I'm totally going to dig into anyone and everyone's past that I have to. There has to be a way to find out who would have wanted Jules deader than Nick would have. I didn't even know they had issues with each other until you said something."

Goldy took my hands in hers. "Sweetie, they had quite a few run-ins. I know you aren't going to want to believe it, but the police do have a right to be suspicious of your brother. I know it's not him too," she said when I opened my mouth to protest, "but they're just doing their job. We're going to have to give them a better suspect than Nick, though."

I bit my top lip.

"Don't do that, dear, it makes you look like a bull dog," Goldy said absently as she looked out the front window. Sheila and her friend were no longer visible, so I wasn't sure what she was looking at, but maybe it would give her some idea of a direction to go. I'd take whatever I could get at this point since I was running low on ideas of where to start and how to get people to tell me what I needed to know.

She kissed me on the cheek. "Go out and use your charm, take your proverbial shovel with you and let's get to the bottom of this thing. Whether Nick could have done it or not is not the issue. The issue is who would have actually done it instead of just threatening the guy." She nodded her head as if agreeing with herself. "Okay, you have your marching orders. Go do the thing, and I'll hold down the shop. You have an hour until my ideal sun-sitting time will be gone, and I need to get my vitamin D in today."

"You're going to end up with skin cancer." I poked her about that often, but I actually was truly concerned that it would happen. She'd always been a bit of a sun worshipper, but this everyday thing was going to have some consequences.

"You just worry about you and clearing your brother's name. We have too much stake in this island to have our reputation sullied." With that she literally shoved me out of my own shop and closed the door behind me. When I turned back to her with a look of dismay on my face, she simply waved at me, then flapped her hands for me to move along.

Marching orders indeed!

But she probably wouldn't let me back in until she decided I'd done a good day's work, or until my hour was up and she headed to the beach to bathe in the sun.

Okay, then. I hitched up my shorts, straightened my cap-sleeved shirt, and decided where to go first. Turning in a full circle, my gaze landed on the ice cream shop to my left. Garry Templeton, owner of the Daily Scoop, was always good for a big old helping of the local gossip to go along with his glorious cones of homemade ice cream and delish toppings.

I sidestepped three bicyclists and a whole host of walkers to make it to his shop. Where the air was hot outside, the inside of the ice cream shop was frigid in a refreshing way. Of course, there was a line. I figured if I was going to try to press for information I might want to go ahead and order a cone to make it worth his time. Yeah, I was going with that logic even though I still hadn't eaten today.

As I waited, I listened to the chatter running through the store. Few people were talking about the murder, and of course those who were stood too far away for me to catch anything but every third or fourth word in their hushed conversations. Especially when overlaid by children bargaining with their parents about having three scoops instead of one. One young teenager even took it as far as saying that since they were on vacation, it only made sense to let go of the rules for sugar intake.

Smart girl, and I liked her thinking, but I really wished I could hear what Erica Braden was saying over in the corner near the toppings.

"Whitney! How's it going?" Garry's face shone with so much happiness and contentment that he could probably light up a whole town in the right circumstances. He'd moved here about twenty years ago and had nestled himself right into the culture and the vibe of this place.

"I've had better days. Thanks for asking, though."

A slight frown marred his brow. "They're not giving you trouble about that unfortunate incident on your boat, are they?"

By *they* I assumed he meant the police, but I also wanted to address the fact that the murder hadn't happened on my boat, or even under it, but the aftermath had definitely been a big surprise.

"He wasn't onboard so much as under sea. I don't know what happened, but they've got Nick in for questioning, and it doesn't look like they're going to try to look for anyone else. I'm worried."

He reached across the counter and squeezed my hand. "It was just a little fight. I don't know why everyone is making such a big fuss about it. So Nick punched him in the mouth and he fell in the water. I would have too if he'd said horrible things about my family. One can only be expected to take so much before one lashes out, you get me?"

Hold the phone, were we talking about the same thing? "But that doesn't mean he killed Jules."

"What? Jules is dead?" The clang of metal against metal made me peek through the glass to see Garry's hand open and his trusty ice cream scoop spinning on the counter in front of him. "Jessie, can you step in?"

"Dad, the line's out the door," his young daughter complained, but Garry was already at the end of the counter and motioning for me to follow him.

I wished I'd gotten my ice cream before saying anything. My mouth had started watering for the creamy treat when I saw chocolate peanut butter ripple was on the menu today. But I couldn't pass up the chance to hear whatever the ice cream shop owner might know or share.

In the end, I gave in to my desire to know more rather than my desire to eat. I could always come back for the ice cream. I splayed my hand over the glass and whispered a goodbye as I walked away from my place in line without the sugary goodness.

I sighed when I got outside behind the store and stood with Garry. He chuckled, the evil man. "I'll get you a cone of the Choc PB when we're finished. I have an in at the shop, if you don't remember, and can get it for you without a problem. I could even add an extra scoop, if you're so inclined."

Well then, I was all ears. "Did you not hear the news from last night?" I asked, knowing it was a redundant question, but I just wanted to clarify to get the conversation rolling.

"No, I had no idea Jules was dead. How bizarre. We just talked the other day about some . . . business things."

I opened my mouth to jump on that but he steamrolled right over me.

"I can't believe he's not here anymore. He wasn't my favorite person, and honestly I don't know who votes for that Person of the Year thing with the Chamber of Commerce, but I don't know many who would have voted for him even if he was the only person on the ballot."

"I—" But he had more to say.

"I could have sworn he took all precautions, but I guess he didn't. Did you say they think Nick did it?" Garry leaned up against the wall with his hands in the pockets of his knee-length, dark green shorts.

"If by *they* you mean the police, then yes they do." I thought it best to clarify because I felt like we had been talking at cross purposes since we'd started this conversation, back when all I could think about was a cone of ice cream and clearing my brother's name. And what did he mean by precautions?

"Of course I mean the police, girl." He cupped his chin with his hand. "There have to be more viable suspects than Nick. I mean, come on, he's not the only one who's had a kerfuffle with that man in the recent past."

"Kerfuffle, I like that word."

"Word a Day—look it up, good site and something fun to do while I'm waiting for the cream to freeze." Then he frowned. "There has to be someone else. Unless your brother accidentally killed him? Maybe he thought he'd just hit him again and instead didn't realize he killed him. Where was he found?"

So much information and so many questions and theories all at once. This would have been much easier if my brain was going through brain freeze while I tried to follow along with the mazes in Garry's mind. But I tried, even without the shot of ice cream. "Why do you keep saying Nick hit Jules? I didn't hear anything about that."

Garry whipped his gaze to mine and clamped his lips shut.

"No, don't go silent now. What's going on? When did this happen, and why did it happen?" And how bad must this look to the police? No wonder they were gunning for Nick.

"I don't have all the details . . ."

"But you saw it."

"No, I only heard about it."

Hearsay or not, third-hand account or not, I wanted to hear this newest story. "Then just give me the ones you do have." I crossed my arms over my flowery top and waited in the rising heat of the day.

He whistled one low tone. "All right, here's what I know, but I can't tell you how I heard it. So don't ask."

I crunched my arms closer. I was going to want to ask, of course I was. I had to know all the details, but if I wouldn't get any info because I'd asked and made him tell me nothing, then I'd be worse off. "Fine, but I reserve the right to revisit this and ask again at a later date."

"And I might give you the same answer, but at this point, this is what I know for certain." He lowered his voice and leaned in to my space. "Your brother and Jules had it out because Jules was supposed to invest some money in Nautically Yours so Nick could get another boat without having to get a loan. Instead Jules decided to go behind Nick's back and have his own cruiser built and start a new arm of his own company so that his wife's nephew, or cousin, or something could come work over here and have a business all set up and ready to make some serious money. They're launching in ten days, but I guess that might be put off now that he's gone."

"What? Why don't I know about any of this? How could he go behind my back like that? We've been doing fine, and I have money to invest if he wanted to expand our business." Shock and irritation and complete bafflement ran over me.

Garry shrugged. "Not sure what to tell you, darling. But when Nick found out, he went after Jules pretty hard core. I think he took out a tooth or two."

Well, no wonder the police weren't moving away from pinning this on my brother. I was having some doubts that they didn't have the right person myself.

This was not good. What were Goldy and Pops going to say?

Wait, wait, wait, I needed to bring it back and find only facts. And facts started with Nick.

So the real question was what was Nick going to say for himself, and had he already said it to the police? More importantly, where on the blessed island of Catalina was the fool?

After that Garry wouldn't say anything more. I grabbed myself a double scoop of my favorite ice cream and snagged a root beer float for Jeannie. She was next on my list. But first I needed to cool off.

I called Nick's cell phone in hopes that maybe this time he'd pick up. When he didn't, I left a scathing message. "Nick Brentwood Dagner, you'd better call me back right now. I do not have the time or the inclination to play games with you. I'm trying to help you, which means you have to give me all the information, not hit people and make deals behind my back. Please call. Please."

As far as messages went, I thought it was pretty succinct, but it made me sick to my stomach, especially since it was the fifth time I'd called him and the fifth message I'd left him. And no one had seen him since he'd left the police station and I'd dropped him off at home last night. Had he gone in and then promptly come back out and run away?

How was I supposed to help him when I was completely in the dark, like all the lights off, underground, and covered-by-a-blanket dark?

I'd figure it out. No matter what happened, I'd figure it out.

That settled my stomach a little. Nick and I had talked on and off for months about me moving out here and starting my own gift shop. Maybe the fight and the backstabbing were before I made the solid commitment and quit my corporate job for a gift shop at the ocean. I suppose that would make a certain kind of sense, but I would have thought Nick still would have said something last night when I was frantically trying to figure out why the police would even think for a second that he was the killer.

And now he wasn't answering his phone, and I hadn't found anyone who had seen him despite my treks into almost every store on Crescent Avenue. Where was he?

Without running around the island on my golf cart I was not going to get any answers. Obviously my threats on his voice mail were not moving him to actually call me back, and I had about twenty minutes before I had to go back to the gift shop. In the meantime, having finished my ice cream cone, I was going to check in with Jeannie in hopes that whatever she had to offer me was worth a filet mignon and scallops topped with crab and a margarita for lunch.

Add the root beer float in my hand and she had better have something not only good but outstandingly incredible.

When I opened the door to the candle store, the scent of magnolias and smoke overwhelmed me. Jeannie had a huge pillar of a candle burning in the center of the store. A cloud of candle smoke hung in the air above my head, all the way up to the ceiling. Who knew I would ever be thankful for being short?

Setting the root beer float on the ground, I still had to duck under the cloud and then wave my free hand in the air to clear it enough to see what was going on. It couldn't just be that candle, though I did snuff it out, just in case. I couldn't imagine anyone would buy it unless it was supposed to be an outdoor candle, but then why was Jeannie burning it in the store? More smoke billowed from somewhere else but I couldn't pinpoint where.

"Jeannie! Jeannie!" I had reached yelling by the second time I called out to her, but I heard nothing and saw no movement in the store. "Jeannie!"

Still nothing. I put the root beer float down on the counter and braced myself to go have a look around for any new issues.

It didn't take me long to find her as she was humming to herself in the back of the store as if nothing was wrong and she hadn't heard me come in.

"Uh, you have a smoke issue up front." I tapped her on the shoulder when she didn't respond.

When she jumped, screamed, and turned around, it was obvious why she'd heard nothing but not why she hadn't smelled the mess up front. She had earbuds in. Seriously, how were you supposed to run a store by yourself and listen for customers if you were rocking out to your music? Even I knew that, and I was still pretty new at this whole store thing.

"You scared the heck out of me!" Her hands shook as she smoothed her graying hair back.

"While I'm sorry about that, I'm not sorry that I stopped in. You have a smoke issue up front you might want to take a look at."

She stared at me but didn't move.

"Seriously. Smoke. Lots of it. Out front. *Now* would be a good time to go." When she still didn't move, I dragged her behind me.

"Oh my gosh!" She ran around flapping her hands above her head and doing nothing but moving the smoke around.

Heaving a sigh, I opened the front door of the store, then went to the back again and snagged a fan I'd seen when I'd gone hunting for her. After I set it up to draw the smoke out, I moved her along through the door and to the sidewalk.

"You have your cell phone?" I asked.

She patted herself down, then shook her head.

At least this time I could talk with the fire department instead of the police department. I placed the call and gave the details. I didn't see an actual fire but this was an island and fire and smoke were not taken lightly.

They arrived within minutes, but they didn't find anything on fire, just the smoke and no idea where it was coming from. To say I was baffled was an understatement. How had smoke gotten in the store without a fire?

Stepping up to Mike McGrath, one of the firefighters, I pulled him aside. "I don't know if this will help, but that candle was lit when I came in and throwing off some smoke, but maybe not enough to have caused all this." The top half of Jeannie's store was black and sooty now, and it would take a lot of elbow grease to get it back up and running, especially with the smell.

"Thanks." Mike called a couple of guys over and they started looking lower and put the candle in a plastic bag. For what, I wasn't sure, but they probably knew and just weren't sharing it with me. Not that they had to, but my curiosity was definitely running rampant.

"And you say you didn't see or hear anything?" Chris Jennings, the leader of the squad, asked Jeannie as I walked over to them.

"No, I didn't."

"She had earbuds in, though."

Jeannie's face creased. "I did, but that's because I'd closed for the day. How did you get in, anyway, Whitney?"

Everyone stared at me to the point where I took a step back. "The door was open."

"But I had locked it." The frown on her face deepened into a scowl. "Is this because I got the most expensive thing on the menu?"

If this weren't so serious, I would have laughed. "No, Jeannie. I was happy to pay for whatever you wanted to eat, but I'd still like to talk to you. I swear to you that the door was unlocked and slightly ajar when I came in to find you. The candle was lit and throwing off some serious smoke. How long ago did you close the store?"

"Well, I never opened it again after I had lunch. That was hours ago."

"And how long ago did you light the candle?"

"Good question, Whit." Chris stood to my left in full gear, looking every inch the complete fireman package. Why couldn't I have fallen for someone like him?

Jeannie dropped her head and rubbed the back of her neck. When she raised her gaze again, there were tears in her eyes. "Only about twenty minutes ago. Do you think this is because I was going to talk to you, Whit? Maybe someone overheard me say I had information, and this was their way to silence me?"

The tears flowed in earnest now. I moved in to put an arm over her shoulders. She turned into me, and I held on to her and caught the look on Chris's face.

"I don't know, Jeannie. I'm sure we can get this sorted out, though."

"Hey, Chief." Another firefighter came in from the back. "We got a rag stuck in the vents and some kind of machine pumping smoke into another vent."

"Excuse me, ladies." Chris followed behind the other firefighter, leaving me with Jeannie.

"Why don't we sit over there on the bench?" I took her shaking hand in mine and led her across the sidewalk.

"Do you think this is because I wanted to talk to you?" Her voice shook as much as her hands.

"I don't know, Jeannie. Honestly, I don't know much right now at all, but if you can tell me what you wanted to tell me before, I'd really appreciate it." I was willing to beg if I had to.

She took a deep breath and then let it out. "Tracy came by this morning and told me she wanted to buy my shop now that she has money. I was going to just brush it off as a ridiculous offer since she's asked to buy it before and never followed through. Jules always told her he needed her at home, and he had helped me out several times financially. He knew how much this store means to me. But this changes my mind. Do you think she's trying to smoke me out?"

That thought had definitely crossed my mind. Should I be worried too, since Tracy had said she wanted to buy my store on the cruise before her husband died?

"I don't know," I said. "But if she's the one who killed him, I guarantee I'm going to catch her and hand her over trussed up in the biggest black bow I can find in my store."

Jeannie laughed sadly. "She's wily. Be careful of her. She seems to not have a thought of her own, but honestly I think she's just been waiting for him to die so she can live the life she says she's always wanted to lead."

Tracy Tisdale was so going to the top of my list. Now I just had to find her and get her to confess.

Chapter 10

After checking in with my grandparents, who were at dinner, I was out of sorts and not sure what came next. I wanted to find Tracy and confront her, but what was I going to say? And I had only suspicions to go with, not any facts. It was possible she was just taking advantage of the situation.

And if I laid all my cards on the table now and she got spooked, she could go back to L.A. and be out of my grasp.

But how to get information without seeming like I was coming for her?

I hustled back to my store and went out back to get my autoette. I hadn't had time to tell anyone about that customer Sheila yet, but I didn't want to face the police for the fourth time in such a small span. While I was considering how to confront Tracy, I could deliver the blanket. Perhaps I could find out more information, so I had a more complete picture to present to the police when I felt up to facing them again.

The Waterman Mansion was one of the most beautiful places on the island. Surrounded by lush gardens and playful fountains, it was situated up on a cliff overlooking the harbor. It had the best views and the prices to match. I'd been in and out of it a few times over the years. Especially when I was younger. Nick and I were both born in the summertime, and Goldy and Pops were big believers in celebrating birthdays.

The mansion put on a magnificent brunch and every year on each of our birthdays we'd do brunch and be treated like royalty. With my birthday coming up in two weeks, maybe I'd take myself to brunch up there. I could check into pricing as I delivered the blanket, and it would be one more legitimate reason for me to stick around after the delivery, when in reality, I was snooping around. I highly doubted the police would appreciate my interference, but at this point I was beyond caring.

If Tracy had a hand in that smoking-out of Jeannie, I would go after that next. First, I had to find out what Sheila knew, and if it fed into the reason Jules was now at the morgue.

Since we had so few cars on the island, the front of the mansion was not a big arching driveway but a broad footpath that began at a shallow pool and ended at the cliffside. I parked my autoette in the small paved parking area around the side at the service entrance and grabbed the blanket. I'd stopped at the store to wrap it in a beautiful sheer pink bow and put a little gift tag on it with my business card attached.

With the heat, the blanket was like a heating pad on my arm. I kept switching sides so I didn't sweat on the thing. My interaction with Sheila earlier had been strange enough, but to buy a blanket in the beginning of July was even stranger. I was pretty sure she had just been avoiding any questions about how she knew Jules and why the thought of him being gone had caused her to faint.

I opened one of the massive front doors and was hit by a wave of air-conditioning that was downright frigid. Not the nice shift in temperature of the ice cream shop at all. More like an arctic blast. My first thought was that their electric bill was going to be horrendous. Especially when I knew that most times they just kept the big windows open to let the balmy breeze through to keep things cool.

Yolanda, the front desk clerk, stood at her post in a sweater with a steaming cup at her elbow. I couldn't say for certain, but it looked like there was a slightly blue tinge to her lips.

My teeth had started to chatter by the time I made it to the huge teak desk set in the middle of an expensive rug. "What the heck, Yolanda? It's freezing in here. Why don't you turn down the air-conditioning instead of wearing a sweater?"

Her gaze darted to the left and the right before settling back on my face. "Keep it down, Whit. I'm doing the best I can with the restrictions of our current guests." She kept her voice down to an almost whisper. I could have sworn I saw a curl of breath escape into a fine mist in the air. Much like the time I went to Big Bear in the mountains above San Bernardino and it was so cold I could see my breath.

"Your guests want it this cold? Where are they from? Alaska? The North Pole?"

She snickered. A door opened to the left, and she cut off her laughter abruptly by pressing her mouth into a smile. A statuesque brunette walked through the lobby without glancing our way at all.

"Good afternoon, Priscilla," Yolanda said with the smile firmly in place.

The front desk manager glanced over and nodded, then continued across the floor. I got the feeling I shouldn't try to talk again until Yolanda's boss was gone.

As soon as she opened the door to the management office and then slammed it behind her, Yolanda released a big breath. "This is right up there with the worst week of my life."

"What's the deal?"

"We have very specific instructions on who to talk to and who to avoid. What temperature to keep the whole building and when things can be done. I'm exhausted. So exhausted."

"No doubt. Is Sheila one of the people you aren't allowed to talk to? I forget her last name, but she's blond? Has sort of a tanning bed bronze glow?" I held up the blanket. "She bought this at my store earlier and then let me know I could have it delivered. Since I don't have delivery service, I thought I'd run it up myself."

"Oh, that one." Yolanda rolled her eyes. "Sheila Graystone. She's probably the nicest one out of the bunch, and that's not saying a lot. She bought a blanket? She's the one who wants the whole hotel at subzero degrees. Maybe she should buy us all blankets."

Another door opened and then closed. Yolanda straightened at her post, but no one came through the lobby.

"I'd better go check to see if anyone needs anything. You can leave the blanket up here. I'll get it to her room."

"Uh, she asked me to deliver it to her." Not entirely true, but since I was here I thought it might be a good idea to see if there were any clues I could glean. Maybe a snippet of conversation or catching a murderer red-handed. I'd take either, to be honest.

"Are you sure?"

I fidgeted but fortunately it was out of Yolanda's view. "Positive. If you could just tell me which room she's in, I'll drop it off and be on my way."

Another door to the right opened and slammed shut and then yelling started.

"I have to go take care of whatever is going on. They don't pay me enough for this. She's in room 122. She should be there." And then she left me to my own devices.

I absolutely could have just chickened out, leaving the blanket up front. But her fainting kept playing itself over and over again in my head, and I felt it was significant to follow up on before taking any suspicions to the police. They were going to automatically think that anything I gave them would just be in an effort to throw suspicion on anyone but Nick, so I had to make sure it wasn't a wild-goose chase before I said something.

Concrete details would be my best friend. Maribel would understand if she were replaced just for the next little while.

So I walked around to the left, away from the yelling that I could hear but not decipher any of the individual words. Part of me wanted to see what the issue was, just in case it might have something to do with the murder, but it could be nothing, and the blanket delivery was at least something I knew might net me an idea or two.

Making my way down the hall past priceless antiques and art that cost more than I used to make in a year, I walked softly along the runner as I counted doors.

Finally I arrived at 122. All was silent, and I was sorely disappointed that I couldn't hear anything through the door. Though now that I thought about it, I wasn't sure what I had been expecting to happen. Sheila railing at the injustice of a man being killed? Admitting she knew why, or how, it had happened in front of anyone who might be walking by her room?

I was so not suited for this whole clue-finding thing.

Maybe I should have researched her online. I had her credit card information from the purchase. I could have at least looked into who she was before I started trying to get her to talk to me.

I was just about to knock on the door when a guy in a tank top and running shorts threw it open, standing in the doorway with his back to the hallway. Quickly looking around for somewhere to hide, I saw a column to my left and hoped that my decision to forego that third scoop of ice cream would pay off by making me thin enough to not be noticed.

"I don't know what you want from me, Sheila. I gave you all this and everything you wanted for the last two years. I thought you'd finally gotten over that jerk, yet it's obvious from your sobbing that you haven't. I'm thinking we should call off the wedding until you figure out what you want."

The wailing in response to that was so loud I wondered if the rooms were soundproofed. I'd heard nothing even with my ear up against the door.

"When you're ready to talk, let me know. I can understand still loving someone after all that time you spent with him, but I can't understand why you can't tell me you aren't *still* in love with him. I'm going to the beach for a run. Hopefully when I get back you'll have some answers that make sense."

The guy stalked out into the hallway. I sucked in my stomach just in case it made me more invisible behind the column.

He didn't even glance my way until after he'd passed me. Then he looked back. "We need more towels and tissues when you have time. And if you could see if there's an extra room that I can have my things moved into, I would appreciate it."

He stalked off without closing the door. Obviously sucking in my stomach had not made me invisible, but I hadn't realized I looked like the help around here. Instead of trying to explain that I wasn't the one to talk to, I simply nodded, and he started his jog right there in the hallway, aiming for the veranda and continuing down a path that I knew wound down to the sea.

So the question now was, did I try to hand the blanket to Sheila and see if she'd talk to me in her grief and say something that would help me? Or did I just go back to the front desk, drop the blanket off with Yolanda, and then look Sheila up before I tried to talk to her again?

It felt like it would be a missed opportunity to walk away without at least attempting to talk with her. But then it also felt horrible to intrude on what sounded like a breaking heart. In the end, I just couldn't do it and bent again to put the blanket up against the wall.

I felt more than saw a presence above me.

"Oh, the blanket that I bought. Thank you, thank you so much. When did it get here?" She scooped it up and held it against her face like it was an old favorite that brought her comfort.

"I finally had time to run it up to you. Sorry it took so long." I shrugged and tried not to stare at how ravaged her face was from her obvious crying jag.

She rubbed her cheek against the fabric over and over again. "I can't thank you enough. I will treasure this forever."

"Okay." I should have had something prepared to say. Some question to ask her to get her talking with me, but I had nothing. "If there's anything else you need, just let me know."

She sniffed and used the edge of the very expensive blanket to dab at her tears. "No, I think you've done enough. I wish I'd known that you'd have to bring it up yourself. I'm sorry for assuming you had a courier or someone to run it up for you."

"That's okay." I felt horrible for this woman who looked so incredibly distraught, like her whole world was falling apart. And maybe it was. "If there's anything I can do, please don't hesitate to let me know." I didn't really know what I thought I could do, but it seemed like the right thing to say in this situation.

"Actually, would you mind running up front and telling management that we might have a few changes to make? I'm going to go lie down, but I should be up in a few hours." She unwrapped the blanket from my bow and then wrapped it around her neck like a shawl. "At least I have this now. My last memory of a man who changed my life."

It was a perfect opening to ask her about Jules again.

"Was Jules that important to you?" I asked. I tried to soften my voice to make it more that I was asking in sympathy than on a fact-finding mission. I wasn't sure if I'd taken the right tack until she fell into my arms, blanket and all, and the wailing started again.

Now what was I supposed to do? I wished Goldy were here, or even Maribel. They both had experience with comforting people. I wouldn't say I was bad at it, just awkward and not the one people normally came to. I'd get life stories and information I didn't need, but rarely things that came with crying.

So I did the only thing I could think of. I patted this woman on the back and tried to channel my best friend while I murmured all the words I could think of that had to do with being sorry.

"He just was so special," she said, then hiccupped. "I thought we'd be together forever, and then he got married and things fell apart."

Another young one Jules had made promises to? I remembered when Tracy had told me she was marrying Jules a few years ago when I was here visiting Goldy and Pops. Tracy had been very verbal about his proposal and all the things he promised her. I had been skeptical, especially since she'd been drinking at the bar and not really telling me so much as telling the entire restaurant in a really loud voice that I just overheard. But if he'd made the same promises here and then had gone on to marry Tracy instead, wouldn't Sheila be less upset about Jules getting what he deserved for playing with hearts?

"I'm going to miss him so much. We had so much fun together."

I cut her off before she could start wailing again. "Was he your boyfriend?"

That got me a watery chuckle. "Jules? A boyfriend? Oh, heavens no. He was my godfather, and then that horrible woman

stepped in and told him that he wasn't allowed to talk to me anymore. She was so jealous of anyone she thought would take his
attention away from her."

"Are you talking about Tracy?"

"Yes, that's her name." Her head snapped up and her eyes
blazed. "I bet you she was the one who killed him. My brides-
maid, Ariel, said she saw Jules two days ago and reminded him
how they used to play the card game War, and how he'd always
cheat. They laughed and laughed. He used to cheat all the time.
But his wife was not amused. She told Ariel to back off, that he
wasn't interested in reminiscing with anyone but Tracy."

"Was he Ariel's godfather too?" The more I learned the more
I realized how little I knew.

"Oh, no, he was her sugar daddy until he married Tracy. She
didn't realize there's really no sugar and most of what he had was
all built on his reputation and his credit. He had more debt than
anyone I know." She laughed derisively. "I hope Tracy's ready
for the bill collectors to come knock on her door. I almost wish
I'd be there to see it." She sounded like she'd relish the prospect,
but now I was confused.

"But the guy who walked out just said that he was okay
with you having loved someone but not still being in love with
someone."

"Were you eavesdropping?" She pulled back from me and
hugged the blanket like it was a barrier between her and the world.

"Uh, it was hard not to hear him with how loud he was talking when I walked down the hallway." I hoped desperately that
she'd buy that excuse.

"Okay, I'll have to tell him to be quieter with his accusations. I'm sure I'll have time to do that once he gets back from
his run. He's always better after he runs."

"He requested to be moved to another room."

She just laughed. "Oh, he does that all the time. He'll settle down once we're married."

I highly doubted that, but never having been married I didn't feel like I had any experience to give. "So you're going to get married even with his anger. What about the person you're still in love with?"

She narrowed her eyes and suspicion radiated off her like the scent of dead fish on the beach. "You *were* eavesdropping."

"No, really, just walking down the hall." I held up my hands like that would prove my innocence. Not that I was actually innocent, but if it got me answers . . .

"Are you sure?"

I felt bad lying to her, but I had to if I wanted answers. "Absolutely."

She didn't entirely look like she believed me. Thankfully, she talked anyway. "The man I'm in love with is dead. It doesn't matter if I'm still in love with him, and Dave knows that. He's just nervous about tying the knot and so he's testing me every time I turn around."

"Then what was the crying about?" Since anyone in the whole hotel could have heard her wailing once the door was open, I didn't think I would get called on eavesdropping again.

"That's a whole different story." She backed into the room, beckoning me to follow. I took two steps into the suite as she settled onto a couch and curled her feet up under her. "Jules was going to walk me down the aisle. I don't know what to do now that he's gone. I'm without someone to give me away."

"Oh." In other words, a total and complete dead end. Now what was I going to do? Escape was the first thing that came to mind, but now that Sheila had started talking, she wasn't going to let me go until she was done.

"Jules was a wonderful godfather, always giving me things I wanted before I'd even said anything. Always so generous. His wife not so much, but then she was jealous of our relationship. She couldn't stand that he'd bought me a car and wouldn't get her a new golf cart for the island. And when he bought me a diamond pendant, she wanted a bigger one. She didn't get it." A little smile played across her lips, and I wondered if anything she said was actually the truth. Was she really in love with a previously dead man or a freshly killed one? Was Jules just her godfather? Were they one and the same and she was playing me?

I just couldn't tell. "Well, I should get back to my shop. I hope you'll love that blanket. It's handmade and very well-crafted."

She tossed it aside and it slid to the floor as she got up. "I'm sure it will be fine. Thanks for bringing it by. If you see Dave on your way out, tell him I'm ready to take him back. Also, he's not getting another room. There aren't any left, anyway." That tiny smile grew into something a little broader, a little more sinister, and all I wanted to do was run.

"I probably won't see him." I backed toward the door, desperate to get out now.

"But if you do." She clasped her hands under her chin and it looked like she was trying to be innocent as she batted her long eyelashes.

"Yes, if I do, I'll let him know."

"Oh, thank you so much! And maybe if I have time, I'll come down to your shop again. It might be the perfect place to get all my bridesmaids' gifts. I'm sure they'd love something from your store."

Well, I certainly wasn't going to turn down business as I was just getting started, but I almost didn't want her to come in. There was an underlying vibe there that I just wasn't feeling good about. She'd started out seeming innocent and nice, but that edge was showing more and more as we talked. Much like the difference between before the fainting and after her friend, Jasmine, had slapped her in the face.

Instead of saying anything else, I waved goodbye and stepped out the door, pulling it closed behind me.

And I almost walked smack into Dave, who'd either ran like the Flash or hadn't gone far. He was also the one who'd run and who she said would come back. She hadn't been lying about him, but that didn't mean she was telling the truth about everything else.

Chapter 11

"How is she?" Dave rocked back and forth with his hands shoved in his pockets and then took them out to cross his arms, then uncrossed them and stuck his hands back in his pockets. Nervous much? But why?

I had to tread carefully here. I had no idea what the right response was. "I'm sure it's fine." That was innocuous enough while not saying much yet still answering his question. Kind of. "Excuse me. I have to get back to my store."

"Wait! What do you sell? Maybe I should buy something so she'll forgive me for being a jerk."

I honestly did not feel he owed her anything, but again I wasn't going to turn down business. "I sell art and baubles that are beach-themed."

"Can you pick something out for me and bring it back up here? I don't think I should go in until I have an offering of peace."

I barely kept myself from groaning in disgust. He really hadn't done anything wrong that I had heard. To be honest, I'd be just as frustrated if I were marrying someone who played emotional games at the level Sheila hinted at being able to play at. What kind of start to a life together was that?

"There were a few things she was looking at when she was down there earlier. I can pick one of them and send it up."

"Send them all. She'll like anything that is an apology from me. That makes her happy."

"I can only send the things that she looked at before she fainted."

"She fainted? Was she okay? Did she fall to the floor? What happened?" After taking his hands out of his pockets, he rolled them over and over each other.

"My grandmother saved her before she hit the floor. Sheila said it was low blood sugar, but it was right after I said Jules had been killed." I was fishing for a reaction and finally got one.

Those hands that had been rolling over each other, clasping and unclasping in nerves, now fisted in anger and his ears were tipped in red. "Jules."

"Yes, Jules. Did you two know him?" He had no idea what Sheila and I had talked about previously. Here was an opportunity to find out if she'd been lying. I was totally taking it.

"I knew him by sight and by deed, though we'd never met, but he'd been stringing Sheila along for years, promising her all kinds of things if she'd wait for him. And then when he married someone else, she finally came back to me."

"I'd heard he was her godfather."

He burst out into quiet laughter. "Of course you did. I'm thinking she told you that. Did she also tell you she was going to let him walk her down the aisle?"

"Uh yes."

"That's just great. She's ridiculous. I'm going to get another room. I'm guessing you don't work here so my request was not communicated to the right people when I left." He looked me up and down.

I remembered the shirt I was wearing and the clam diggers

and compared them mentally to the more upscale outfits the women and men wore here on staff. "No, I was just delivering a blanket."

"A blanket? Seriously? She's the one who wants it at subzero and now she wants a blanket?" He squeezed his fists until his knuckles turned white.

"Why don't I walk with you up to the front desk? I'm sure there's someone who can move your stuff to another room."

"Let's go. I'm also calling off this wedding and going back to the mainland. Do you happen to know anyone who has a plane? I need to get away before I do something stupid like change my mind again. I'm done."

Yikes. I so did not want to be in the middle of this. "I can give you the number for the airport, but I don't have anyone in particular to recommend for flying you back." I could have given him Nick's name if my brother wasn't hiding.

"I'm sure they can figure something out for me up front." He shrugged and I wondered for the first time how old all of these people were and how they had the money to not only have a wedding at the mansion but also stay here for some length of time. Who'd paid for that? Especially if Sheila was going to have her godfather, Jules, walk her down the aisle. It made me think no parents were in the picture for her.

It wasn't really my business. My business was to find out who killed Jules and hand them over to the police so Nick could come out of hiding. I highly doubted it was Sheila who'd put Jules in the water, since that meant her income stream would be cut off. Even more so if Tracy inherited and was in control of all the funds.

I walked with Dave to the front desk, then approached Yolanda. She raised an eyebrow at me.

"Dave would like to get a ride back to the mainland," I said when he stood there in awkward silence.

"He's not going anywhere until he pays me back all the money my husband spent on this farce of a wedding." Tracy Tisdale stood in the wide-open front door with thunderclouds behind her in the sky and an equally angry storm flashing in her eyes. I involuntarily took a step back. I found I wasn't the only one as all three of us shied away like she was going to bite.

"I'm leaving and you can't stop me." Dave brought those fists out again and balled them at his side. "I didn't ask for any of this in the first place. You want money? You talk to Jules's darling, Sheila. And while you're at it, let her know it's over and I'm out." He turned to Yolanda. "Just pack up my things and ship them to me. You have my address. I don't need this noise, anyway."

And he stormed off with the three of us watching him walk away.

Which then left Yolanda and me to awkwardly avoid looking at each other while Tracy growled as he tried and failed to slam the French doors behind him. He tried again and the left one bounced, then he tried again and the right one swung open, almost smacking him in the nose.

Tracy laughed when he stomped off down the path, and then she turned to Yolanda with no awkwardness at all. "What room is she in? And don't tell me you can't divulge that information. I won't believe it, and if you don't tell me, I'm just going to go around yelling her name until she comes out to face me once and for all."

While I had always thought Tracy was nice if a little vapid, there was absolutely no vapidity here. She was fierce and forceful, and I didn't want to leave before I saw what would go down between her and Sheila.

I almost felt like I should get some popcorn.

And then Sheila came trailing the blanket behind her along

the floor. She was humming to herself while smiling. "Did Dave get back yet? I thought I heard his voice. Didn't you tell him to come in and tell me he was sorry for being stupid?" she asked me, apparently either not seeing Tracy or ignoring her. Either one did not sit well with Tracy. A door behind us opened as Tracy went for Sheila, with her hands clawed and a growl erupting from her mouth.

"Not here, Tracy," a familiar voice said quietly from the doorway two seconds before Tracy would have made contact with Sheila.

It was as if time froze. Everyone stopped, even Tracy. We all turned to the man silhouetted in the doorway. The sun shone behind him and almost blinded me. There were no more clouds in the sky. I couldn't tell who he was for certain until he stepped in closer, but I knew that voice, and I was going to be the one with my claws out and howling if it was who I thought it was.

Tracy ran for the man and fell against him. "We need to go. I'll deal with this later. Take me away, Nick. Please." The imploring gaze she sent his way made my stomach turn while confirming my worst fears. What the heck was going on?

My stomach might have been turning but not enough to cut my voice off. "Don't you go anywhere, Nick. The police have a warrant out for you. You need to turn yourself in."

Saying nothing in return, he and Tracy whisked out the door and then slammed it behind them. When I tried to open it to follow them, they'd made it impossible. Looking out the window next to the door, I saw a chair wedged under the doorknob.

"Where's the nearest exit?" I barked at Yolanda, who really didn't need to be barked at. She pointed a finger to the right and picked up the phone with her other hand.

"I sure hope you're calling the cops. Tell them where we are and get them on Nick's tail. I don't know what the heck he's doing, but this is ridiculous." I took off to the right. It was the service entrance that led right out to my autoette. Jumping in, I cranked the tiny engine over then zipped into reverse. I didn't care where they went or how they got there, I was going to find my brother, and I was going to give him a dressing down like he'd never heard before. And then I was going to drag him to the police.

But first I had to find him.

I pulled to the end of the pavement and sat for a moment. No one was in sight in either direction, but to the left there was only the cliff a few hundred feet away. To the right was the way down to town. I figured I had a better chance to the right and took the turn, not sure if I was going in the correct direction but unwilling to just sit there and do nothing.

I had complete faith that Yolanda would have already called the cops and maybe I'd meet them on the way down to the harbor, or wherever I found the unlikely couple.

But fifteen minutes later, I hadn't seen the cops and I definitely had lost any trail on Nick. I sat at the dock with my arms crossed over my steering wheel, staring out at the sea. I hadn't just lost them, I hadn't seen a single trace of them, and now I'd have to keep looking for the real killer, even as my brother romped around with the widow.

Why was he with her? How did they know each other?

As the breeze ruffled my short hair, I ran back through our summers. I had known Tracy but Nick had his own friends, and I'd had mine. I didn't remember Tracy and Nick ever meeting.

Had he found her, or had she found him? Why did she think he was going to save her? Why *had* he saved her?

That stomach churning happened again, and I took a few deep breaths to calm myself.

Even if I felt like an idiot, I knew I was still going to look for the real killer. It couldn't be Nick, no matter what the circumstances. A small doubt in the back of my mind bloomed. "Go away!" I told it, not realizing that I was not alone on the strand.

"I know I might not be your favorite person right now, but I'm thinking I don't deserve that."

Squinting, I looked up to find Felix sitting in the passenger side of the autoette. I closed my eyes, dropped my head, and drew another of those deep breaths. How long would Felix believe that Nick hadn't had anything to do with Jules's death if I told him that my brother was apparently the widow's knight in tarnished armor?

"I already heard. It's the talk around the station." He rested a hand on the back of my bowed neck and massaged. Despite my best intentions, I leaned into that touch and blew out the breath I'd been holding.

"What is he doing?" I asked of no one in particular.

"I have no clue, but we'll figure it out." He gave one final squeeze and then let go. "Do you want to grab something to eat, and we'll talk about it?"

I wasn't sure that was such a great idea. If people saw me out with a guy on the island the rumors would start flying. And Pops would want to have that talk with Felix about his intentions a lot sooner than I was ready for. "I have to get home. I don't know what else I can do down here, and you pretty much know everything I do." That wasn't the whole truth, but I didn't even know where to start with the things I didn't know, and what I did know was miniscule compared to what I wanted to know. Namely who had killed Jules, and how my brother was connected to Tracy.

"I have info to share too, if you'll give me a little time. I don't know if out here on the beach is the best place."

"And you think a restaurant would be better?" I asked, chuckling in disbelief. "I doubt it. Everyone who knows about the death is looking for the gossip, and anyone who doesn't is just going to get in my way."

"But I heard you were asking questions this afternoon. Get any answers?"

I sighed. "Other than the fact that everyone seems to owe Jules money in some way, and Tracy is not nearly as soft as I thought she was, I don't have much more." My phone pinged, and I excused myself to look at the screen. It was Maribel asking me what we were eating, along with when I was coming home.

I totally forgot that today was her day off. We always hung out if we didn't have other plans. I quickly let her know I'd figure something out, and I'd be home soon.

A thought struck me, one I hesitated over. I didn't know if it was my most brilliant one or would turn out to be the worst one yet.

I blurted it out before I could stop myself. "Why don't you grab a pizza and come to the house? I need to hug my cat, and Maribel is home. Maybe if we pool our information we can fill in some gaps for each other."

At least that way I wouldn't be alone with him, and we wouldn't stray too far off the topic of what to do about this murderer.

Because, the more I sat next to him, the more I remembered that he'd been the best guy I'd ever had the chance to meet. I did not want to start berating myself for walking away from him, as he seemed to think I did. I also didn't want to clutter up my clear focus on Nick and what the heck he was up to.

He smiled, which made me pretty sure he'd gotten the message that this would not be "us" time. It would be working time. He was either on board or not.

"Still like that pineapple-and-ham thing?" he asked.

That surprised a laugh out of me. I appreciated it more than

I was willing to say. "That was only one time and no, I learned my lesson. Pepperoni is fine for everyone. Meet us in a half hour." I gave him my address and then he jumped out of the passenger side.

"See you soon."

"Yeah," I said, but inside I was hoping I had not just opened myself up to something I wasn't really prepared to handle.

Chapter 12

"Okay, so when he gets here, don't mention anything about us having dated before." I moved Whiskers from the small couch we had in the living room to her bed in the corner. She was not happy about being moved until I laid her toy in the bed with her, and then she still gave me the stink eye but stayed where I'd put her.

"Really?" Maribel scoffed. "We've met at the station a few times. Now that I know who he is, how am I not supposed to mention the connection? And while we're on the subject, why didn't I know about him in the first place? I thought we shared all our secrets."

Oh man, I did not have time for a pouty Maribel. With how fast Marco put out pizza from his brick oven of yumminess, Felix could be here any minute. I needed her on board with not talking about dating and not giving me lip that I hadn't told her. "Can we talk about this later? I just wasn't ready to talk about it and then it was over, so it wasn't a big deal." I fixed the pillow on the oversized chair for the fifth time, and she put her hands over mine.

"I'm not going to chase you for this one right now. But just know that there will be talking, even if it has to involve wine. And that talking will be about why I never heard about this one, and how he seems to be making you nervous just because he's coming over with pizza."

I gave her a quick hug in appreciation, then promised we'd talk later just as the doorbell rang.

Patting myself down, I checked to make sure everything was where it was supposed to be and then ran my tongue over my teeth. I should not be this nervous but I was, so I just made peace with it and moved on.

When I took too long answering the door, Maribel rolled her eyes and opened it herself.

"Come on in, and please tell me that's pepperoni." She laughed so easily. I wished I could do the same.

Instead, Felix felt bigger in the house than he had outside it. I was going to have to get over this issue until we found my brother. I'd just have to let Felix help like he said he would. I was not some teenager in junior high hoping to get asked for the last dance, for goodness' sake!

I grabbed napkins from the breakfast counter Maribel and I had set up instead of a dining table and brought them into the living room. In the meantime, Felix had opened up our two TV trays and then sat on the floor to eat at the coffee table.

I barely stopped myself from making him use a tray. He could eat wherever he wanted, and we had important things to do, not play musical eating spots.

He'd even thought to bring paper plates and napkins and handed them out, making my napkins from the breakfast counter unneeded. Why had I left him again? Right, I wasn't thinking about that.

We each took two slices and settled in. I figured I should probably lead off the conversation since I was the one who had the most at stake here, but I wasn't sure where to start.

"The department hasn't been able to find your brother yet, Whit," Maribel said between bites and hums of appreciation. "Thanks for bringing this up, Felix. It's delish. I don't know why I didn't know about you before now, unless you were too close to Whitney's emotional wall and she got scared. Just my two cents."

I almost choked on my slice and had to hold my hand up when they both came at me to pat my back.

I got my breath back finally. "I'm okay, no worries. And as to your statement . . ." They both looked at me expectantly. "I figured they haven't found my brother yet since I haven't gotten a call to come bail him out."

Felix chuckled and Maribel rolled her eyes. Fine by me as long as we didn't go back to the forbidden topic.

"Now we need a plan," I said. "Who's got info? I have some but I don't know how it all fits in with everything." I took another bite of my pizza, then waited for someone else to say something. Whiskers chose that moment to come over from her bed to bat at the cheese hanging from my pizza. She meowed loudly as I pushed her away.

"We're doing important things," I told her. Of course she didn't care. She curled up in my lap, probably waiting for the next drippy piece of cheese.

"I can't talk about much, Whit," Maribel answered. "I don't want to lose my job, but I will tell you that they've at least started looking at some other people. It seems Tracy's been a little busy since her husband died, and I don't mean grieving."

"I heard she was over at the ice cream shop demanding that the owner pay her back the money that Jules loaned out." Felix leaned back on one arm and crossed his legs under the table.

"That's what he was talking about," I said. "I need paper."

Conveniently, Maribel reached behind her to grab my tablet

off the bookshelf we'd put there for our board games, books, and a couple of candles. "You need electronics for this, not paper. That way you can share it with us instead of having to make copies."

"But—"

"Look, girl, if you think you're going to be the only one looking into this, and the only one who needs to have it at your fingertips, then you are completely wrong. I never got to finish that forensic degree and so I took the next best thing, working at the front desk. But I want in on this. You're not going to keep me out in the cold."

Felix took his phone off the end table and swiped his finger across the screen. "And if we use a doc program then we can all just add things in and make connections that we might not see with one of those notebooks stuffed with notes."

His excitement flowed through the room. What had I gotten myself into? We weren't exactly in one of those case-cracking mystery shows I loved to watch on television when I had time, especially since one of us actually worked at the department, the other one only helped, and me, well, I was the epitome of amateur.

What would we do if we actually did figure this out?

I'd worry about that once it happened.

"Okay, so using a computer program is the best method, I guess. Do you think we'll get in trouble? Should we use code words?"

Maribel had the gall to laugh. "Absolutely not. I have a hard enough time remembering my passwords to things I have to access every day. I am absolutely not going to figure out a secret language."

"We could use Ye Olde English," Felix said. "Isn't that what you studied in college?"

"As a minor," I mumbled.

"Oh yes, those were the days." Maribel leaned back and chuckled. "Our girl Whit here dives right into whatever she sets her mind to. You should have seen her when she was reading Shakespeare. I couldn't get her out of this ruffled collar one time. It got knotted around her throat, and we couldn't cut it because it was part of the theater department's props. So she had to walk around with it on for the whole day until we could borrow a screwdriver to wedge the knot open."

Felix looked at me with a huge smile, his white teeth gleaming in his tanned face, and I felt the blush rush over my face.

"I would have loved to see that," he said.

"But not hear it," Maribel went on. "You should have heard some of the language this girl was using but it was all Olde English and insults that Shakespeare had used in his books. It was hysterical."

I laughed even though I wanted to use that ruffled collar on Maribel right now. But that wasn't going to get us any closer to the murderer, so I put it aside. "Let's get back to why we're here." I said it despite my blush and the way my voice wanted to tremble. "I saw Tracy today at the mansion." I filled them in on the bill Jules had allowed the bride to rack up, how he was supposed to have walked her down the aisle, and the fury with which Tracy had come in. I tried to gloss over the way my brother had whisked her out the door, but in the end I couldn't.

Not if I wanted to solve this.

"She called out for my brother to save her, and I'm assuming he did. I wasn't able to find either of them when I jumped in my autoette. As far as I know he still doesn't have one—unless he's driving hers?" It came out more as a question because at this point I really did not know what to think.

Maribel flicked me in the arm. "Don't even worry about

how this is going to end up. Your brother might even be mixed up with this, but I can't imagine he actually killed Jules. I wouldn't pass up looking at Tracy, though. I heard she's already talked to the lawyer and is trying to get the estate closed as soon as possible. Jules set it up here instead of in L.A."

"It's probably easier here to do certain things, and those lawyers on the mainland can charge an arm and a leg." Felix switched arms to lean on. I wanted to offer him a spot on the couch, but there wasn't enough room for all three of us.

"Okay, so she might be stuck here until that's settled, and Nick can't leave unless he tries to take off in the plane. Which he shouldn't be allowed to do," I said.

"They've already locked it down." Maribel picked a pepperoni off her pizza. "It's literally locked in a hangar. Buckey has very clear and strict orders to not let Nick off the island, or he'll be charged as an accessory." She popped the pepperoni into her mouth and smiled.

"But will he actually listen?" I asked. "He seemed to have something in his background that would make him help Nick if he wanted to get off island." I told them about my conversation with him.

"That's something to think about." Felix got himself another piece of pizza and so did I. I could eat just as much as he did if I wanted to. I wasn't out to impress anyone. I still took a smaller piece, just in case. But then he plopped the biggest piece on my plate as he chuckled.

"Go ahead and eat it. I asked them to cut one side bigger since I know how you like to fold your pizza in half."

We'd only eaten pizza once together. Apparently that had made an impression on him.

I shrugged, took my pizza, and sat back down. I would not think about how that comment from him made me feel.

We got down to eating and I wished for just a second that this was not a night trying to investigate a murder but a night simply hanging with the people who were important to me. Of course Nick would be here too, but now I wasn't sure how much I really knew him. Maybe we'd grown apart over the years with him here and me in Long Beach. Maybe I hadn't considered that he might have strayed that far from the path.

I gulped the last bite, trying not to choke. Gathering my courage, I balled a napkin in my hand and went for broke. "Do we all still believe Nick didn't do this?" I held up my hand as they both started to speak. "If you don't know, or don't want to offend me, please just be honest, and go from your gut. I'm having my own doubts, so I am not going to be upset if you two do also."

There, I'd said it, and no matter how much it made the pizza want to come back up, I couldn't ignore the fact that Nick could very well have done this. Maybe by accident, maybe on purpose, maybe for the widow, if they were together in some way. But I couldn't drag Maribel into something that might make her lose her job, and Felix too, if they didn't really believe that my brother was innocent.

Maribel took my hand. After a second, Felix took the other. I didn't pull away from either of them.

"I don't believe Nick did this," Maribel said first. "We might not yet know what happened, and we might find that he knows more than he's sharing, but I really don't believe he was the one who killed him. I'm in for the truth, Whit, right there with you."

"What Maribel said." Felix squeezed my hand and then let go. "It's just a little too convenient that he's the one everyone is pointing the finger at so quickly. As outsiders I think we have a better chance of getting to the bottom of this because you don't have all that red tape to get through."

With the hand Maribel wasn't holding, I took a gulp of the

iced tea at my elbow. "We need a plan, then. I don't think I'm covering enough good ground by just going around and asking everyone to either divulge their secrets or hoping I hear something I shouldn't. I also don't really know where to go next, so . . . a plan."

"A plan." Felix leaned back on his hand again and crossed his legs. "How about if we divide and conquer? I heard that there might be one of Jules's old rivals on the island, and you keep hearing about how everyone seems to owe Jules money. We also need to look at the widow and hopefully find Nick. So who wants to do what?"

"I can probably go by La Fluencia, the spa that Tracy uses all the time, and see what gossip I might be able to gather. I thought she was the quiet one, just in it for the sugar daddy, but seeing her in action today makes me think that perhaps she's more than I considered. And if she had to tell someone her stories, I bet you anything it's a masseuse or a hairdresser. I know most of the people in both of those positions. Conveniently enough, Goldy has been bothering me to use the gift certificate she gave me, so that's as good an excuse as any." Again I shrugged because I wasn't sure what else to do. To say I felt out of my depth was like calling the Pacific Ocean a puddle.

"I'll take the possible rival guy." Maribel keyed something into her phone. "I can do some research and then let you know what I find."

We both looked at Felix. "So I guess that leaves me with what? I don't know the people around here. They're not going to tell me about any money they owed to Jules."

"Why don't you see what the guys at the station are talking about? Go in and just do some locker talk. It can't hurt. Oh, and I'll give you a list of people to do some research on." I wasn't sure what else to give him, but I appreciated that he wanted to help.

And I was incredibly grateful they were both still on board, despite the facts that seemed to be presenting themselves.

What was I going to do if I'd been chasing other people, and it really was my brother? I couldn't go there in my mind and still be okay. Not right now. It couldn't be him. Once I got a hold of him I was going to make sure he told me why I should believe that without a single doubt.

In the meantime, we wound down the evening with more pizza and more talk. It moved to living on the island, and I was able to see that I was not wrong for asking Maribel to come with me, and also see that Felix was possibly where he belonged for the first time in his life.

"You were pretty quiet after the murder talk," Maribel said after Felix had left. We dumped the paper plates into the trash and put the soda away in the apartment-sized fridge.

I shrugged. "I enjoyed listening to the two of you. I've been worried about encouraging you to move out here with me and hearing how much you love the area makes me feel better, though this murder thing is probably not in the plus column for living here."

"Oh, please, don't even worry about that. It's never going to have the amount of crime from where we used to live. We'll figure this out and then smack your brother in the back of the head for running when helping would have been so much easier."

I wiped down the counter, even though we hadn't used it with Felix's thoughtfulness in bringing all the things we'd need to have dinner without having to wash any dishes.

"But what if we're wrong?" I said it in a small voice, mirroring what I'd been thinking earlier. I just couldn't help it. Sometimes my gut was not the most reliable, and I did not want this to be one of those times where I should have run instead of ducked.

"We're not. There has to be an explanation, and someone we

just don't know about yet. We'll get it. Don't give up just yet, Whit. What the police have is weak, but they're so used to guarding celebrities and settling little skirmishes that a murder for the first time in a long time is making them antsy. Being able to close it fast and early would make the commander happy. But we're not here to make him happy, we're here to see justice done." That last part rang through the kitchen with conviction.

I nudged her with my shoulder. "Think you might go back for that degree in criminal justice?"

She was the one who shrugged this time. "Who knows, maybe Avalon is just waiting for a Latina who can get things done."

"You'd blow their socks off."

"You know it. Now move so we can start doing some research. I think we have quite a list of players in this game. Once Felix has some insider info that I can't access from the front desk, we can make a murder board and see what connections we can make."

"I should have thought of that."

"Eh, you have other things on your mind and you're more the connector than the set-upper. That's why we work so well together."

"Well, let's not fail now, okay?"

"Never, and I'm sure your Felix will be doing his best to get some more info for you."

"He's not my Felix," I said quickly.

"Oh now, let's not start lying to each other. You know better than I do that he is, but I guess we can all just wait until you figure that out."

I left the room without answering, but it wasn't like I had far to go. We'd table that whole discussion until after this was all settled. I didn't have time to do anything but try to keep my shop running and figure out where Nick was, and then also find a murderer. Piece of cake, right?

Whiskers wound around my ankles and then rubbed her head against my calf. I reached down to pet her as I opened the web on my tablet and prepared to dig into all the things I knew and all the things I wanted to know.

I had a feeling there was far more of the latter than the former, but maybe I was about to flip the ratio.

Chapter 13

The next morning, I snuck out of the house again. Maribel and I had stayed up late into the night and had dived back into the leftover pizza about midnight. I'd gone to bed shortly after with more questions than answers, but at least we had a couple things to look into. Actually, more than a couple of things and that at least made me feel better, even if I still couldn't get a hold of my brother.

Making my way down to my gift shop, I guided the autoette around tourists and locals alike. I didn't stop to talk to anyone this time because I had to be open in an hour. I had finally gotten in touch with Lacey Cavanaugh, and I now had the wonderful local pottery maker coming in to throw bowls in the front window. I was not going to let a murder investigation that I shouldn't even be involved in stop me from keeping my promises.

Later I would go to the spa and start my focused investigation. Right now, I had my own business to mind.

Soon after I opened the door and got money put into the register, my pottery lady showed up.

"Lacey, thanks so much for agreeing to do this." I went out to her autoette and started unloading things, including a portable kiln that I'd envy if I was more craftly inclined.

"Are you kidding? This is one of my favorite things to do. I appreciate you not cancelling on me with all the drama going on in your family."

Speaking of family, Goldy picked up the next box and winked at me.

"Where'd you come from?" I asked.

"Everywhere and nowhere, my love. Let's get this going and see what we can do to help this lovely lady. Then you can tell me what you've been doing to clear your brother's name." She winked again. I wasn't sure how to take that one. Was she joking with me? Did she know something I didn't know?

I went with it, though, so that maybe I could pull her aside and ask her after we got Lacey set up.

Moving the table and wheel into the shop proved to be a little harder than I had anticipated and just for a second I wished that Felix were here to help me.

Maybe we had some kind of psychic connection, because suddenly Felix *was* there, his hand taking the wheel out of my hand. It wasn't as if I couldn't have moved it myself, but I was just over five feet tall and he was over six. I had all the muscles it took to lift my porky cat, Whiskers, up onto the couch if she was too lazy to jump up, or if I just wanted a cuddle and she chose to ignore me calling her name. Felix, on the other hand, was built like the swimmer he was and had arm muscles that reminded me of one of those modified superhero suits.

"Thanks," I said when he had everything in place. We'd moved the display at the front window to make room so that passersby could see Lacey doing her thing.

I should have been prepared for her with everything moved out of the way yesterday, but being caught up in finding a killer was leaving me behind in a lot of other things.

"Sure thing." He tucked his hands into the pockets of his shorts. Crabs played across the material of the shorts, wearing sunglasses and holding plastic sand pails.

"Nice attire." I took him in from head to toe, from the flip-flops on his feet to the shorts and up to the red T-shirt covering his chest, and then to the sunglasses resting in his dark hair.

He looked down at himself and then grinned. "I was teaching kids to swim. These are always one of the best icebreakers. They like the shorts and think my wardrobe is cool, so then that translates to also thinking I'm cool."

I nodded. "Right, and that's the only reason you wear them?"

That got a laugh. "Nah, I also think they're pretty kicking, but that's just me."

I thought they were kicking too, but I was not going to say that in front of Goldy. Next thing you knew she'd have us walking to an altar on the beach and pouring sand into a vase together to show that our essences were mingled and could never be sorted out again.

"Oh, Felix, thank you so much for all your help," Goldy gushed. "It's always nice to have a strong man around. What would we have done without you and those muscles?"

I had been smart not to compliment him on his clothes. She would have been even worse if I'd admired his shorts openly. As it was I had to intercept her hand as she went to rest it on his bicep.

"Don't you have some sunbathing to do or something? Or maybe Pops needs help with the boat?" I raised my eyebrow at her and narrowed my eyes.

She tittered like a little bird as she swatted at me. She landed a hit that was harder than it looked like it should have been. "Sweetie, if we don't thank those who help us, then what's this world coming to?"

I rolled my eyes and waited for her next move. It could be anything. I wanted to be ready for whatever that anything was.

She tucked her arm through the crook of Felix's elbow before I could step in to stop her. She pulled him along with her out of the store onto the sidewalk outside. "Whit, you stay in there and help Lacey. Felix and I have a few things to talk about. We won't be but a minute and then I'd like to talk with you."

Lacey called me over, looking for a plug for her fan, so there was nothing I could do but watch helplessly as Felix was ensnared in the Goldy net.

I sighed and went to help the other woman.

Once I had her settled, she pumped the foot pedal under her table a few times and the wheel on top began spinning. She put water on the surface and then dipped her hands into a short barrel at her side and pulled out a ball of clay.

"Any requests?" she asked.

"A vase might be nice." I looked back outside where Goldy and Felix seemed to be in a deep conversation that excluded every other person walking past them.

"A vase it is, then. And if you need to leave to save your boyfriend from your grandmother, I totally understand. I'm good to go on my own for now." Her smile was gentle so I decided not to fight her about the boyfriend thing.

He wasn't my boyfriend, and I didn't know if he ever would be again, but I certainly wasn't going to leave him in Goldy's clutches for longer than necessary. There had been a reason I hadn't asked him out to the island to meet them before now.

"So we'll do it like we agreed, then?" I caught Goldy saying right before Felix nodded and then they both turned to me with huge smiles on their faces.

"What are we agreeing to?" I asked.

"Oh, nothing, dear. Just a little business talk about the boat. Now, Lacey is in the store and hopefully that will bring people in to talk about something other than murder for right now. I'm tired of hearing the same story over and over again. I wish you'd find your brother and get his name cleared, at least."

"I saw him yesterday and clearing his name might be a little more complicated than we thought." I walked her through seeing him at the mansion and how he refused to come with me, running off with the widow.

"Oh, that is not good. He needs to stay away from her and come clear his own name. If he didn't do it, then that shouldn't be too hard."

"I'm not sure you understand quite how this works, Goldy." I placed my hand on her arm and pulled her out of the flow of traffic. Felix followed along with us like we were all tethered with the same rope.

"Of course I do. We find him, he tells us what his alibi is, we take that to the police, and they leave him alone."

"Ideally, yes, but he doesn't seem to *have* an alibi. To be frank, this all feels like a great big setup." I dropped my voice to a whisper. "Do you think maybe the widow did kill Jules and she's using Nick to be her scapegoat?"

Goldy drew back for a second, then dipped back in to our little bubble. "You know, that might just be the ticket to what we need to get Nick to confess he didn't do it." She tapped her chin with one manicured fingernail. "How can we get the inside info about that, then? Who do we ask about how things were in her marriage and if she's capable of this? We have to be certain."

"I already thought about that." Last night after I had gone to bed with way too much pizza in my stomach, I'd lain there for an hour trying out scenario after scenario, and it just made sense that if Nick thought he was protecting someone he'd do whatever it took. That was the brother I knew. Not a possible murderer, but someone who'd stick their neck out even if someone didn't deserve it.

"And what did you come up with?" Felix asked.

"I'm thinking it's very possible. She was not her usual mousy self on the boat when they came on for the cruise. She was bubbly as usual, but there was something just underlying the words coming out of her mouth. And then she said she had to get something up at the house, but she had heels on, and I hadn't seen their golf cart that I could remember at the end of the dock. They were all supposed to be dropped off as a party. So how was she going to get home in those shoes and then back to the party? And what was so important that she needed to head out that very minute?"

"Good question. Very good questions." Goldy paced away and then came back. She seemed unable to stay still. "Here's another one for you. I've been trying to remember any small detail about the day, and one of my questions would be what time did he die, and did he ever make it to the dinner at all?"

"Wow, I'd never even thought to ask that," I said, feeling a bit stupid. That should have been one of my first questions.

"You're not trained to think like that, Whit. But I am, and your grandmother is right." Felix drew us back out of the way.

I waited for the explosion at the word *grandmother*, but it never came. Maybe Goldy was so enamored with Felix that she let it slide this time. I wasn't going to be the one to correct him.

She did narrow her eyes at him without saying anything. Perhaps that was going to be the end of it.

But she also stepped right into his space and I knew she wasn't going to actually let the slip pass. "It's Goldy, not Grandma, not Grams, not Grandmother. Goldy."

Felix stepped back, probably taken off guard by her vehemence. He wasn't the first one and he probably wouldn't be the last.

"Goldy, he doesn't know the rules. I'm sure he didn't mean anything by it. We have very important things to talk about right now."

"This is also important." She harrumphed.

"Would it help if Felix apologized? Can we move on after he says he's sorry?"

I expected another harrumph and got it.

"I'm so sorry, Goldy. I had no idea how much that meant to

you. Whit and I never really talked about our families. I'm sure that would have come up if we had."

Well, that was a masterful jab in my direction. But I was going to ignore it for now because Goldy was happier. Or at least she wasn't frowning at him anymore. Now she was frowning at me.

"Can we move on?" I said.

More people were starting to congregate along the sidewalk to look at Lacey doing her work. The noise ratcheted up, which made good cover for what we were discussing, but it also made it harder to hear what everyone else was saying.

I leaned in to make sure I didn't miss anything.

"From what the mayor said, Jules showed up for a little while and then took off before Tracy got back," Felix said. "He was seen walking away with a redheaded beauty who was dressed all in black. I was told she looks like Bonnie Raitt, with a very distinctive silver stripe of hair directly over her left eyebrow."

Man, I did not know if I could handle another player. Why did they all seem to be women except Nick? And another redhead? At least this one had a silver streak, which would distinguish her from Shelia's friend, Jasmine.

"Was anyone able to find her after that night? Or do they know who she is? Why don't they think it's her instead of Nick?"

"Honestly, I just think they want it done and Nick had motive and no alibi. No one else seems to have both. I'm looking into it after my lessons, but I just thought I'd keep you up to date. And I guess help with getting a very primitive-looking pottery setup into your store." His smile melted me more than any hot day on the island. In defense, I stiffened my knees. No melting allowed.

"Okay, well, thanks. I guess let me know if you find out who she is and if she's even worth considering. I'll put the notes in the document if you haven't already."

"They're already there. I'll add to them as soon as I get some more info." With that he waved and was off.

Goldy and I both stood and watched him trot away in his flip-flops with those ridiculous crab shorts.

"You know, when I met your grandfather I had no idea he was the one," Goldy said, tucking her arm through my crooked elbow. "I held him off for months and thought there was no way he was ever going to stick around, so what was the point in setting myself up to get hurt?"

"I'm not . . ." I trailed off because I wasn't even sure what I wanted to finish that sentence with.

"You are. And as long as you don't make any definite decisions, you can continue to do so. Life is short but not so short that you shouldn't savor it just a bit before you commit to anything." She bussed me on the cheek. "Now, let's see what Lacey is throwing down and then maybe we can put our heads together over this file you say you have. I'm sure looking into this with your friends is great but don't forget the wisdom of your elders, or at least the fact that we've lived a lot longer so we've had time to make more mistakes to learn from."

As we walked back into my gift shop, I thought about what she had said. I wanted to ask for her advice on a number of things, but I also didn't want to create any waves. I'd had enough of those to last a lifetime before I'd moved here.

Lacey was holding court when we got through the front door. Business had picked up while we were talking outside and the store was full. I stationed myself behind the counter and left Goldy to work the floor.

She answered some questions, pointed things out to treasure seekers, and sent those looking for maps to me. We were a good team. Sometimes I wished I could steal her from Pops to help me out full-time. But for one thing, I couldn't afford her, and for another, I wasn't sure that I'd want her in the store every single day.

I could do this on my own. This was my chance to show myself what I was made of.

Right after I found Nick and pointed the finger at the actual killer.

I blew out a breath as one more person stepped up to the counter and asked for a map.

"Dave?" I couldn't stop myself from wondering what on earth the guy who was supposed to marry Sheila and had stormed out of the mansion early was doing in my shop asking for a treasure map.

"Oh, hey. Uh, yeah . . ."

"Whitney." I introduced myself since he seemed to be looking for my name and had never asked for it before.

"Right, right, Whitney." He looked everywhere but at my face. "So, um, I thought maybe if I did a treasure hunt for my soon-to-be bride that we could work things out."

"But I thought . . ." The fierce look on his face at my words stopped the rest of that sentence from tumbling out of my mouth. The customer was always right. Right? "Of course, I can get you a map. I can have everything ready by tomorrow afternoon if you want to do a treasure hunt."

With how many maps I'd sold today, I didn't want Pops to be running himself into the ground trying to hide all these treasures. Thank goodness he had several different spots that were standards. I had the maps all stored in a chest behind the desk but waited to hand them out until closer to the hunting time. I'd staggered the times so that he'd have the opportunity to do that and not have people crossing paths.

"Is there anything in particular you'd like at the end of the map?" I asked. If it was a parent buying for a child, I didn't ask anything more than what kind of things they liked, but for an adult there was usually some big reveal they wanted or something more specific than that the kid liked pirates.

"I have it in my room. I'll put it out there tomorrow and then we can hunt for it."

"Let me get the location. We'll go from there." I pulled up the maps on the computer and sorted through which one might work best. "Something close to the mansion?"

"Oh, well, we're not staying there anymore." There was a thump near the floor and I wondered if he'd just kicked the counter.

"Something near the harbor, then?" I desperately wanted to know where they were staying instead. It wasn't like we had discount motels around here, and with it being summer I was pretty sure everything was booked for the next few months.

"No, if you could put it out near the campground. Sheila and I are staying in a teepee until we figure something else out." His ears flamed, and I looked away so he couldn't see the way my eyes rounded with his answer.

For the woman who demanded that the air-conditioning be put on arctic, I couldn't quite see her being comfortable in a rawhide teepee with a sleeping bag and not a single comfy couch in sight.

"Near the campground it is." I tapped a few keys just to keep my eyes averted without seeming to avoid his gaze.

How was Sheila taking her move? Was it because Jules was no longer paying for their accommodations? Could Tracy do that without the will being read?

"She's not thrilled, in case you were wondering, but she feels so much better now that everything is settled. We might not have the money to have a big wedding right now, but we will soon enough. When that comes in, we'll do it up big, the way we want to, instead of at someone else's whim and want."

Now I was totally afire with questions. But I couldn't exactly ask him. Maybe I could ask Yolanda up at the mansion what she knew.

After that I couldn't get him out fast enough. I promised him the treasure would be placed by four tomorrow, then watched as he scuttled out the door.

Goldy leaned against the counter. "Pops is going to be busy this afternoon." She peeked at the computer to see the receipts. "Yikes, very busy."

"Sorry. I'm sorry. It's just that everyone kept asking. I didn't want to have to say no. I hope this is okay. I could probably help, if you don't mind hanging here for a little bit?"

"That's probably for the best. Lacey and I will hold down the fort. You go make some kids' dreams come true."

Since Whiskers hadn't been out of the house for a few days with all this investigating going on, I decided to grab her and take her with me while I delivered treasure chests to the designated spots.

The sun was high in the sky when I stopped by my house to get her. She purred and purred and went right into the harness for walks. Then she sat in her basket on the front seat of the autoette while I made my way to Goldy and Pops's house.

All the treasure chests were kept in the shed next to the house and were stocked with all manner of things. I'd kept the options pretty narrow after the first two chests so we wouldn't run the chance of not having something on hand and having to make the treasure chest before delivering it. For custom things, we usually had a two-day wait to make sure it was truly special. Same thing for anything that had to be brought in from the mainland.

But for these, the kids mostly just wanted to find something, anything. From plastic baubles to fake gold coins, they just wanted the beauty of discovery, and we gave that to them. In spades.

But as I picked out five chests to match the maps I had sold, I wondered what Dave was going to be hiding for his bride-to-be. And what the heck did she have going for her that made him come back and treat her like it was his fault that he'd had to walk away?

A movement out at the curb caught my eye, and I turned just in time to catch Nick running around the corner of the house.

Chapter 14

Of course, I had a mess of treasure chests at my feet that I had to stumble over to get to where I'd last seen Nick running around the corner of our grandparents' house.

I picked my way through as best as I could, and when I came to the corner, Nick was nowhere in sight.

"Nick!" I yelled, not caring who could hear me. If the cops were staking out the house I frankly did not care at this point. Nick needed to turn himself in and then wait for justice to be served, or at least stop running from me.

"Nick Dagner!" I yelled again. I was so angry I couldn't remember what his middle name was, or I would have used that too.

"Whit, you've gotta keep it down," a voice said behind me.

I whipped around, ready to grab Nick's arm to keep him from going anywhere. I came up empty.

"I do not have to keep it down," I said to the bush behind me. I couldn't see him, but he had to be close by if he could talk to me.

"Please. I think I'm in big trouble, sis, more than before, and I don't know what I'm going to do. I need your help."

"*Now* you need my help, when I've been trying to save you since we found the body and you were more than happy to just traipse off with the widow? Honestly, Nick, you can't be that stupid." I crammed my hands on my hips and Whiskers yowled from the autoette. If she went on too long she'd try to jump out of her basket—unless she was being incredibly lazy today. But I couldn't count on that.

"Yes, Whit, please. Can we talk? I can't be seen until I clear my name. I can't do it all by myself."

"Fine. Let me get my cat. I'll meet you on the deck."

"The house would be better," he whispered.

"I'm not letting you in until I know what you're about, Nick. Don't look this gift horse in the mouth because it might just bite you."

He sighed, but I did hear him break through some of the brush and head toward the back of the house.

So now it became a question of did I listen to what he had to say and then see if I could help him? Or did I just use the time to grab my cat to actually call the cops and have them come get Nick?

The conflict sat with me as I took Whiskers out of the basket and held her close to me.

I couldn't do it. I couldn't just have the cops pick him up.

So I walked back to the deck around the side of the house. In the process, I hoped against all hope that Nick would wow me with a story of his innocence and how there was no way he was involved, along with proof that we could give to the police. Proof that for some reason he'd chosen not to hand over before. Proof that I was not being an idiot for believing him.

I found him sitting with his back to the cliff behind him and crunched in on himself like he could make his six-foot football-player frame small enough to not be seen.

I plopped down on the metal patio chair across from him and waited. I was not going to be the one to start this conversation or lead him along to the answers I needed. He'd have to do that on his own and be pretty darn convincing in the process.

When he glanced up, I took in the way his eye was still black and blue. It also looked like he had yet to clean the gash on his chin from the supposed golf cart crash.

But he looked so sad that I couldn't help but reach a hand out to him. He grasped my fingers like they were a lifeline.

I sighed. "You know I'm here for you. I've been trying to run around and gather as much info as I can but I'm missing pieces. And with the cops trying to find you everywhere, I don't know where else to go or what else to do. You have to help me help you, Nick."

"I know, Whit. And I know I screwed up, but I don't know how to fix this. I need your help."

"I'm all ears. Lay it out for me and we'll make a map like Pops does." Oh man, that reminded me that I was supposed to be out hiding treasure chests. I could not sacrifice those kids' happiness on the hope that Nick might finally be honest with me. But I really didn't want to leave him here because I just couldn't be sure if he'd be here when I got back.

"I don't even know where to start." He spread his hands out before him and then clasped them together hard, so hard that his knuckles turned white.

"At the beginning, and you're going to have to be quick, or you'll have to come with me to get these treasure chests buried."

"I'll be quick and then I'm going into hiding again. But I promise I'll answer your texts from now on."

"No, we can't do that. That's going to make me an accessory in whatever you're up to your ears in. If the cops check my cell phone records and see that I've been talking with you or texting you that makes me complicit. Just talk fast and talk now."

He blew out a breath. "Okay, so a few months ago, Tracy contacted me."

"How do the two of you even know each other? I remember her from the island summers, but you weren't around when she and I hung out. That's exactly why I hung out with her."

"This is going to take a long time if you interrupt every sentence with a question." His eyebrows creased over his eyes, and I sat back and petted my cat.

"I wouldn't have to ask all these questions if you had told me what the heck was going on in the first place." I waved a hand in the air like Goldy liked to do. "It doesn't matter. Continue and let's see what we can do."

He blew out another breath and seemed to be collecting his thoughts.

"Tick tock, Nick."

"Okay, okay! Look, Tracy called me a few months ago and told me that her husband wasn't being very nice to her. Actually, he was abusing her verbally and physically, and she needed help to get away. We used to fool around when I came here. I always thought maybe we'd end up together." He paused and looked down at his hands. "To be honest, it was more than that, but I can't get into all of it in the time we have."

I stayed silent because this was a lot to take in. I had never seen Jules abuse her, and I'd never seen any bruises. But that didn't always mean anything. Cosmetics could do wonders.

"Anyway, she contacted me in L.A. when they were there, and wanted to know if we could get together to talk. She came with this huge shiner and abrasions on the backs of her hands and on her knees. I couldn't turn a blind eye. I didn't leave the island the night Jules died because she and I were making plans to get her off island before the cruise. We were going to let him leave and then she'd forget something at the house and come back out and we'd escape while you had him on board. But she never came out. When I texted her, she didn't answer. I came down to the dock to see if something had happened, but didn't see her there. I met you at the end of the last cruise because I was going to ask you if she'd come aboard, but then we saw Jules floating by, and I just didn't know what to do except be thankful that someone had made it possible for Tracy to actually be free now."

"And then you got taken for questioning."

He grimaced. "And when they let me go I ran and hid with Tracy."

"Where did your face injuries really come from?"

"I really don't—"

"If I were you, I would think long and hard about how you want to finish that sentence, brother mine. I'm putting my neck on the line for you here and could get into some serious trouble. If I ask a question, you answer it, and you answer it honestly, or I just call the cops and have them take you in. They can figure it out themselves."

"Harsh."

"It's been a rough couple of days while you've been living in the lap of luxury. So lay it on me. Where did the face injuries come from?"

His shoulders drooped and so did his whole demeanor. "I really did wreck the cart when the cops came for me, but the damage to my face came from getting into a fistfight with Jules the night before. When I hit the wall, all the scrapes and bruises that were healing tore open and I had bruises on top of bruises."

"Oh, Nick, what am I going to do with you?"

"Save me? Like you always did when we were kids? Please help me, Whit. Please."

There was no other answer than yes, and I knew it. So I got up, leaned in for a hug, and told him I'd do everything possible, all while wondering what exactly that entailed—and also wondering if I could actually believe his story.

Sitting back down, I settled Whiskers on my lap and brought out my phone. I'd synced the file from my tablet into a cloud and pulled up everything I had up to this point. I didn't see any changes from Maribel or Felix just yet, but it could be that they were working on things and would input anything they found once they had their thoughts in order. That didn't help me, but it wasn't going to hinder me either.

"What do you know about Jules?"

"He was a Class-A jerk."

"That's not helping. Other than your feelings toward him for thinking that he mistreated your girlfriend from when you were a teen, what do you know about Jules?"

"Not a lot, unfortunately. It's not like I've been following along behind him this whole time. I'd let Tracy go when I found out she'd gotten married. I wasn't going to try to destroy a marriage. It wasn't worth the time or the pain."

"So why now, then?" I scrolled through my notes and kept an ear open for his answer.

"I guess I just didn't want her to be hurt, and thought that if I could save her then maybe there was a chance for us."

"I'm pretty sure she'd want another sugar daddy, one who actually paid out this time. I don't think you're in a financial position to give her everything she wants to keep her. Especially when I hear you asked Jules to fund a new boat."

His head ducked and his shoulders rose. We used to call it doing the turtle. He did it whenever he was embarrassed or upset. I wasn't in a joking mood, so I didn't bring out the old memory, just waited for him to answer.

"I was just putting out feelers to see if he'd be interested. I didn't actually ask him for the money."

"And what about us having competition now when he launches his new boat?"

Nick scoffed. "He wasn't going to launch anything. He didn't even buy one. He just told Tracy that so she'd stop bugging him."

"Hmmm. Are you sure?"

"Absolutely. I talked with Cameron down at the boat builders. Jules never even contacted him for a quote."

I tapped a few things into the phone and waited for more information.

"So why did I hear that the two of you got into a fistfight about the money?"

He shook his head and leaned back in his chair. "This is all a huge misunderstanding."

"So you didn't get into a fistfight?"

"We did, but it was because he was talking crap about you and your shop. Saying that you'd never make it work. That you might as well just hand it over now. They were going to wait until you failed and then swoop in and 'save' you. I told them you were going to make it shine more than he ever could, and then he threatened to give me a shiner and threw the first punch. I just defended myself."

"Ahhh."

"You don't believe me?"

"Hmmm."

"Knock it off, Whit. This is serious." Nick sat forward in his chair and pounded his fist on the glass.

"Don't break it. Goldy would have your hide."

"Then stop making noncommittal noises at me. I know what you're doing. You don't believe me. You're not going to agree with me until I tell you something you think you can actually believe. You used to do that when we were teenagers. It drove me crazy then, and it drives me crazy now." He thumped back in his chair and crossed his arms.

I petted Whiskers and thought how I wanted to say this. "You aren't giving me much to work with, and I still don't know where you were before we found Jules under the boat. All that time when you should have been flying to Murrieta. And I have a hard time believing that you fell for Tracy's schtick and ran to her after one phone call."

"Whit, I'm serious. Tracy's better than that."

"She went ballistic on a bride-to-be about money Jules was spending on the wedding of his goddaughter. She went after her like she had claws and was going to rip her to shreds. Or did you not see that part before you came in and saved her?"

His sigh was huge and seemed to deflate him altogether. "No, I saw it. I just didn't want to look at it that way."

"Look, I don't want her to be a villain in all this, but if it's not you then it has to be somebody else. I haven't come up with a ton of names of people who'd want him dead unless his will says that whatever money they owe him never has to be paid back."

He took to staring at his hands again, and I wanted to bop him upside the head.

"I have to go soon to get these deliveries done. What else can you tell me?"

"She's happy, happier than I've seen her in years, and it's connected to money, the money she says she's going to get now that someone was nice enough to knock off her husband."

"Well, that doesn't exactly sound like a grieving widow, now does it? Has she been taken in for questioning? What did you do when she was?"

His face flamed red. "I hid in her closet, behind a rack of shoes."

"Seriously, Nick? A rack of shoes?"

He shrugged. "I didn't have any other choice. They were coming for me, and I didn't want to get caught."

"And why didn't you just tell them that you were with Tracy before the cruise, and why you fought with Jules?" Just the thought of that made my stomach churn. So many things were stacked against my brother. This particular fight to clear his name was going to be a big one.

"Because Tracy sent me to their house before the dinner. I was supposed to be at the house waiting for her. She was going to make her excuses and not go to the dinner, instead coming to the house so we could leave. But then she never showed up. I came down to make sure they'd taken the ride and had gone on their way."

"But she said she had to go back to the house. She never actually showed up?"

"Not that I saw."

"Then where was she?" I tapped on the tablet and my doodle pad came up under my fingertips. I liked to practice ideas of frames for my logic puzzles on the pad and save them to see how I could make them work in real life. The sunflower theme I'd left there last time wasn't helping me at all so I ignored it.

"I went to her house the night you dropped me off at Goldy and Pops's but she wouldn't answer the door. I ended up spending the night on the *Sea Bounder* and then being on the run from there, until she called me and told me to come up to her house because we had things to talk about."

A clock flashed on my phone. I was not going to be able to get all the treasure hidden in time if I didn't leave right now.

"Okay, you've given me a lot to think about and a lot to go over. Where are you going to stay now? I don't think we should randomly contact each other unless something big happens, but I might need to be able to get a hold of you. I don't think you should stay here." What I really thought was that he should turn himself in and *sit there* until I could give the police someone else to focus on.

I started to mention it, but he looked so dejected and so confused that I just didn't know if I could do that to him.

"I know you'd probably rather I just turn myself in, but I
can't until I figure out what happened. They won't look for
anyone else if they have me in custody. That cop I talked to
the first night said that he had to fight hard to be able to let me
go. The sheriff wanted this taken care of within twenty-four
hours and was willing to book me just to look like things were
done. If they get me now, we might never know who actually
killed him."

Sighing was the only thing I could think to do. "But they
might not look for anyone else if you're on the run, either. It's a
no-win situation. I'd let you stay at my house, except Maribel
works for the sheriff's department, and I can't put her job at
risk." I considered Felix too, since he was more of a part-timer
with the diving for the force, but I wasn't going to do that to him
either. Not to mention he lived on a boat, one that Nick would
know how to sail to get away if he really wanted to leave.

We had a dinghy that he could take out to sea and just hang
in the water, but that wouldn't work for any amount of time.
And I wasn't going to ask Goldy to let him use their personal
boat. He couldn't stay on the *Sea Bounder*.

Which left me with just about nothing.

I didn't know what to do. I took another second to scroll
through the rest of my notes and then came to a decision I didn't
think I ever would.

"You're going to the hangar. Go to Buckey and tell him to
hide you. I talked to him when I was looking for you and he'd be
the one I'd absolutely trust to not turn you in. I'll come get you
once I have a plan in place and some other way to get you off the
hook. Please do not tell him anything, just ask him to hide you,
and tell him I sent you."

I wasn't sure that was the right decision, but as I heard a

siren sound off down the street, I didn't have a lot of choice. It was either the hangar or go on the run again. Or I could have dragged him down to the police, but I had a bad feeling in my stomach about Tracy and the way she was manipulating things.

There were several pieces I wanted to have in place before I put my brother in the police's hands again.

Chapter 15

Step one of putting the new plan into place was to go to La Fluencia as I had planned to do and see if I could get some hint of who Tracy was now, and why she'd want to drag my brother into her problems. As much as I was not a Jules fan, I also needed to know the truth.

After I'd hidden all the treasure chests, I went to find Goldy to talk her into continuing to cover the store so I could head toward the one place I didn't really want to go.

When I got to the store, though, it was closed with a sign that said WENT SUN-WORSHIPPING, MIGHT BE BACK LATER. Lordy. I was hungry and felt like if I didn't keep the store open, people wouldn't know when to come in to shop. But right now, finding the real murderer was more important. So I went to find Goldy. And I *was* hungry. Breakfast had worn off hours ago. Right now I wanted something light and a smoothie sounded about right.

"Goldy, can you please come over to the shop and help me for another hour or so?"

I'd found my grandmother at the beach, of course.

"You're blocking my sun, honey. Back up or stand to the other side. I want even tanning, not a crosswise shape of you over my thighs and a back that's lighter than the rest of my body."

I moved left and then right, trying to find a spot where I wasn't casting my shadow on her but was also not so far away that I had to shout to her over the rest of the beachgoers.

In the end I sat in the sand and figured I'd just brush myself off when I was done.

"Please, Goldy. You want Nick's name cleared. I want Nick's name cleared. He doesn't seem to care in the least since I can't find him." That part wasn't entirely true, but Nick and I had agreed to keep our grandparents in the dark for just a little while longer. "There is more going on than I had been aware of. Despite what you seem to think, this isn't going to be a simple 'oh, he didn't do it' thing. I know you said Nick and Jules got into a fight, but you didn't tell me what it was about and that it actually got physical. That's a lot more than I was led to believe had happened."

"It was just a little altercation, Whitney, nothing to get all fussed about." She shielded her eyes with the flat of her hand, frowning at me.

"He knocked some of his teeth out." I sat back and waited to see if that was something she also knew.

Apparently not, as she shot into a sitting position on her towel, quite the feat considering she'd been lying on her stomach with the back of her suit undone. Fortunately, there was no flash of anything indecent as she sat and turned toward me. "That boy! What is wrong with him?"

"Garry at the Daily Scoop said that Nick and Jules were supposed to go into business together and buy another boat for Nick to run under the company, but then Jules decided to buy one for some relative of Tracy's instead and was going to take business from us."

She growled low in her throat. "I'd kill him myself if he were still alive, and I might go after the one who's still alive for being so irresponsible with my business," she murmured.

I put a hand on her arm. "Please don't *say* anything like that. I already have one person I'm trying to defend and he's not helping. I don't need to add you to my 'needs protection' list. Please."

"Oh, sweetie, I can take care of myself, and of course I'm not going to do anything rash."

I raised an eyebrow at her and she lowered her sunglasses to stare me down over the rims. Right, I was never going to be able to win in a staring contest with the Queen of the Stink Eye. I hadn't when I was younger, wanting to go against her rules and she told me no. Despite being older I still wasn't in a place where I'd take her on. Especially when ultimately I needed her help more than I needed to be right.

"Can you tear yourself away from sunbathing and run the store for a little while, then, to give me some time to talk to a few more owners of the surrounding stores without losing even more business?"

She did up her swimsuit and raised her hands, and I grabbed her forearms to pull her to her feet.

"I'm not a shopkeeper," she said, dusting any stray particle of sand from her body.

"And I'm not a detective. So where does that leave us?"

"Sassy, that's what you are." Taking her wildly colored sarong from the towel, she wrapped it around her bathing suit and smiled at me.

"Not so smart, that's me. Why am I trying to defend some-one who can't even have the decency to return my calls when I'm trying to save his hide?"

"Because he's your brother."

"And he's ungrateful." I was feeling grumpy and she'd just have to deal with that. I was also trying to play up the fact that I didn't know where he was in case anyone was listening.

"Maybe he doesn't think he needs your help. And it's not like you asked him if he wanted you to clear his name. You took that on all by yourself."

That got me to laugh. "Or it could have had something to do with a certain someone telling me that we couldn't sully our reputation. That she was certain Nick hadn't killed Jules. That I needed to use my charming personality to get people to talk to me. I don't know when she thought I'd do that if I'm tied to the store all day."

"Touché."

"I thought you might feel that way."

She chucked me under the chin. "A chip off the old block, there, my girl. Now go use your smarts and wits and I'll go use my sunny disposition to sell the merchandise in your store." She hooked her arm through mine. "Things are going well at the store? Are the receipts adding up to what you need?"

"Well, I won't be asking anyone to chip in to fund my venture, if that's what you're asking. It's paying for itself, at least."

"Okay, well, maybe we'll need to come up with some new advertising, once we clear our name."

"Now it's *our* name?"

"Are you not a Dagner? I know that the island is often populated with tourists, but even they can get wind of a place to avoid if no one ever seems to go in the store or takes the boat rides. Or if the other shop keepers never recommend people stop in and see what you have to offer. Don't forget that."

"I promise not to. Now are you ready to sell, or do you need to go get yourself gussied up?"

She looked down at herself. I gave her a once-over, too.

After chuckling, she said, "Oh no, I think this will be fine. Everything's covered that's supposed to be. I'm following your shoes-and-shirts-required sign, so I think I'll be fine."

We stopped at the edge of the sand for her to step into her sandals. These at least only had a three-inch heel. She towered over me now. Where most of the women in my family were over five feet seven inches, I hadn't quite managed that at just over five feet. Well, at least she wouldn't have any trouble getting anything off the top shelf.

"I'm running a sale today, so don't forget to do the discount from this morning. Oh, and make sure you listen to anything that's being said. Maybe we can get together tonight to go over any rumors that might have something to do with this." I didn't need all the rumors, but I hated not to ask.

"Whitney Sheridan Dagner, I have run a business for years, even before you were a twinkle in your mother's eye. You do not have to tell me how to make a sale or three." She huffed and walked two steps in front of me no matter how much I sped up to catch her.

Soon we were at the store and she had to wait for me to unlock the door. It was lovely inside and out. I'd taken a weekend when I'd first gotten here and painted it a beautiful robin's egg blue with white trim. The front windows shone with twinkly lights and a very cool display of mermaid art and blue cellophane and tulle to create the illusion of being underwater. I'd also installed a shelf to represent the beach and put up the miniature furniture Leslie Moore created on her sunporch. The tiny beach chairs with the little checkered blanket and picnic set rested on some sand that I'd stolen from the beach. Goldy must have set the whole thing back up after she'd moved Lacey out to her autoette and helped get her on her way.

It all said welcome and come on in to check out the best the island had to offer, including hand-thrown pottery and stained glass that made your eyes travel over and over it just to take in all the marvelous detail. I carried the wares of those who made awesome things and some souvenirs, too, but mostly the awesome things.

"I have to say, you've got quite the eye for displaying things. I enjoyed reconstructing that little ocean view after Lacey left."

It was surprisingly one of my talents here. I thought I'd be really good at keeping the books straight and inventory and organization since that had been my job for the railroad. Sure, I used to make tiny fairy gardens out of clay pots on the balcony of my apartment in Bellflower, but my apartment had always been very simple and everything had its place. Here my creativity seemed to have exploded like a supernova and I had chairs draped with afghans, placemats spilling out of hand-woven baskets, and candles built into pyramids with their fat bottoms making a colorful flower if you looked at the whole display instead of just the top.

I was pretty proud of myself, but it was always nice to have the person you'd admired and loved tell you that you weren't ruining what called to your heart.

"I've got this handled, Whitney darling. Go see what you can find out. And in the meantime I'll blow up Nick's phone. He has to be out there somewhere, right?"

Oh, he was, but I had to keep that to myself for now. "Yeah, as long as Buckey hasn't let him take his plane and escape, or Nick hasn't taken the boat out and gotten lost at sea very deliberately." How had life gotten this complicated in such a short time? Another question to add to my impossibly long list that just kept growing every time I thought I might be on to something. Now I was also lying by omission to top it all off.

Still, it made my skin crawl and I just wanted to be done with all this so I could go back to the life I'd moved here for.

Since I hadn't hit the seafood delicatessen yet and I was suddenly hungry again, I stopped in at the Crabby Situation to talk with Cindy Jones first. I was avoiding the spa, but I'd get there eventually.

Actually, I could kill two birds with one stone at the seafood place. Maybe that was the wrong phrasing during this current issue, but it was the first thing that came to mind for me.

I wanted to get with Maribel later on if possible and discuss what she knew, or at least as much as she could tell me about what she knew after her shift at the station today. And Whiskers would be happy to sit on my lap while Maribel and I talked. I'd let the cat walk along with me while I'd delivered the treasure boxes and then had taken her back to the house, where she'd promptly fallen over into a deep sleep.

Walking into the shop, I found myself pretty much alone at the counter. No one came out from the back and a low hum was all that I heard in the whole store. Normally, Cindy had some kind of island music playing—either a reggae she loved from a band that had come through here when I'd been here one summer, or that smooth jazz WAVE stuff, but not today. Today there appeared to be complete silence—except for maybe the refrigerator? I couldn't tell where the hum was coming from. I wasn't willing to wander around to find out. Cindy could love all of her free-love, hug-trees stuff, but she could be fierce if you tried to cross her, especially on her territory.

"Hello?" I waited a beat for someone to call back then tried again. "Hello? Anyone here? Cindy?"

"Arrrh, matey! Whatchya be doin' here, lassie?" James Scervin came out from the back, smoking his pipe and staggering like he was still on a boat on rough seas years after he'd made landfall.

"James." I wasn't sure what else to say. He was one of the last people I expected to see here at Cindy's shop. They were often at odds about any number of things, from the tourist trade to whether or not the lines on our roads should be repainted. Cindy was hugely against it since it created fumes in the air that would then affect any endangered species on our island. James thought she was an idiot, which he happily told her as often as possible right to her face.

So what was he doing in her shop and by himself from all appearances? Also how had he gotten in the back?

"Aye, Whitney Dagner, 'tis I, Captain James, trying to find the lady proprietor of this fine shop. I'd like to swab her decks for her latest fiasco."

I wasn't sure that he meant exactly what he thought he'd just said but I decided to let it go for the minute because it had nothing to do with my current mission. He was as good as anyone to talk to about Nick. And this way I didn't have to go to his bait shop down the way and deal with looking at a ton of creepy-crawly live things that were solely purchased to be eaten by fish that people would then eat.

"I was just in the area and hoping to talk with her about my brother. I'm trying to find him. He's not answering his cell."

His eyes lit up with some kind of gleeful light that I didn't understand until he opened his mouth.

"Ah, the young scallywag be takin' off for parts unknown now that he's been caught at his nefarious game, has he?"

I had never been able to figure out why this man, who was obviously from this century and had been born and raised in Arizona, felt the need to talk like he was some Victorian-era sea-farer with a penchant for long sentences.

"I don't think he's been nefarious at all. Why do you say that?"

"Och, right, right, course ya don't. He's your kin, after all."

Now we'd moved to some sort of Scottish brogue. It was obvious I was not getting anywhere with him, and I still would rather speak to Cindy. "Well, if you see Cindy, please let her know I'm looking for her."

"Will do, wench, but I think I hear her scurvy self coming this way now. Just wait for another click or two and you should be able to talk with her yerself, don't you know."

What I didn't know could fill the hull of a huge shipping freighter, but I sat tight as Cindy breezed into the room, her long tie-dyed skirt swirling across the floor over her Birkenstocks.

"Oh, Whitney! I heard about what's going on with Nick!

Have they been able to catch him?" She tittered out a giggle. "Sorry, I meant find him?"

Oh, this conversation was going to be just awesome. I don't know why I had thought either of these people could help. Instead, they were making me feel like I was on a wild-goose chase looking for anyone except my brother.

"Uh, no, I was looking for him but I can see he's not here. Thanks anyway." I made my exit just as James started in with his shanty talk, cutting Cindy down to the ground for her business practices, and Cindy was shooting back with her laid-back attitude of none of it being his business so he could just go take a long walk off a short plank.

I sighed as the door closed behind me. Nothing there, but at least I'd tried. Taking my phone out of my pocket, I thumbed on the screen. Nothing new from Nick, nothing from Goldy. Pops, however, was letting me know he was taking a hike today to put up more treasure chests, and if I wanted to join him we could shoot for after the store closed.

At least that would be something to look forward to.

In the meantime I had a spa to go to and perhaps some more information to find.

Chapter 16

La Fluencia, the day spa to the island stars, was one of those places I figured I might go once a year and only if someone gave me a gift certificate for my birthday or Christmas. It was posh, a haven for the people who could afford to have their toes wiggled and polished by a professional. It was also a little out of my price range. I knew a few of the girls who did the toe polishing and they'd offered me discounts, but I just hadn't had time to take them up on it with getting the store up and running.

I still had no idea who might have killed Jules, but hoped to get some idea of Tracy here. On those crime shows I watched, it was often a lover or a spouse. Tracy seemed to have plenty of reasons to want to take her husband out, and the attitude to match. She and her husband seemed to barely be able to understand each other, and she was the most viable person I could think of at the moment. Plus, she'd called Nick in to save her. I couldn't discount that.

So why not follow that path until it ran into a brick wall?

I felt a little lost as I drove my golf cart to the spa, though. Why was I out looking for a killer when I should be selling my baubles and smiling and laughing about some local mishap, or attending one of the concerts on the beach with Maribel?

I'd traded corporate life for a chance at frivolity and a slow pace. I'd left the world of backstabbing and time schedules and annual reports to relax and give myself a break. Yet here I was instead, running the tread off the tires on my golf cart to help someone who wasn't helping himself much.

I exited the autoette at the curb, figuring I wouldn't get a ticket for the few minutes I planned on staying. I had decided to just go in and ask some questions instead of using my gift certificate. I had other things to do and a business to run.

At the front desk, I smiled at Annaliese, with her bleached-blond hair and her overly whitened teeth. They shone even more when set against the intense and unnatural brown of her skin, reminding me of a baked potato. She was a big believer in the tanning bed in the back room. Me, I owned the fact that I burned whenever the sun touched me and was a big believer in the wonder of sunscreen, SPF 100, please.

"Whit, how's it going? You finally going to use that gift certificate your grandma gave you? She has such a lovely skin tone. I wish I looked like her." She said the words dreamily as if it was her biggest wish to give herself skin cancer.

"Ah, no, not yet. I'm putting it off maybe until winter—you know, when the sun isn't so bright and I need to touch up the pigment." A total and complete lie as not only didn't I need more sun, but this being California, it rarely went a day without at least some sun. Maybe the temperature would drop a few degrees, but it wasn't like the east coast. We didn't actually have all four seasons, at least not normally. It was one season with some rain thrown in for good measure.

"Right, pigment touch-up. Got it." And she scribbled something down on the notepad in front of her.

I peeked over the counter to see what I'd said that she had to remember and found the words "pigment touch-up" on a notepad emblazoned with the spa's logo: a seashell with a mermaid, her hair wrapped in a towel turban and admiring her nails, in the center.

In my corporate job I had not been the graphics person at all, but even I found it to be eye catching.

I wondered if Pigment Touch-Up was about to show up on the menu of services for La Fluencia Day Spa.

I didn't have too much time to contemplate that because the owner, Merry, came out of the back, laden with towels and full of smiles. "Whitney! Such a pleasure to see you here! Are you finally going to take me up on my offer to get those nails back into shape? You always had such panache, such style when it came to your hands."

Had being the operative word, I thought, as I folded my hands in on each other to hide the fact that I didn't even have nail polish on. It wasn't that my nails were ragged or unkempt, it was simply that with starting over, the need for makeup and nail polish and gel and hairspray and all those other products had kind of disappeared along with my suits and heels. I still had everything in storage, just in case, but in my daily life I no longer needed that kind of thing, and I was happy about it. Tremendously.

What I was not happy about was the fact that I was hiding my brother in an airport hangar, and I hadn't yet found out anything to help me find the real killer. I still had more questions than answers. Frustrating, to say the least.

"Hey, Merry, I'll get around to using the gift certificate soon enough. I'm just here to see about some, um . . ." I had to think fast. Why was I here? I couldn't say it was to try to get the dirt on Tracy. Improvisation was not something I was adept at and the almost nonexistent skill was completely escaping me. "I, um, am here to see if you wanted to put some of your business cards

in my shop!" I probably shouldn't have used the full-throttle exclamation point at the end but I couldn't help myself and so my
words ended up coming out like I was announcing some kind of
lottery win instead of offering to swap services.

Towels still in hand, she rocked back a step, probably at my
overenthusiasm, but regained her composure far faster than I regained mine.

"That would be great, thanks for offering. Let me get you
some."

I heard the door open to the spa and Tracy's voice a split second later. I did not want to be caught in the same room with her
right now.

"I'll come with you." I smiled at Annaliese, who seemed not
to know quite what to do with me. She wasn't alone. I didn't
know what to do with myself most days.

Trotting along after the unknowing Merry, I kept far enough
away that she wouldn't turn and tell me to go back to the front
counter, but also close enough that I didn't lose her in the maze
of hallways and rooms in the spa.

They performed just about every kind of service here having
to do with tanning and sculpting and relaxing, not to mention
haircuts and manicures, pedicures and waxing—all kinds of waxing. I shuddered to think about someone pulling all the hair out
of my legs with one yank, but some people swore by it. Goldy
being one of the many.

After several twists and turns and almost losing sight of Merry
at least two times, I watched as she opened the door to her office.
I caught it before it closed behind her.

"Hey, sorry to stalk you. I had a question after you left." My
improv was lacking, but at least it wasn't as horrible as the
overuse of exclamation points.

"Sure thing, what can we do for you?" She sat at her desk,

which was as big as a lake and held all manner of computers and monitors big enough to outsize the television hanging on my living room wall at home. She also had piles of paper stacked precariously to the point where I was afraid one would fall if I breathed too hard in its vicinity.

She laughed. "This desk. I swear if I didn't know where everything was already, I'd take the time to actually organize the thing." She laughed again and I laughed along with her, though just looking at it reminded me of my last job and how much it drove me crazy to have piles.

I had been a huge fan of stationery stores and folders and binders and had had a huge bookcase to house all of the information in. Now I had a laptop and a calendar in my phone and that was about my extent of paperwork.

"Okay, so business cards." She reached down below the level of the desk and pulled out what I figured was a drawer since I couldn't see over the mounds of things.

"A small stack would be great. I figure since I'm going to have my official grand opening in a few weeks when they have the golf cart parade on the Fourth of July, I'd go around and ask people if they wanted to be set up in a rack I plan on keeping at the front counter." I'd thought no such thing, but the idea actually made a lot of sense if I did say so myself.

"It's really a great idea, and I appreciate it so much. I'd be happy to return the favor." She smiled as she handed over the cards, her gold bracelets sliding down her arm and making a kind of tinkling music as they hit each other.

"Oh, that would be wonderful. Starting out is not easy. You have a lot of years under your belt, though, so it's probably not as hard for you."

Another laugh, this one full of derision. "Oh honey, it's just as hard if not harder. At least your overhead isn't astronomical and you don't have a ton of employees. It's not easy keeping this place up and running when most of your money is made in a short period of time that has to last you through the leaner months. I don't know what I'd do without Jules to tide me over sometimes."

And there was the entrance I'd been looking for, though it didn't resemble anything I'd tried to prepare myself for.

"Did you not hear what happened to him?" For an island so small I was really surprised that it wasn't all over town already. It had been over forty-eight hours since he'd been found. Then again I rarely heard much of anything unless it had to do with me specifically, so I guessed it wasn't too hard to believe.

"I didn't . . ." She trailed off as a knock sounded on her door.

"Merry, we need to talk. Like, as soon as you can. Right now would be good. I need my money back." Tracy stalked in. The look on Merry's face said that she'd very much like to leave if only a hole would open up in the floor and swallow her.

I was so tempted to excuse myself. I was not a big fan of drama or awkward situations. But then I remembered Tracy had put my brother in an awful position and that I needed to find out what was going on before anything else bad happened. And so I stayed.

"Can we do this another time, Tracy?" Merry picked the towels up and then set them down on her desk, looking at me then back at Tracy. I had a feeling that she'd like me to leave if she couldn't manage the hole in the floor swallowing her, but I wasn't going anywhere until someone specifically asked me.

"I don't think we can." Tracy twirled a lock of her hair around her finger and gave a little smile. "I went through some files this morning and it turns out that my dearest Jules has quite a few bills that have to get paid. I'm thinking I am calling in all his markers. I hope you don't mind."

I sat in the visitor's chair and crossed my legs, wishing for some popcorn. What would Merry do? It was high season around here so she shouldn't be in one of those dry spells. But had Jules been making her pay him back every year? Or was Tracy talking about a wad of money that Merry was not going to be able to come up with?

"Can we talk about this later?" Merry darted her eyes toward me again. This time, I decided to take the hint instead of hanging around. I might need her later, and I didn't want her to keep people from coming to my store.

"I'll see you later, Merry. I hope everything turns out okay." It was the best I could do.

But I didn't get two steps before Tracy called my name.

"I'm going to need Jules's money back from you too, Whitney. Don't go running off. I'm calling in his debts, and I'm not going to take no for an answer. My dearest deserves the kind of burial that's reserved for people who are the Person of the Year, and our account—or rather my account now, since he's dead—doesn't show a balance that reflects what I want to do. I'll expect a cashier's check tomorrow from both of you."

She scooted around me and exited the room that was suddenly filled with a deafening silence. Merry and I looked at each other and then away. I didn't know who was going to be the first one to speak, but I knew exactly what I wanted to say.

"I didn't borrow money from that man. I'm going to rake Nick over the coals when I see him." I groaned and sat back down in the visitor's chair. It was actually quite comfy, and if I hid out here for the next few days maybe this would all blow over. Nick could be caught for all I cared right now.

What had he done, and how much did we owe? The bigger question was would I have enough to cover it without tanking our business and my bank account at the same time?

Merry gulped. "I can't pay right now. I just got a new set of chairs in and had to pay the insurance. And I have a suit against me from a woman getting a wax in an area we won't mention that she didn't like."

"Oh, wow." I wasn't sure what else to say, and my mind was awhirl with all the things wrong with both our statements.

"Yeah, I took the wax off the service menu. I have to redo it anyway because now someone thinks we should put pigment touch-up into the menu. Who says things like that? And I can't refuse her because her daddy owns the franchise I work under."

"Yikes." To tell or not to tell on myself? "Uh, that was my phrase to get out of having to use the tanning bed."

At least she laughed instead of groaning at me. "God, Whit, now I'm going to have to figure out a way out of that too. I just don't know if I can take all of this and cater to the wedding party that's set up tomorrow morning."

That zinged something in my brain. "That wouldn't be the wedding party with Sheila, would it?"

"Yes, Sheila Graystone. Do you know her?"

I bit my lip, then remembered that it made me look like a bulldog, according to Goldy, and relaxed my mouth. "Well, she came in to my shop the other day and fainted when I told her Jules had died. She tried to play it off as low blood sugar, but I didn't believe her and neither did the friend who was with her. And now I wouldn't be too sure that she's coming in at all. She was being funded by Jules too, and as you can see Tracy's calling in all debts. I doubt she's going to pay for another woman to get dolled up. Not to mention that I don't know if the wedding is happening now or not. The groom came in to the shop to get a treasure chest, but said they'd moved from the mansion to a teepee out at the campground."

"Interesting." Merry tapped a pen on the blotter situated in the center of her desk. The piles of papers surrounding her reminded me of Scrooge counting his money, but if she was worried about paying back a small loan then it could be that the paperwork was more debt than credit.

"What do you know?" I asked because that word had to mean something.

"Just that when Sheila made her arrangement, she paid in advance with a credit card. I can't imagine that she won't come in anyway since it's already paid for."

"Oh, that makes total sense. Do you think Tracy will try to stop her?"

"Not if she doesn't know. And if she doesn't know and the bride-to-be shows up, then I'm going to handle her myself."

"Can I be here to watch? I could hand you towels and stuff."

"I don't think that will work if she already knows your face. From what you said, I'm pretty sure you're going to be one person who would absolutely stand out to her." She tapped the keyboard in front of her and I remembered doing that just a few hours ago when I was still trying to find Nick and avoiding looking at Dave the groom.

"I know this is probably not something you want to do, but I'm going to put it all out on the table for you. Nick is going to be taken in for Jules's murder if I can't figure out what happened. I swear to you that I think Tracy did it. She has her hand out too much and has been very quick to start calling in money. Plus, she was livid up at the mansion when she threw that girl out and said she wasn't paying for anything."

"Go on."

"So." I licked my lips, knowing I'd have to make my way around this as discreetly as possible. "I just have this feeling that she's using Nick as a scapegoat. Why would the police even be looking at him? Why, when they hardly ever interact, would it be Nick?"

She stopped tapping and looked at me straight on. "I'd like to know that myself. Your brother was my favorite boyfriend when we were younger, and I'm not going to see him go down for something he didn't do. Be back here tomorrow at eight in the morning and we'll see if Sheila shows. I have a closet or two that I'm sure we could fit you into."

I smiled, but not at the prospect of being shoved into a closet. I had some time until tomorrow and I knew how I was probably going to be spending it.

Putting on my deerstalker hat.

Chapter 17

I uploaded some notes to my tablet sitting out in the autoette and then drove off to meet Pops. I hadn't talked with him much today, but at this point I wasn't even sure what to say. I had so many theories and questions and suppositions that I didn't even know where to start.

A nice walk through the canyon could be just what the island ordered.

He was already there when I made the final ascent to the plateau.

"You're looking spry in your outfit there, darling."

I looked down at the cargo shorts and the T-shirt with the Nautically Yours logo plastered across the front. I'd tied my tennis shoes a little tighter, knowing we'd be hiking, and had pulled my hair back into a messy ponytail. I didn't think *spry* was the right word, but I wasn't going to fight with him.

"You're looking spry yourself, young man."

He laughed at that and slung an arm over my shoulders. "So this is a bridegroom-and-bride thing, huh? He's going to come up and put the prize in the box tomorrow?"

"That's what he told me. I'll get it up here in enough time for him to hide it tomorrow."

"Makes sense. We'll put it on that fountain; down along the bottom should be safe. As long as it doesn't damage the flora and fauna, the park doesn't mind."

I followed him as he stepped along the path. I couldn't have told you the names of even half the plants; I was much more an underwater garden girl than one who knew dry land. But I could still appreciate the vibrant colors and the way the air was scented with a fragrance that just caught the edge of your senses.

Something floral and something else a little more pungent. It wasn't a bad smell at all, and as the afternoon heat wore down in the lowering sun, it was very peaceful up here.

Trooping along, I kept feeling like I really should say something to Pops about everything that had been going on. Goldy could be the hothead, but Pops was more the thinker before doing. Where Goldy would stomp off and demand answers, Pops would think his way around every conceivable possibility and then ask the one question that ended up being the answer to them all.

It could be frustrating to wait him out, but in the end he was generally the one who did not run off into the melee and leave me hanging.

I took a deep breath and then sat down on the edge of the fountain. "You have a minute?"

"For you? Of course. I have many minutes for you." He sat next to me and took off his hat to rub his sweating head. "What's going on other than Nick and death and getting pinged by your grandmother about everything from cleaning to not having the hair she wants you to?"

I laughed softly, grateful for this man. "Everything but that last one is what I need to talk about."

"Spill it, then, and let's see if we can go Perry Mason on it."

"I think Nick is in a lot of trouble. I sent him up to the hangar instead of turning him in to the police. Did I do the wrong thing?"

He crossed his legs and took out his pipe. He never actually smoked the thing, but he liked to have it in his hand. "I don't know if it's the wrong thing, but I don't think it was the best thing to do. He needs to go in and talk about what he knows so that they can find the real person and you can go back to running your shop and not doing the cops' job."

I groaned. "But Goldy wants me to protect our good name, and I didn't want Nick to get railroaded."

"Honey, our name is going to be fine no matter what. We need to go get Nick and figure out what to do to get him down to the police and get things sorted out."

"But how do I ask him to do that when he's so scared and I promised I'd help him?"

"I can ask him if you want."

I got up to pace and wondered how I'd gotten myself into this whole thing. Right, trying to do the sisterly thing.

"I have to get him down the mountain and into police custody without having him feel like I've given up on him." I bit my nails and Pops got up to take them out of my mouth.

"You've got this, sweetheart. You'll figure it out. That might be the Perry Mason way, but I think it's better that way. He needs to turn himself in voluntarily and then deal with the consequences."

I rested my head on Pops's shoulder. "I wanted him to be all the way innocent."

"I know you did, and he might still be, but we have to get him to the police, where at least he'll be safe. What if whoever really did this thinks their scapegoat isn't playing by the rules and decides to take him out too?"

I hadn't even thought about that. And see? There was that question that I'd been waiting for. Maybe if we had Nick turn himself in, then we could lure the real murderer into the open. It wasn't my first idea, but it might be the best.

"You're the best." I kissed him on the cheek.

"Nope, you are, but we'll keep that between us. Now go get your brother and twist his arm until he decides to do the right thing and we'll go from there. I'll handle Goldy."

"Ha! Good luck with that."

"It hasn't been forty-three years for nothing, little lady. And then, once this is all over, I'd like to talk to you and your beau, Felix."

Man, I had so hoped to get away without touching that subject.

"I'm not making any promises."

Looking out at the ocean, he took my hand. "I'm not asking you to. I'm just asking for a conversation, that's all."

Giving him the side-eye because I knew that it was far from all, I let it slide. I had a plan and I had to execute it before something worse happened.

Walking back down the trail alone, I had time to think about how to approach Nick. Carefully. Cautiously. He was more volatile than I had ever known him to be, and I didn't want to set him off. But I had to take him into the police.

It was getting late and I needed to check in with my cohorts to see if they'd found anything on their missions. I didn't think I was up for another cozy dinner in my house, so I texted Maribel and then called Felix.

"Anything yet?" he asked after we exchanged hellos.

"Not really. I did get to talk with Nick, but I sent him into hiding again."

"*What?*"

"Wait. Before you get angry, I'm going to get him now and turn him in to the police. I still don't think he did it, but my signals are all pointing to the widow. She had the most to gain, I think, and has been using my brother to save her." I went through everything Nick had told me, and when I was done, Felix blew out a big breath.

"That would be a hard one to turn your back on, especially if she was an old girlfriend and you'd thought you'd have more with her someday."

Was there a hint in there for me? I glossed right over it even if there was.

"So I have to get him and then turn him in. Any ideas on how to do it peacefully?"

"Would he go for the fact that it's the right thing to do, and if he doesn't and they catch him it would be far worse?"

"Probably not, but that's going to have to be my best guess." I heard sirens wailing in the distance. "What on earth is going on now?"

"I have no idea, but I'm being texted so I should go. Let me know if you need anything. Anything at all."

I sighed, turning in a slow circle and wishing I knew which direction to point myself. "I will. See you later. Take care."

"You too, Whit. We'll talk soon."

And then he was gone, but the sirens got louder and louder and cop cars whizzed past me up the road to Airport in the Sky. Oh, that was probably not good.

I abandoned my edict not to text with my brother and sent him a quick message to please stay calm and to not fight. I doubted it would do any good, but I was more interested to know how they'd found him and what it meant that they were going after him with such a vengeance.

I had a feeling I might end up back at the sheriff's station. Perhaps I should set up a cot there.

I didn't want to arrive unannounced at the station, though, just in case they weren't going after Nick but something else, so I went home instead and sat down for a minute to just breathe. Whiskers curled up in my lap and I closed my eyes.

* * *

When I opened them again, it was to find Maribel calling my name and shaking my foot. The sun was shining right in my eyes and my mouth felt like a desert.

"What time is it?" I croaked.

Maribel smirked at me. "Seven-thirty in the morning, Sleeping Beauty."

"Seven-thirty? In the morning? Wow, I must have been more tired than I thought." I stretched and cracked my neck. Couch sleeping was not for the broken-backed. Man, I was going to be hurting today.

Something niggled at the back of my mind, but it was just out of my reach. It would come to me.

"So, what was going on last night at the airport?" I asked, hoping that my voice sounded innocent but afraid I hadn't nailed it.

"Someone pushed a golf cart off the cliff at the airport. I'm not sure why, but the deputies were able to verify that no one was in the cart when it went over the edge."

I sat up to make room for her and she curled into the corner. "Have you heard from Nick? They still want to talk with him."

So either he didn't get my text or he'd ignored it and ran anyway. I gave her the rundown and then waited for the scolding for not just turning him over. But to my surprise, she simply sighed.

"Yeah, I wouldn't encourage him to go in just yet if he can keep out of their grasp. Something is going on there and they're desperate to close the case down." She bit her bottom lip. "I was able to get some information about that rival we were talking about and there might be one other person we should look at, but I probably shouldn't tell you. And I definitely don't want to put it in the spreadsheet, just in case someone can access it."

I folded my legs under me and sat forward. "What? What

did you find? Please, Maribel, I don't want to put your job at risk, but I'm trying to save my brother."

"Well, the rival has some serious issues and he was gunning for Jules on the day he died. Marvin Goldberg arrived at noon that day on his yacht and then came into Two Harbors. It appears that he went right to the police and wanted to know what it would take to get a warrant to toss Jules's home for something that was stolen from him."

"And what did they say?" This could be good stuff.

"Since he wouldn't tell anyone what he thinks was stolen they couldn't do anything, but they did warn him against doing anything on his own. Then he has a ton of unaccounted time from about two until he checked into the mansion at ten o'clock that night."

"Oh! This is awesome. Where's paper?"

"We can't write anything down, Whit. We're just going to have to keep it in our heads."

I deflated a little but understood her reasoning. "And what about the other person?"

"Well, you know those burglaries?"

"Yeah, the mayor had mentioned that it was a good thing that the cruise went well because he doesn't want people to think we're all about crime."

Maribel sighed. "Not much chance of that right now. The sheriff's station is usually pretty silent except for a mishap here or there, but they're running around like the island is on fire."

"Felix got called to the thing at the airport when we were talking."

"Talking, huh?" She had a sly smile on her face and I groaned at her.

"Yes, talking. So what about the burglaries?"

"Well, it seems that the mayor hired a woman to look into them and she appears to be an old flame of Jules's. He was not

happy to see her on your cruise, from what I heard, and he threatened her. She used to be special ops and looks like she could karate
chop your toupee off. I don't know what he said to her, but she
was angry and stormed out of the party about the same time Jules
did, and now they're not sure where she is."

"Hmm, two very good possibilities. I'll have to sneak around
to see what I can find out about each of them. Thanks!" And
then it hit me—that niggling something was that I was supposed
to be at La Fluencia in less than thirty minutes to hear what
Sheila had to say for herself.

I jumped off the couch, dislodging Whiskers, who was not
happy at my abrupt departure.

"Whit! What's going on?"

"I'm off to the spa for a massage," I called from the bathroom, and then closed the door. I had three things to follow up
on today and hopefully by tonight I could clear my brother's
name. It was going to be a good day. It had to be after all the ones
that had not exactly been pleasant lately.

Before I entered the spa, I scoped out the premises. I did not
want to get caught in the cross fire if Sheila saw me. Plus, I'd
only had time to run my fingers through my hair, quickly change
my clothes, and brush my teeth before hustling down here, so it
wasn't like I could walk in like I owned the place.

Though I was sure that any number of the spa workers would
be happy to make me look better, I just wanted to get in and listen for anything that might help me and my brother.

I put my finger up to my closed lips when Annaliese greeted
me. She looked confused but I stepped in close and said, "I'm
here gathering info. Can you discreetly let Merry know I'm late
but ready for the closet?"

That confused the poor woman even more but she scurried
away, hopefully to do what I had asked.

In the meantime, I had just stepped into the hallway behind

the desk and flattened myself against the wall when I heard someone walking in the front door.

"Hello! Hello!" Oh boy! It was Tracy! "Why isn't anyone here for my appointment?" She pounded on the bell on the counter.

"So sorry, Tracy. I'm here, just had to do something really quick." I was not a fan of how meek Annaliese sounded when confronted with Tracy's attitude. I almost came out of the hallway to confront the widow over all of her shenanigans, but I held myself back.

"If you'll follow me," Annaliese said.

"I know where I'm going. I do not need you to lead me. God, when I own this place, you'll be the first one to go."

Oh my. Now she thought she was going to own the spa? Did that put her at four or five businesses? Between wanting my shop, the candle shop, the spa, thinking she owned a boat that some relative was going to run, and whatever it was that Jules owned, I'd think she was going to be up to her eyeballs in debt. If she wasn't already.

I heard a door close and Tracy's muffled voice so I figured it was okay to come out and look for my closet abode. But the front door opened again and someone else walked in. Could it be Sheila? Or was she already here? I should have checked before I asked Annaliese to let Merry know I was here.

"I have an appointment this morning, Annaliese, if you don't mind letting the masseuse know?"

I knew that voice. Rebecca was here, Jules's cousin. So now we had the trifecta of women who might or might not get along in the same building. I was interested to see how that was going to work out for everyone, and also wished I could split myself in three so I could hear everything that was said.

I contemplated texting Maribel and asking her to take a closet, but she was sleeping after her overnight shift and it wasn't like I could ask Felix to walk in and take up space. Goldy, though,

I could probably count on her. I sent a quick text and she agreed to come down, but she was going to get a massage not hide in a closet. I wished I had followed my first inclination instead of this hiding thing.

Annaliese poked her head around the corner. "Merry said you can come on back. Sheila's in the bride room and there's a closet in there." She shrugged and I so wanted to explain myself to her so she didn't think I was some Peeping Tammy or something equally gross.

"I hope they say something that will get Nick out of the cops' sights. He's a nice guy and I don't want to see him take the fall for something I know he never would have done."

That made me feel so much better.

"Thanks, Annaliese."

"Hey, we need to watch out for our locals. There had to be someone else and Nick's lucky he has you to look out for him."

He might not think so if I couldn't get some hint of what was actually going on around here. And though I had promised Felix and Pops that I'd get him last night, I hadn't had a chance because I'd fallen asleep right after I'd warned Nick to just go silently. With the incident being a tossed golf cart, and no mention from Maribel that Nick had been brought in, I had to believe that he'd gotten my text and ran.

Hopefully, before I had to get him, I could clear his name.

I was led back to an empty room where Merry was setting up a nail station.

"I hope this is going to work," she said as she laid out a file and acetone and a few other implements on a gleaming white counter. The soft gray of the walls stood in a beautiful contrast to the way she'd bought all-white furniture. It looked clean and inviting but still cozy.

"Me too. Thanks for letting me in."

She shrugged. "Your brother's a good guy and he shouldn't

have to be on the run because someone is using him as a scape-goat. Now get in quickly, Sheila's due in here any second."

I stepped into the closet and found that there was a door on the other side too. Cracking it open, I realized I was peeking into the room where the waxing happened and I could hear Tracy coming down the hall, her voice at full volume as she told the poor waxing girl exactly what she'd be waxing and exactly how to do it, then she threatened her if she hurt her.

Uh, there was no way she wasn't going to be hurt. It was waxing, after all.

Could I keep both doors cracked and listen to both conversations? It was worth a try. I'd just have to make sure I could keep the two separate and pay attention to both.

I could do this. I had to. Nick's life depended on it.

Chapter 18

Taking a spot up against a rack of towels in the closet, I settled in on a small stool and cleared my head, then took out my tablet. I dimmed the backlight because I didn't want the closet to be glowing if someone looked over, but I could type a lot faster than I could handwrite. And I didn't think the microphone would pick up both conversations, or even one, unless Tracy was going to continue to be loud.

Then I settled in as Merry introduced a nail tech to Sheila, and Tracy continued berating the woman who was soon going to be pouring hot wax on her body. She wasn't the smartest cookie in the box.

Even though I'd gotten a lot of sleep last night, I either needed more or I hadn't slept well on the couch because the fluffy towels were calling me to just rest my head back and be cocooned in their softness. I caught myself dozing and snapped to attention when I heard Tracy's first scream.

"What is wrong with you? Don't you know how to wax?"

"I do, ma'am, as I told you before, it's going to hurt a bit, but I'm going to use a soothing cream afterward. I can go get Merry for you, if you'd prefer."

Tracy harrumphed but must have settled back in and only

made short, sharp sounds for the next minute or so. I checked in with Sheila's side of the closet.

"And so Dave said he was surprising me with something awesome this afternoon, and I'd be super excited about it. I hope it's a car. Or a new house. Or maybe a puppy."

I held in my snort because I was pretty sure that all three of those were not going to be on the island, and if they were staying in a teepee, I highly doubted he could afford any of them. Not to mention that even the puppy wouldn't fit into the treasure box. I quickly wrote a note to remind myself to place the box later today.

This sitting in the closet and hoping for that one piece of information that could help was going to be a waste of time. I thought I'd sneak in and solve everything because most people talked to their stylists, but these two weren't saying anything I needed to hear.

I sighed, quietly.

"So when I call in the debts for this place, I expect you'll want to stay and keep your job," Tracy said between pants of pain.

The technician made a noise that could have been an agreement or dissent. Tracy chose to take it as a yes. Of course she did.

"We'll speak about pay after everything's called in and paid back to me. I'm sure we can work something out. You're not too horrible at your job. I suppose I'll need to keep some staff since the island is small, and I'm not paying for anyone to move here."

I was going to get a headache from rolling my eyes. She was ridiculous. I couldn't imagine that Merry owed that much money to Jules. And even if she did, if it wasn't in writing, how was Tracy expecting to get it back? Did she even know what she was talking about, anyway? Why would she think I owed her money? And Nick had said he hadn't taken anything from Jules before the man had died.

I wasn't sure I could believe that last one, but I desperately wanted to. And since I was stuck in a closet for the moment, I chose to go with it.

"I'm hoping he's going to surprise me with something nice, though, because I'm so sad about Jules dying," Sheila said from my other side.

Her technician also made the vague sound. It must have been something you learned in beautician school. I would have to ask Merry about it.

"He really was my best friend. And even if Dave doesn't get it, I really do miss him. He was kind and nice, and he always explained things to me in a way I could understand them. I'm going to miss him."

That was more the Jules I remembered. He might not have always had a lot of tact when explaining things that could sometimes come off as mansplaining, but for the most part he'd done a lot of good around here. And if he'd never asked for any of the money he loaned people in order to keep their shops up and running, then that was a good something, right?

I mainly didn't like his attitude and his highhandedness, and my opinion of him had only worsened after I'd found out that he was trying to strip Nick and me of our business.

Although the more I thought about it, was it true? Rumor wasn't often reliable, and I hadn't seen a single new glass-bottom boat out on the water or in the yard at the boat builders. Plus, Nick had said Cameron hadn't built him one yet. Per his information, Jules had never even asked for a quote—unless Cameron had lied to Nick so he didn't know competition was coming. Something to think about. I tapped it on the keyboard and got back to listening.

"Jules used to love my eyebrows," Tracy said dreamily from the next room. "He was the gentlest, most wonderful husband I could have ever had. I wish he was still here, but I'm not surprised that he's gone. He had enemies. Did you know that?"

The vague response that was neither yes nor no didn't deter Tracy.

"I wish we hadn't fought that last night, but I got myself into trouble. I'd lied to one man to get the other one to notice me, and I think it backfired on me."

What was this? I scooted the stool over closer to her door and leaned in, careful not to accidentally nudge the door open and expose my hiding place.

"I'm sorry to hear that." The technician spoke for the first time and I realized it was Carissa, the woman who had cut my hair for years.

I texted her quickly. Then I texted her about ten more times that I was in the closet and I needed her to ask a question.

I had my eye up to the crack in the door and saw when she finally checked her phone. I figured if I texted enough, she'd think it was something wrong and check, and I was right.

But her gaze zipped up when she read my text and her eyes widened.

I texted her to ask how it backfired. Carissa shook her head after reading and I texted the word *please* in all caps.

She frowned as she turned back to Tracy. "How do you think it backfired on you? Will you be okay?"

"Oh, yes, I'll be fine. In the end it happened just as I had hoped, but now I have a different problem, one that keeps hiding from me. I need to get it taken care of so that no loose ends are left."

Carissa looked back over her shoulder and I texted again.

"Are the loose ends here on the island? Will you be here for a while this time? I know you like to travel back and forth between here and Long Beach. Now that Jules is gone, will you pick one place?" She smeared another daub of wax on Tracy's upper lip and pulled. I heard the rip all the way over in the closet and squinted my eyes in empathetic pain. No, thank you.

Tracy squeaked. "Um, yes, yes, I'm going to be here for a while. I have debts to collect. Jules let too many people slide with his generosity. I want that money back in the estate. When it closes and I can get the lawyer to actually answer my calls, I'll spend the next few months getting affairs in order and then everything will change. Just you watch."

My question was, what was going to change? So I quickly texted that to Carissa.

She shot me a look through the crack in the door and I shrugged, though she probably couldn't see me.

"What will you change first?" Carissa slathered on another layer of wax and got out a small piece of cloth. She smoothed it over the wax and grabbed the corner to rip it off again. Since this one was on an eyebrow, Tracy didn't make much noise. Either that or she was so numbed with pain that she didn't feel it anymore.

"My first order of business is going to be buying that witch Rebecca out of my house. I know she owns part of it, and I want her name off. I'm having it appraised today and then I'll pay off the appraiser to make it lower so she can't charge me too much."

"That's good to know."

My eyes almost popped out of my head, and I nearly tumbled out of the closet. That was Rebecca's voice. When I steadied myself enough to get the best angle possible of the room, I saw that Goldy was trailing behind her.

Tracy jerked to a sitting position. She looked ridiculous with wax over one eye and another strip of cloth stuck to her face. But her fuming rage was anything but funny.

"What are you doing here?" she seethed.

"Well, Merry and I have been friends for years. In fact, I once worked the front desk for her. I think I have every right to be here. And you?" Rebecca was cool as the cucumbers they probably used on your eyes when doing a mask here, but the gleam in her eyes said something more was going on.

"I'm getting ready to see the lawyer."

"And you need waxed eyebrows and other parts before you can see the lawyer? Interesting."

Tracy sputtered. "No, but I want to look nice when I take over control of all Jules's accounts. It benefits a woman to look professional when dealing with people she'll do business with again."

"And what other business will you be doing? I don't think he defends against civil suits for bribery."

Oh, burn! And Tracy seemed to understand that she was in a bad position.

"I wouldn't really have lied to you or bribed anyone. Of course I want you to get fair market price for your share of the house."

I could tell she was totally lying. Surely everyone else in the room knew it too.

"Again, I find that interesting, since I don't believe there is any part of the house that isn't mine, to be honest with you." Rebecca smiled and there was little to no gentleness in that look. "In fact, I believe the lawyer isn't calling you back because I specifically asked him not to. I wanted to tell you myself that Jules left you nothing. So I hope you have cash for your services today because I shut off your card."

Tracy scrambled off the table and then just stood there with her mouth open.

"Coming, Goldy?" Rebecca asked. "I believe our massages are waiting for us. In fact, it'll be my treat."

And they exited the room in robes with the name of the spa emblazoned on the back.

I had no idea what I expected Tracy to do, but it certainly wasn't for her to storm out of the room in the opposite direction with the cloth still attached to her eyebrow with the wax under it.

"Tracy, wait!" Carissa called and then ran after her. And since

I wasn't really supposed to be here, I was stuck in the closet while Carissa sorted out Tracy. Shoot!

I leaned my head back against the towels and tried to figure out my next move. I certainly wasn't expecting the door to open from the nail side. So when I fell through and ended up on the floor, I was staring up at Sheila.

I shrugged and waved at her. What else was I supposed to do?

After dusting myself off and apologizing for scaring the nail technician, I quickly excused myself and went out to the front desk. There was no need for secrecy at this point as far as I was concerned. I was much more interested in what Tracy would do when she found out her card truly was cancelled.

Was Rebecca the sole inheritor from Jules?

Oh man. This could be a huge blow up.

And in fact it was. I wasn't two steps from the front desk when I heard Tracy yelling. I wasn't the only one hauling tail to the front reception area. When I arrived, I was joined by women in turbans, women in bathrobes, and one woman with just a towel wrapped around her glistening body. She stood out to me not only for the towel and sweat but because she had beautiful red hair with the most intriguing silver stripe in the front.

Wait. Hadn't Felix mentioned something about a woman who looked like Bonnie Raitt who was involved in all this?

Was every woman who had been attached to Jules in some way here at the same time?

Interesting would be an understatement if that was true.

"Put it on my account, then!" Tracy yelled, bouncing on her toes as if she wanted to vault over the counter at Merry, who had replaced Annaliese. The poor receptionist was hovering behind Merry like she was afraid of bodily harm. But when I looked a little closer, she actually seemed more to be hovering over Merry's shoulder so as not to miss the show. The mischievous smile on her face spoke volumes.

"I'm sorry, Tracy, but you don't have an account here." Merry folded her hands on the desk in front of her and leaned in, almost daring Tracy to take a swing.

"Then put it against the money you owe Jules back from all the times he's bailed you out."

Rebecca stood on the opposite side of the room, still in her robe. "That won't be happening either. Perhaps you didn't completely understand me, Tracy, but you have nothing. That prenup that Jules had you sign will hold up in court. You walk away with nothing more than you started out with two years ago, when you tricked him into marrying you because your boyfriend was supposedly beating you up and you needed his protection."

It was like déjà vu. "Wait, she's used that one before?" I blurted out. I hadn't meant to call attention to myself, but I couldn't help it.

"Why do you ask it as if she's using it now?" Rebecca asked, crossing her arms over her chest.

I darted a glance at Tracy and then went for broke. "She told my brother Jules was beating her and Nick had to come save her. He was supposed to meet her at her house so they could escape, and then Jules was dead, and Tracy never came to the house, and Nick came to the dock, and we found Jules under the boat." This was exhausting, but it got everyone's attention.

"That's rich." Rebecca shot a death glare at Tracy. "Did you do that fancy makeup to make it look like you had a shiner again? I know Jules fell for that, but *I* also know you used to take classes in movie makeup before you decided you wanted to be a kept woman."

I would have sworn Tracy's head was about to explode off her neck. She turned a horrible shade of red and screamed like her hair was on fire. Then she ran out the front door, still with the cloth and wax on her face and only a robe covering her body.

Hopefully she found someone who would be kind when they ripped the wax strips off.

All the women in the lobby just kind of stared at one another in stunned silence. Then tiny groups began talking quietly, mostly the technician or stylist and their client.

Merry took control of the situation before it got out of hand. "Please go back to what you were doing. I'm sorry for the inconvenience. This is not normally how things work at La Fluencia, and for the trouble I'm willing to give each of you twenty percent off your services for the day. Again, I'm sorry."

She stepped back into the hallway where I had hidden earlier and took Annaliese with her. Everyone else slowly went back to their respective business except Goldy, Rebecca, and Sheila, who was standing like a bison when you approached it too fast in your autoette.

Sheila stared at her nails, then down at her toes, then back at her nails before lifting her gaze to Rebecca. "I'm pretty sure Jules had prepaid for our salon services, but I'll figure something out if you need me to." She gulped.

"No, dear, that's fine. Your mother was a good woman and I'm happy to help out with this."

"Oh, wow, thank you. Thank you so much. I'll leave now in case you need to get back to your own spa day."

Rebecca nodded to her and then blew out a breath as soon as Sheila left the room. It was like Rebecca deflated in on herself. Goldy was quick to catch her, and then put her in a chair so she didn't fall to the floor. What was it with the women connected to Jules fainting?

"Do you need a glass of water? Something stronger?" Goldy patted Rebecca's hand and gently pushed her back into the maroon oversized chair. Those things were plush and Rebecca sank in with a groan.

"Can you see if they might have a mimosa? I know it's early

for drinking but I feel it's warranted, and the orange juice makes it breakfast, right?"

Goldy chuckled and patted her hand again, then went in search of Merry.

"I guess I should get out of your hair too. You probably need to rest after that." I hooked a thumb over my shoulder and pointed it in the direction Tracy had just stormed off, like Rebecca didn't know what I was talking about.

"Actually, do you mind staying for a sec? I don't want Tracy to get herself all fired up and come steaming back in here when I'm all alone." She sighed and rested her head back, closing her eyes. "I didn't want it to come to that. I did want to tell her myself in private because I knew the news was going to be devastating to her. I was almost certain that she didn't know when I heard she was going around to various stores and claiming they were hers. She was making waves and I wanted to keep her from embarrassing herself, but when she was yelling at Merry, who I've known forever, I just lost it and went corporate-lawyer on her."

I sat in the chair next to hers. "Honestly, I would have blown a gasket. You were totally cool and calm and collected. You held it together pretty well from what I could see. And with the way she's been acting lately she deserved to be brought down a notch."

"Or four." Rebecca sighed. "I'm not sure what Jules ever saw in her, and I was so concerned when they got married that things wouldn't go well. I tried to be there for him, and I'm glad I encouraged him to get that prenup signed. I have a feeling I have a lot to clean up once this is all settled."

Goldy came out with a tray of mimosas. I tried to pass up the glass she handed to me, but she shoved it into my hand and tipped it toward my mouth. "Drink up, my lovelies. I think we have a suspect to give to the police and we can get Nick to come out of hiding. I'd say that was almost as good as a massage."

* * *

I put in another call to Nick as soon as we got out of the spa, but I couldn't get a hold of him. I left him a message letting him know not to interact with Tracy, who might have gone off the deep end, and then waved goodbye to Rebecca and Goldy. I'd declined lunch to go with the mimosa so I decided to leave my autoette at the spa and walk, though, just in case. There had been more champagne than orange juice in that thing, and I certainly didn't want to get pulled over by the police for drunk driving in a golf cart.

Especially when I was heading to the very station they'd take me to in order to sleep off my buzz.

The walk did me good and gave me time in which to figure out what exactly I wanted to say and how I wanted to say it. In fact, I brought out my tablet and started a new spreadsheet to detail what I felt they'd want to know. Like the fact that Tracy had said she was heading to their house after the cruise but never showed up. How she was sure she was inheriting. How she already had plans for the money and was calling in debts. How she had roped Nick into the whole thing with her fake makeup and false sob story. How she'd used that sob story before.

It all fit. And it had also been nagging at me that the body had drifted in from the opposite direction of the harbor where Jules should have been.

Did she have Jules meet her at the house, kill him after Nick came down to the *Sea Bounder*, and then roll his body over the cliff from their house? I couldn't see how she'd be strong enough to carry the body down to the beach and roll him in. With the currents that night he would have drifted from that direction. If she'd killed him at the harbor, he would have gone the other way.

But, honestly, that was no longer my problem. I was only supposed to clear my brother's name. And as far as I was concerned, that was done and signed and sealed and delivered.

Was Nick the loose end Tracy had alluded to that needed to be cleaned up, though? And had I missed anything by not talking to the woman with the red hair and the silver streak?

As much as I was currently not a Tracy fan, that didn't mean I wanted her to be falsely accused either. Shoot! Now I was going to have to rethink things. I picked a bench on the edge of the sand and sat. The clues all seemed to point to Tracy. It had to be her. I bit my lip, not caring if I looked like a bulldog. But what if Nick had helped her roll that body? What if he was the loose end?

What if he was the one she was going to throw under the bus?

I was still sitting on the bench when the woman with the red hair walked across my path.

I ran after her and tapped her on the shoulder. She was far taller than I had thought in her high heels.

"Ah, the troublemaker. I'd know your face anywhere."

"Troublemaker? Hardly." I took offense to that.

"Oh, I think you might be more of a troublemaker than you let on. I heard you at the salon earlier, and I've been watching you." She said it with a smile, but the words creeped me out.

"You've been watching me?" Totally creeped out.

"I've been watching a lot of people. Your brother, for example, might want to make sure he can explain being up at Jules's house around the time the man was killed."

"What?"

"Surely he told you that when you all had your little chat on your grandparents' deck. I was wondering why you didn't let him go inside and then I thought that perhaps it was best to not interrupt."

"Wait, how do you know all of this?" And what kind of trouble was I going to get into for aiding and abetting a man wanted for murder?

"I have my ways, but you might want to be a little more careful in the residential areas. We have a burglar running around, and I'm the one tasked with finding them. I have my fingers in a lot of pies." She adjusted the backpack slung over her left shoulder and leaned in. "I can tell you this, though. Tracy was at the house that night, but she was hiding from Nick. Jules was also at the house, but they didn't cross paths. Maybe that will help you." She waved to someone behind me and when I turned to see who it was, the woman walked away and melted into the afternoon crowd.

Who was she, and how on earth did she know so much? And more importantly, how much had she told the police?

Chapter 19

Being in my gift shop, the Dame of the Sea, with the air-conditioning running was at least one way to cool down to some extent. Normally, the ocean breeze was enough, but I felt on the verge of a panic attack and I didn't want to plaster myself to a screen if it got to the point that I overheated.

A few customers wandered around in the store and asked a question here and there, but nothing that needed too much of my attention.

I took the time to work on my spreadsheet. I was careful to keep the info about the rival off the sheet, but at this point I needed everything else at least in one place. I hoped to talk with Goldy and Pops and then Maribel and Felix at some point soon to make sure I had everything organized to the best of my ability.

I still thought the murderer might be Tracy, but I had no proof and probably no leg to stand on. If I just walked into the police station and told them it had to be her, they would assume I was only trying to save my brother.

I tapped my stylus on the counter in time with my racing thoughts and it sounded like a metronome set on high. Was I missing something? Had something today passed me by because so much information had come at the same time?

It was obvious from Tracy's reaction that she had had no idea she wasn't inheriting. And a part of me felt for her—only to the extent that I hated to be taken off guard. That was far overshadowed by the fact that her whole attitude had been shut down. If she'd killed Jules then she'd only shot herself in the foot because now she had less than she'd had before.

Would that send her over the edge? She'd run off and had no home to go to if Rebecca was going to kick her off the estate Jules had purchased years ago. So where would she go and how would she pay for it? Should I be out looking for her to see if she was so unstable that I could get her to admit what she'd done?

My tapping sped up with that thought until Goldy came in and took the thing out of my hand.

"You have a line in front of you and you might want to make sure that you're taking care of your customers." She glanced to the line at the register and I flushed with embarrassment.

"I'm so sorry," I said to the first person in line.

"That's okay, if my brother was a murder suspect I'd be off in la-la land too." She put two shirts on the counter and one of the pots Lacey had thrown the other day. My word, was that just yesterday? It seemed like forever ago.

"I'm going to clear his name. He didn't do it."

"I hear you. I don't think he did either."

I peered at her. I didn't know her that I could recall, so how did she know about my brother? Or was she just fishing? I'd listened to a podcast the other week about people who just liked living vicariously on the edge and frequently became pen pals with men in prison because it intrigued them to talk with an inmate.

"Do you know Nick?"

She giggled and blushed. "Yes, he flies for my dad sometimes. He's so nice and I just can't believe he'd do anything so awful, no matter how much that woman pushed him."

"What do you know about a woman pushing him?" I asked. The customer behind her cleared her throat and looked at her watch. "Sorry, sorry. I'm almost done." The customer harrumphed. Fine by me.

"All I know is that he was grumbling up at the plane the last time about some old girlfriend bothering him. My dad told him to not pay attention to old girlfriends. There was a reason why they never worked out and he should respect that."

"Who's your dad?"

"Marvin Goldberg."

My brain zipped into high gear. "Goldy, can you take the next customer?"

I didn't wait for her reply, I simply stepped out from behind the counter and grabbed the girl's elbow. I didn't drag her behind me, but it was a close thing as I shepherded her to my small storage room at the back next to the bathroom.

"What are you doing?" She yanked her elbow away from my grip.

"Please, I need your help. I need to know if your dad had anything to do with Jules dying. Not that he'd kill him," I said quickly. "But does he know anything about it? His name came up recently as having a beef with Jules, and I'm just trying to eliminate people as best I can so the police have one solid suspect that's not Nick."

Leaning back against the wall, she took me in from head to toe. "And if I told you my father had him killed, but I couldn't tell you how or when?"

Was she kidding? Testing me? "Well, if he had Jules killed then I would hope he would turn himself in and get a really good lawyer. This is totally not fair to Nick to have to be the fall guy for someone else."

"He didn't do that. I can guarantee you that. He's said he wishes Jules would just fall off a cliff, but I don't think he actually made that happen. If he wanted revenge for ruining his first engagement and his business prospects years ago, I don't think Dad would have waited all this time to make it happen."

"You never know, revenge is said to be best served cold." I wasn't sure where that phrase came from or why people thought it was true, but I'd have to look that up later.

"All I know is that Jules took him to the cleaners and broke up his engagement at the exact same time. I don't know how they were connected but I can tell you my dad wasn't even on the island when Jules died. He got called away to San Francisco and didn't get back until the next day. I'm sure there's a log of his flight if you need to check it out."

Dang it! Not that I wanted it to be her dad but I wanted it to be anyone but Nick. "You might just want to tell him to have that alibi ready if they start looking at people other than Nick."

"Will do. He wasn't totally heartbroken when it happened, he was more angry that she listened to Jules instead of the guy she said she was so in love with, but I guess that happens sometimes." She shrugged in the tight confines of my storage closet. Another closet. I should be used to this by now.

"Yeah, not everyone is smart about love." Myself included, though for different reasons.

"Anyway, he said it was really hard to see her when he got to the island, but when he tried to touch base with her, she seemed really distant. Ever since my mom died last year he's been lost. Maybe he thought reconnecting would make sense, but she was having none of it. I guess she thinks she's about to be independent and doesn't want to get involved."

"And you don't know who she is?"

She shook her head just as someone banged on the storage door. We both jumped and I whipped the door open.

Goldy stood there smiling. "Sorry to interrupt, but you have a longer line and more boxes to hide. If you need more from Jessica, then I think you're going to have to do it later."

"I don't have anything else, sorry. I'd better head back to my dad. He's going to wonder where I am. I just wanted to let you know I'm thinking of Nick and hope he gets out of this."

Jessica left the store without signing her credit slip, but I knew where to find her if I had to. I looked at Goldy and she looked back.

"Watch who you talk to and who you talk in front of," Goldy said. "That little angel causes quite a bit of trouble herself and her dad is always trying to get her out of it. I don't like her for Nick, but if that information will help you at all then I guess we might owe her something."

"She just said it wasn't her dad."

"Why would you think it had been?" She looked completely surprised and I forgot that I hadn't had a chance to fill her in or invite her to share the document on my tablet. Not that she'd know what to do with it, but still.

I gave the brief rundown and she chuckled. "That marriage would have never worked no matter what either of the parties wanted. Rebecca had a lot of living to do before she would be ready to settle down. She's still not ready, if you ask me. We talked over lunch and while she's sad that Jules is gone, she's also looking forward to spreading her wings. That marriage was arranged by her dad and would have tanked within months. She hadn't even gone to college yet."

"So another dead end." My shoulders sagged. I tried so hard not to feel like I was fifty steps behind the ball. Or maybe on a whole different field altogether.

"You'll figure it out, and it really could be as simple as being the wife, sweetheart. Sometimes the solution is right in front of your face when you get done ignoring it."

"But why would Tracy have taken out her sugar daddy without being sure she was going to inherit?"

"I don't believe it would have occurred to her to check. She was always so sure everything would work out in her favor and really nothing has yet. She needs to get her own business in order."

"Speaking of business, I guess we'd better go back out and ring up customers."

"That's my girl, go make that register sing and then deliver the boxes. And with today's information, I think you have enough to know that Tracy was the one who did it. That will clear Nick's name and your part will be done."

After making a ton of sales, I needed to get the boxes for the treasure hunts delivered. I took an extra one with me so that Dave would have something for Sheila to find. I still thought that situation was very strange, but who was I to judge? His credit card payment had gone through and that was as far as I needed to concern myself.

And Sheila was back on good terms with the Tisdale family. Rebecca might not be paying for her wedding, but she'd at least let her get fixed up today and this afternoon Dave would present her with whatever he had up his sleeve. Maybe there was hope for them yet.

After dropping the first five off, I carried the last empty box up past the botanical gardens and prepared to put it under some foliage by the fountain. We didn't actually dig anything up unless it was sand, and even then it was only a shallow hole so that the box was easy to find. The last thing we wanted was to have a bunch of boxes left behind and a slew of unhappy kids because we were too good at hiding things.

So I parked my autoette, hooked Whiskers up to her leash, and then went into the gardens, meandering along so she could smell anything that caught her fancy. I had considered leaving her with the autoette for the walk because I was running short on time, but I'd promised to take her and she'd been very good at being patient with me the last few days.

Walking along the paths, I feathered my hand along the ferns and flowers that grew here with help from the conservancy society. There were so many things that bloomed here naturally, but this was a place that flourished with life when so many other places on the island were arid and dry.

Under my feet, the dirt kicked up in little puffs and hundreds of footprints marked the fact that this was a popular place to get a beautiful view of the ocean below you.

But I had a purpose here and needed to get this chest into place as soon as possible.

"Whiskers, I wish I knew what the heck I was doing with this mystery thing."

She made this adorable snuffling sound and wound her way through my legs.

"This document thing is great, and I appreciate having helpers, but there's just a part of me that wishes I didn't have to do anything like this. Not the box hiding, you know I love that, but this murder thing. It's so not my forte."

She meowed and purred like a rumbling truck.

"I'm so happy you listen. If only Nick would do the same thing." I sighed. "I think we're going to have to just hand it over to the police. There are too many options and not enough info on anyone. Is it Tracy?" I kicked a rock and Whiskers went after it, tugging the leash. She pounced and I squatted next to her. "Is it Marvin? I mean, sure his daughter says no, but what if she's wrong? What about Sheila? But that would be like Tracy. I mean, the girl had it even better than his wife, but maybe he denied her something and she shoved him off the cliff? Thank goodness Rebecca was nice to her at least, especially after the way Tracy chewed into her. Or is the murderer someone I haven't met? Or someone I've met but can't pin it on? That lady with the red hair?"

I put my hands on my knees to straighten myself and Whiskers's back went up as she howled. "I'll take the rock—" But the rest of the sentence was lost as I was pushed into a gully and tumbled head over heels through rocks and brush.

The sun was still in the same place when I cracked my eyes open and felt for lumps on my head. "Ow."

Whiskers howled from the top of the hill. Well, at least I'd let go of her leash in time to not drag her down with me.

I didn't feel anything broken. Shaking my arms out, nothing hurt too much, and when I stood I didn't collapse on a broken leg. I didn't even seem to have sprained an ankle.

But I had a heck of a climb back up the hillside. I scrambled since there really wasn't much to grab hold of.

And when I got to the top, the first thing I saw was blood on Whiskers's paw. Darting my gaze around, I looked for the person who'd shoved me and prayed they hadn't hurt Whiskers. I was one thing, my baby was a whole other subject.

But there was no one within sight. What the heck? I stood up and tried stretching to make sure nothing was truly broken. Did I really get pushed, or had I just tumbled? The footing wasn't always solid up here and it was possible that in my deep concentration, I had simply stepped wrong. Maybe?

But that seemed unlikely. And where had the blood come from?

Taking Whiskers's paw in my right hand, I petted her with my left. "Just let me look at it, baby. I promise not to hurt you."

She squinted her eyes at me, but she did reach out to give me better access to her paw. I saw some skin caught on the end of her claws. Had she clawed someone after they'd pushed me? Grabbing my cat up, I started worrying about the fact that I was alone up here.

I used my phone to call Felix and ask if he could meet me at the fountain. At this point I just wanted to get this last box delivered and then get the heck home and reassess my whole life, preferably with a cup of tea and a big donut or cupcake. Or both.

My gaze kept darting right and left, looking for anyone up here with me, listening for anyone nearby. I was shaken when I put the cat back down.

And yet, as I walked around a curve, I missed hearing someone huffing with labored breath and nearly overtook Dave.

"It can't be that late already," I blurted out. "I still have time."

"Oh, Whitney, I'm so thankful you're here." He grabbed my hand and made me almost bobble the chest.

Stepping back, I shook his hand off. "I told you I'd be here before it was time to treasure hunt." Glancing at my watch told me I still had over an hour, even with my little trip down the gully.

"I know, I know, but Sheila found the map and took off by herself. She wouldn't listen when I told her that it wasn't ready yet. I lost her because she took the golf cart, and I had to follow on foot. Now I can't find her, and I don't know where the map led to. I just remember that it was somewhere up here."

The sun was going to go down in about two hours and the park would close then. I led the way to where we should find Sheila if she was any good at following a diagram. If we didn't find her, I might be forced to call the police regarding Sheila for reasons other than what I had originally thought.

"We're heading up the mountain. There's a fountain up there and the box was going to be around the back under a fall of flowers."

Dave followed along close behind me, crowding me a few times, but I just picked up the pace and was so relieved I had Whiskers with me. She rubbed up against his leg and his arms were clear of scratches, so I was pretty sure my assailant wasn't him. If there even had been an assailant. As I walked, I noticed a stinging on my calf and looking back, realized the skin and blood were probably mine when I'd stumbled and Whiskers had caught me with her claw.

That didn't exactly make me feel better, but it wasn't as bad as what my overworked imagination had conjured up.

Finally, we reached the summit. Dave was huffing and puffing behind me, which I found strange when supposedly he was a runner.

But that thought flew out of my head when we went around the back of the fountain and found Sheila laid out on the ground, her hands clasped around her neck and her tongue protruding. Dave yelled some incoherent word, and I gasped.

Quickly leaning down, I felt for a pulse, then closed my eyes and exhaled. There was nothing.

Another dead body. I sure hoped that cell service was good up here this afternoon because I was going to be putting in another call to the police to tell them I'd found one of my two best suspects dead.

Chapter 20

Other than a few side eyes from the deputies who'd responded to my call, I didn't get much grief for finding another dead body.

Dave, however, was not quite so lucky. They wanted to talk to him as a "person of interest" and he was escorted down to the station for questioning.

Felix arrived shortly after they followed Dave down the stairs.

"Oh man," he said, taking my hand in his.

"Yeah, I don't know what the heck is going on around here, but I feel like I'm on a roller coaster that refuses to stop."

"No doubt. Any idea what happened to her?"

We watched as they used a stretcher to move the very dead Sheila down the hill and into the waiting ambulance. I turned away when they passed by us.

"Hey, I'm sorry." Felix tucked a strand of hair behind my ear and then tipped my chin up until I looked into his eyes. It was a long way up with our difference in height, but I was happy to have something to concentrate on other than Sheila.

"Can I be done now? There's no way Nick killed this woman. He didn't even know her." But Tracy had, and had threatened her just this morning. Had she found out that Sheila was going to inherit something and had gone after the other woman to make sure that didn't happen?

I had no idea and very little strength left to care. Even though I didn't want to do it, my body decided to droop against Felix and let him hold me up. Just for a minute, no more.

"If you really don't want to do this, Whit, no one is going to blame you for letting the cops handle it. They'll find your brother and make sure justice is served. No matter what the captain wants, the guys and girls on this team are solid. I promise."

I bit my tongue because another deputy was moving past us, and this was not the place to talk about how I knew Nick was not going to be found until he was good and ready.

"Can you meet me at the house in about thirty minutes? We need to talk." I gave him the pleading gaze, hoping that he'd understand without me having to say I couldn't talk about this here.

"I can, but I'm going to need a little more information than that."

I leaned into him again and brought his ear down to my mouth. "Please just trust me."

Straightening, he looked down at me, then up at the crime scene being processed.

"Okay, but this had better be good. There's a lot on the line here."

"Believe me, I know."

I turned to leave and Captain Warrington was blocking my way. "If you know where your brother is, Whitney, you'd better turn him in. Two deaths on my island at his hand are two too many and I want him in my station now. He'll pay for all of this."

I didn't respond because what could I say? He stepped aside and I very pointedly did not look at Felix as I trotted down the hill with my cat in hand. I didn't have time to walk her. I had to tell Nick to hide as deep as possible until we could figure out why the cops wanted it to be him.

I did not want to drive up to my house, but I had to. I knew there were going to be a ton of questions and very few answers, and that the answers I did have were probably not going to make anyone happy. But there was nothing else I could do. If I drove a little slower, stopped for every pedestrian who looked like they might want to step off the curb, and got out to pet as many dogs as possible, I couldn't help myself.

Whiskers was not going to be happy with the way I smelled of dog, but I figured Maribel and Felix were going to be less happy than that when I told them my brother had gone into hiding when I could have turned him in to the cops.

Who was I kidding? I should have turned him in instead of sending him to the hangar. At least then he would have been safe and not in danger, hoping against hope that no one would find him or that Buckey wouldn't tell on him.

Pulling up to my house, I rested for just a moment before going in. I put my head on the steering wheel, almost wishing Felix would come out and massage my neck. Since that didn't happen, it was time to go in.

Maribel and Felix stopped talking as soon as I opened the front door. They didn't start again as I put my keys on the hook by the door, set down Whiskers's basket in the living room, and then petted her even as she backed away from me. I so wanted to yank her into my lap, but that would make for even less happiness, and I had to face what I'd done.

"I should make a phone call before we talk," I said into the silence, and the room erupted.

"Absolutely not." That was Maribel.

"That's probably a very bad idea before we know what we're

dealing with. I already told Maribel about the death. At least as much as I knew. We need details, Whit. Please."

It was that last word that had me sinking into the couch next to Maribel and dropping my head back against the afghan we had draped across the back. "I had Nick yesterday afternoon, right at my grandparents. He talked to me about everything and instead of taking him to the police or telling him to go himself, I sent him to the airport. Then when I heard the sirens going up to the airport, I texted him to ask him to just go peacefully, but he never responded and he must have run." I stared at the ceiling while I talked, not wanting to look at anyone and see the disappointment that had to be on their faces.

"Oh, Whit." Maribel scooted closer and rested her head on my shoulder. "I can't say I wouldn't have done the same thing, but this puts all of us in a very bad place. Is that the call you need to make? Because I'm thinking you need to call him right now to make sure that not only does he not know Sheila, but that he also was definitely within sight of Buckey the whole time."

He might not know Sheila, but he had been part of the scene at the hotel. And if Tracy was the one who was doing these horrible things and trying to throw Nick under the bus for her crimes, then how was I going to prove it was her and not him?

I took a deep breath. "Okay, I'm going to call him. We'll go from there." I looked over at Felix, who had yet to say anything after my revelation.

He merely shrugged and sat back in his chair with his ankle crossed over his opposite knee. Well, no matter what happened, I guessed it was good that I hadn't really thought Felix and I would get back together.

I took my phone out of my pocket and thumbed the screen on. After typing in my code, my notifications went crazy—text after text flashed up along with seven different calls and all of them from Nick. My cell service wasn't always reliable, and this was one of those times I wished I had a different provider. How long ago had he been trying to contact me?

I glanced over everything and called him as quickly as I could.

"Nick, where are you? I told you to stay at the hangar."

He huffed like he was running. "I was going to go back after last night but the cops came back and were there looking at Buckey because he'd known Sheila. I couldn't stay. I'm sorry."

"Are you on the run? Like, literally?"

"Yes, Whitney. I'm going to go to Two Harbors and hide somewhere in the tiny town. I don't know that it will change anything, but I can't be caught yet."

"Nick, I think I was wrong. I think you should turn yourself in to the cops. They're not going to hurt you. They're going to need to talk to you to find the right murderer. You weren't anywhere near the conservancy when she was killed, so you should be in the clear for that."

"I was on my way to meet Tracy. It's time I find out what she is about. But then I heard the sirens, so I wasn't at the hangar, and I'd taken a walk before that to clear my head. Buckey might say I was there. I can't guarantee that since I really wasn't."

Yeesh, when was this going to end? "*Please* just turn yourself in. I'm sure we can figure this out before they transfer you anywhere or charge you." But I was talking to dead air. He'd hung up, and I didn't know what else to do but clutch the phone in my hand and wish that none of this was happening, much less to my brother.

Leaning forward, I dangled my hands between my knees, turning my phone over and over. "I know this doesn't look good, but I know he didn't do this. We have to step up this plan and put the death of Sheila into the mix. Who had it out for both people?"

"Do you think it's a vengeance kind of thing?" Felix spread

his arms out over the top of the big chair in the corner. "Tracy kills her husband, then goes for the woman who was draining his account?"

"But why now?" Maribel hugged a pillow. "Why not months ago? Why not a few months from now? Why not just leave it at Jules? Tracy didn't want to pay for the wedding, okay. But once she got rid of Jules, Sheila moved to a teepee, so it's not like that bill was going to his credit card."

"Maybe they got into a fight again?" I offered.

"Maybe it was the groom," Felix said. "Maybe he killed Jules because he found him to be a threat. Then he killed Sheila because she wasn't going to be happy without her godfather, or with anything Dave would be able to do?"

"The police took him in for questioning. They called him a "person of interest" out of his hearing. I wouldn't want to be called that." I thought my way through what I wanted to say next. Maybe that meant Captain Warrington was rethinking his position that Nick had killed both people. "Should we call the police and tell them to question him about Jules's murder?" At this point I was on board with anything that didn't involve them dragging my brother back in for questioning.

"I don't know if they'll think the two murders are related." Maribel shrugged.

The timer in the kitchen buzzed and Felix smiled. "Let's eat and then we can talk some more. I have a few theories." He got up from the chair much more gracefully than I ever did. It was one of those deep chairs meant for people who were definitely taller than me, and I usually avoided it because a time or two I actually had to roll out of the thing and drop onto all fours before rising to my feet. Not exactly graceful.

Maribel scooched over as soon as he was out of the room. "You had better have one amazing reason for why you left him on the mainland without a backward glance."

"I can't do this right now, and he can probably hear us, Maribel."

"Pssh, don't try to duck out of this conversation. He can't hear us, and even if he can, I'm sure he'd like to know why too."

I bumped her with my shoulder. "It was complicated. I didn't think he'd want to do long distance. We'd just started dating, and I didn't really think it was going anywhere, so I didn't pursue it after he stopped calling."

"Did he actually stop calling, though? He said his grandmother died so he had to go to Mexico for the week we moved here."

My eyes widened and my heart stopped at her words. But I didn't have time to respond because Felix came back into the room with a tin-foil pan in one hand and a stack of dishes in the other.

"Is that what I think it is?" I moved forward on the couch and then snickered when Maribel fell over behind me.

He smiled that smile that made his eyes crinkle. "If you think it's seafood fettuccine, then yes, I believe that might just be what this is. Brain food. We'll get all those vitamins and carbs and other good things, I'm sure, and then put our thoughts together in the spreadsheet. These new developments deserve a new plan."

So that's what we did. The whole time my brain kept going back and forth between Maribel's revelation and my brother's plight. They both deserved attention, but Nick was going to have to come first. If what Maribel said was true, then Felix wasn't going anywhere. We could work on things after this whole debacle was sorted out.

The new plan involved me and the beach the next morning. Felix was giving diving lessons throughout the day and Maribel had been called in early to cover a shift while evidence was sorted through.

That left me by myself on a weekend with the summer crowd. I was on a mission, though, and a mission would keep me focused as I went around street parties, beach volleyball, and yoga on the beach. Pops had the tour-boating in hand so I wasn't needed as back-up.

On was a hunt for gossip and I wasn't going back until I found some—or at least until it was time to take over from Goldy, who had opened the store for me at ten. Hopefully, I'd have something before that.

About noon, I finally had to concede that no one was really talking about the second murder in less than a week. They were talking about the upcoming Fourth of July holiday and related parties, who was wearing what, and which celebrities they'd seen, or which ones they hoped to see.

I stopped in at the Drop of Sunshine coffee shop and sat with my tablet while I waited for the drink to be delivered to the small café table. I didn't have a lot to add to the spreadsheet, but Felix had put a few notes in about Sheila's death. It was sad that someone so young had been cut down. I wanted justice for her too.

Had it been Dave? Felix didn't seem to think so, and neither did the police, after having questioned him. They were still looking for Nick. They did have a few leads that pointed to someone else, but Felix didn't know who.

I was going to have to get Nick to turn himself in. I'd go over to Two Harbors this evening and convince him it was the right thing to do when Maribel was on the front desk. Maybe things would go better if he didn't run, and if we were all there to stand up for him.

I doubted that all of his family and friends being at the station would help, but at this point it couldn't hurt. Could it?

My cell phone rang on the table. Turning away from the crowd, I took the call when I saw it was Nick on the screen. Maybe I wouldn't have to go to Two Harbors, after all.

"Please tell me you're going to turn yourself in. I really think this has gone too far already. I just can't keep up. I'm not going to be able to figure anything out while I'm worried about them catching you."

"I can't, Whit. I just heard they're going to try to pin this Shelley girl's murder on me too. I've never even met her! Why would I kill her?"

"It's Sheila. And she was the one at the hotel who you dragged Tracy away from when she was tearing into her fiancé about the hotel bill her husband was paying for."

"Oh man, this is not good. How did I get trapped in all this crap?"

"Tracy. Tracy is how you got trapped in all this. I think she's pointing the finger at you. I think she's telling the police, or someone who then tells the police that it was you. From what I can gather, she's just letting you swing in the wind, hoping that with you gone it will clear up all her loose ends. She said as much in the spa and insinuated that once you were handled she was free to pursue whatever she wanted."

"You have got to be kidding me."

"I wouldn't do that to you, Nick. I get that there's some long-ago connection-with-a-girlfriend thing, but she's not who she might have been then. She's out for blood. I wouldn't doubt that she killed Sheila just because she was getting money and Tracy was getting nothing. You should have seen her shriek her way out of the spa when Rebecca told her she was inheriting nothing. It was not pretty."

"I just can't . . . I just have such a hard time believing she is that dirty."

"I get it. I do," I said when he scoffed at me. "I do get it, but it's time to save your own neck. Who's going to be next? What if she goes after Rebecca and takes her out so that if Tracy's not getting money then no one is? Rebecca used to babysit us. She doesn't deserve to also fall at the hand of that banshee."

"You're right, but what do I do now? Just turn myself in? What if they don't want to listen to anything I say? They barely gave me time to say more than two words last time, and the only words they wanted were 'it's me.' I can't do that again."

I smiled when Brittany delivered my coffee before stepping back from the table. "I get it, but I spoke to someone on the island. She said something that makes me think we might want to look at the cameras at Jules's house. I'm sure the cops have already looked at them." But had they? "Or I hope they looked at them, but it might be worth trying to get them ourselves. Do you know anyone at the security company? Can you get access that way? Maybe we can prove that Jules was nowhere near you when you went up there, and then see if he came later. Maybe find out who was with him or who met him up there?"

"I don't think anyone is going to play well with me right now, Whit. Can you get them? Or get your boyfriend, Felix, to do it? You know, the boyfriend I'd never heard of? The one who uprooted his whole life to come over and be near you, but I've heard you're not giving him the time of day unless it has to do with clearing my name? That Felix. The one Buckey told me about, who heard it from Goldy. Watch out for that gossip, Whit. I should know."

Would no one leave me alone about that when I was trying to save my brother's life? "I do not need that kind of noise right now, Nick. I know exactly who you're talking about, and we'll have another discussion about that later, after I get your rear end saved. Let me see what I can do, but seriously think about turning yourself in. At least you'd be safe. I don't want Tracy to be able to get her hands on you too."

He made no promises as he hung up. Not that I had expected him to.

I lifted my cup to take a sip of the fragrant brew and something on the napkin caught my eye. My hand started shaking as

I looked around the outdoor café, trying to spot anyone who was watching me, or anyone who was lurking. But I saw no one interested in my table or the fact that on my napkin the words "Mind Your Own Affairs or Die" screamed up at me in crimson marker, like the reddest of blood with swirls of sparkles in the ink.

Chapter 21

I shoved my chair back from the table and waved my hands at Brittany. She wove her way through the tables on the patio, smiling at me when she arrived. "What can I do for you? Do you want a muffin or something?"

"Were you the only one to handle my coffee?"

That seemed to take her aback and she looked puzzled when she answered. "I didn't make it, but I picked it up from the counter."

"Was this napkin under it when you picked it up?"

"Um . . ."

"This is really important, Brittany. Was the napkin under the cup?"

"No. I don't think so. It was already on the table."

"And was there writing on it?"

"Just the logo." She shrugged, looking at me like I was crazy. Maybe I was.

I looked at the napkin again and shivered at the words. Flipping the square over, I found the logo. So someone had written on the napkin and flipped it over and then flipped it over again after the coffee was delivered? How did I not sense anyone so close to me? And who had it been?

I looked out over the crowd again. Plenty of locals strolled around along with people I didn't know. I dismissed the non-islanders and focused on the locals. Who could it be, though? Several waved at me, including Lacey and Jeannie. But why would either of them warn me off?

I asked Brittany to make my coffee to go and then left a tip as I exited the café, looking over my shoulder every other step. This needed to end now. I had an idea on how to get it going in the right direction. I would not be threatened, and I would not be pushed again. Someone was going to pay for the crimes on this island. If I had any say in it, and I did, it wasn't going to be me or my brother.

Taking the napkin with me, I struck out on a fact-finding mission.

Pulling up Felix's number, I texted him to see if he had access to the video. Next I called Maribel.

"Somehow we have to get the recordings from the Tisdale house. Do you have an in with the security company?"

There was a long pause. "Um . . ."

"I can't take any more of that word today. Yes or no? Do you have an in at the security company?"

"Well, I've kind of been flirting with this one guy there."

Oh, thank my lucky stars. "I will take you to task for not telling me after this is all done. For right now, can you please see if he can get you the recording from the night Jules died? Do you know if the police have looked at it?"

"Are you sure you want to talk hidden boyfriends with Felix back in the picture?"

I groaned. "Okay, maybe not, let's call it even. How about that footage, though?"

"I don't really have anything to do with that end of things, but I can ask. What's up?"

"I was just threatened on a napkin, and someone knocked me down a gully last night, I think. I'm not sure about that last one, but I know I was threatened."

"Yikes."

"Yeah, and this is no longer a lark. I want Nick cleared. I want everyone else safe, and Tracy needs to go behind bars for a very long time for her crimes."

"Are you sure it's her?"

"No, I'm not, but she's the only one who makes sense, and I don't have any more time to play games. Can you get the team to look at the footage, then get back to me?"

"I don't know, Whit."

"Okay, just do your best. Let me know what happens. I'm going to get my brother and we'll be in."

And then I hung up because Rebecca was walking into the store next to mine.

As quickly as I could, I ducked in and out of the foot traffic. Pulling the door open, I slipped inside.

"Hey Rebecca, can I talk with you for a second?"

She jumped a little and turned around. "Oh, Whit, I'm sorry, I was just inhaling this lovely candle. Have you smelled the ocean one Jeannie has available? It's so beautiful. I think I'll take it home with me so that I can remember when I'm hip deep in work."

She held the canister up to my nose and I dutifully sniffed. It was good but not as good as the real thing.

I pulled her aside by the elbow and she winced.

"Sorry, I just have urgent news. I wanted to warn you to please be careful."

"What's happened now?" Her narrow mouth dropped into a frown.

"No one has seen Tracy and Sheila is dead."

"Oh, my goodness. Dead? When? What happened? That poor girl!"

"I don't know if she was at the wrong place at the wrong time, but she was looking for a treasure I hadn't hidden yet and someone killed her up in the gardens. I just want you to be careful. If this is about money, it's possible you could be next and that would be awful."

"Well, okay." She cleared her throat and played with the small necklace there. "I was planning on leaving on Friday but maybe I should go tomorrow instead."

"That might be a good idea, unless the cops need to talk with you about Tracy. I'm hoping they get her soon. I asked them to look at the surveillance footage at Jules's house to see if he was still alive after Nick left. I'm hoping that will clear my brother's name and then it will be up to the cops to do the rest. I'm out." I smoothed my hand over the napkin in my pocket but didn't bring it out. The fewer people who knew about the threat, the better. This way I wouldn't have to defend my need to solve this part myself.

"You be careful, Whit. You have so many great things in front of you. Don't get caught up in a way you shouldn't."

"I'm almost out. Let me know if you have trouble getting off the island. When they release Nick, I could ask him to fly you out."

"That would be lovely. Take care of you, Whitney."

"I will, thanks."

I left her in the store, feeling like I'd done my part. Goldy was waiting for me outside my own store.

"You know it's going to be hard to make money at this place if you're never here."

"I'm aware of that, but I think I might have just saved your grandson's rear end, so let's take a breather inside while I fill you in."

She made the right noises and listened intently until I ran out of words.

"Well, what are you doing here? Go get your brother from Two Harbors and bring him back. Let's clear this thing up."

"I was going to let them view the footage first and see what happens there before picking up Nick."

"It'll work out, and if I have to call in a favor from Judy Walden to get that footage, I will do it."

"Judy Walden?"

"Red hair, silver streak? She's been investigating those burglaries on the island. No one is supposed to officially know that she's here watching houses and sometimes breaking in to test the strength of the system, but I used to teach her snorkeling, so when I saw her on the island, I chatted her up."

Judy Walden. Okay, well that answered one question, and I was itching to get that into the tablet.

I put Goldy on contacting her and then called Nick back. "Get ready, I'm coming to get you now. We're finishing this."

The drive to Two Harbors wasn't far, but in an autoette it wasn't exactly fast, even with my foot all the way to the floor on the gas pedal. By the time I got to the tiny town on the upper end of the island, my leg was sore and my brain was zooming faster than the speed of light with information.

Pulling up at Paulie Sinclair's house, where Nick had told me he was hiding, I texted Nick to get out here now and then waited while he peeked his head out the door, looked everywhere like I had brought the SWAT team with me, and then crept out to the autoette.

"Just get in! We're going to get this done. It's got to be Tracy. She had the motive and the opportunity, and even if it didn't turn out the way she planned, she definitely didn't want Jules around anymore. You know she'd done the shiner plea before and that black eye wasn't even real?"

I pulled away from the curb as he groaned. "I shouldn't have fallen for it."

"What else were you supposed to do? You thought she was hurt and hurting. You just wanted to help her. She's the one who turned dirty on you."

We talked about my information and I filled him in on all the things that he had missed while he was hiding out. By the time we got to the sheriff's station, they must have gotten a slew of calls about Nick being out and about because they were there to take him into custody as soon as I stopped the autoette.

"No, he's coming in voluntarily." I stood between them and their prey like a momma tiger. "This will be peaceful. It will be peaceful because he's coming to you and will tell you everything you need to know. Don't make it worse by throwing all your accusations at him without hearing him out first."

Captain Warrington stared me down, but I didn't give an inch. Finally, he nodded once and turned back toward the station. "Come along, then."

Nick and I followed, my arm hooked through his just in case they tried to separate us.

When we passed Maribel at the front desk, she gave me a thumbs-up. I really hoped that was because she'd gotten the footage from the guy she was flirting with and the cops had had time to look at it.

No matter what, I was ready to fight the up-hilliest battle I had to if that was what it came down to. Tracy had done this, and she was not going to get away with it.

Two hours later, I heard Tracy yelling her head off even through the soundproof room where Nick and I sat as he explained for the fifth time how Tracy had called him with her sob story and how he thought he was saving her and had never touched either victim.

Finally, they let him go. The tape I had asked Maribel to get had shown him leaving, and another one at a house down the way had shown him going to the dock and coming to the *Sea Bounder*. There was no missing time in there where Nick could have killed Jules. Thankfully, Judy Walden had told me about it earlier. It wasn't something the cops would have necessarily accessed on their own since it was private property and paid for by citizens, not the state, but I was eternally grateful for how it saved Nick's hide.

My work here was done, and I took Nick to his house, then went by the store to relieve Goldy of her post at my cash register.

"Lots of receipts today. Even for not being open much over the last few days, you've still made a killing."

I winced at her phrasing.

"Too soon?"

I laughed because I felt so light now that everything was wrapped up with a big old bow. The police hadn't exactly thanked me for my help, but I also hadn't gotten in trouble for hiding Nick, so I wasn't looking that gift horse in the mouth.

Nick stopped in just as I was closing up. "Hey, Goldy, do you mind if I borrow your golf cart? Mine's still in the shop, and Rebecca asked if I could fly her back to Long Beach."

Our grandmother turned to me. "Care to give me a lift home?"

"Sure thing," I said, all smiles. I hoped that Tracy was seething in a cell right now. I hadn't seen her at all today and they'd picked her up from the house where she wasn't supposed to be. She had barricaded herself in and hadn't come out all morning, hiding.

But then how did she write on my napkin?

I tried to shove the thought away because really it didn't matter. Things were all wrapped up. Like the treasure boxes I made for kids, the map had led right to the one person who had had all the reason to get rid of her husband—until she realized that she'd killed her money tree.

Nick left and Goldy and I closed up the shop. I was counting out the receipts and making sure that everything was signed when I came across a slip that stopped my heart.

It was signed with a flourish in red sparkle ink, just like the napkin still in my pocket. I took the square out and spread it out on the counter. Could it be?

I was a huge fan of those logic puzzles they used to give us in school. Most people also called them logic grid puzzles. I made them for the shop as often as I could.

For each puzzle you were given a series of categories, and an equal number of options within each category. You could only use each option once. The goal was to figure out which options were linked together, based on a series of clues. Each puzzle had only one unique solution, and each could be solved using simple logical processes.

Using the tablet while Goldy asked question after question, I drew out a grid, put my different suspects down the side, then put the clues I'd found along the top: being unaccounted for when Jules was killed, having a motive, knowing their way around the island, having access to Sheila, something to gain.

The point of the puzzle was to mark which person had each of the top row. Tracy definitely showed strong in every category. Though I had heard that she'd been hiding up at her house when Sheila was killed, she could have lied about that.

I added *red sparkle pen* and *scratch from my cat* to the top of the grid and put Rebecca at the bottom of the suspect list. And she got a check mark in every single column. I'd seen her this morning before my coffee. I'd even waved to her. She had the pen because it was used to sign her purchase receipt for the exact same map that I'd given to Dave the day before. She'd winced when I'd grabbed her elbow. Maybe because that was where she'd been scratched by Whiskers?

She stood to gain the most.

"What do you know about Rebecca?" I asked Goldy.

"She's a sweetie and got the raw end of the deal when it came to family. I'm surprised she had anything to do with Jules at all, though I suppose inheritance can make someone stick around. But he ruined her life years ago. We talked about it over lunch after the spa the other day. She used all the right words, but you could tell that it really bothered her that Jules had a fit and sent Marvin away after paying him off."

I had just sent my brother off with a murderer!

If I could have run faster than my autoette I would have. Thank goodness Nick had taken Goldy's and not mine. As it was, I jumped into the golf cart and prayed it would go the fastest it had ever gone. The Airport in the Sky was up a winding hill and my little putt-putt might not like that, but she was just going to have to do her very best.

I promised her a full-service bath and tune-up just as soon as we were done with things. Starting the golf cart, I hooked my arm over the back of my seat to move in reverse and found Whiskers sitting on the back seat grooming herself.

"How the heck did you get here?"

She meowed at me.

"Well, I don't have time to take you home or take you in to Goldy, so I guess you're along for the ride. Hold on there, girly."

We zoomed off and the whole time I just kept going over the information. I had to be right. I had to be. She fit every single box on that grid. It had to be her. Under that nice, straightlaced façade was a woman who thought her cousin had ruined her life.

* * *

I zoomed into the parking lot of the airport and made my way to Nick's space in the hangar. The whole way up here I'd had time to think about how I should have told Goldy to call in the troops, or at least the police. And why hadn't I shown them the napkin? I hadn't been sure what I could prove with the napkin, though. And calling in the troops didn't occur to me when my mind had been completely set on saving my brother.

He and Rebecca better be at the airport because if they weren't, I didn't know what I was going to do. I couldn't exactly call him over the radio and tell him to turn back with her.

And then there they were. Rebecca waved to me as she handed her luggage up to Nick, but I must not have hidden my anger fast enough because she started backing away, then turned and ran.

Whiskers thought it was a game and scampered after her. I was not nearly so delicate and blew past a very baffled Nick.

"I'll explain later," I yelled as I ran as fast as I could. It might not have been fast, but it was faster than Rebecca in her heels. We came to the edge of the cliff overlooking the sea at the same exact time and I thought for a second she was just going to give up. But Whiskers had ideas of her own and tripped the other woman. Rebecca went sailing over the edge of the cliff, screaming, but that was quickly followed by an "Oof!" as she hit the ledge of rock right over the rim.

"Want a hand up, or do you want to take your chances in the sea like you did to Jules?" I stood looking down at her and almost feeling sorry for her, until she reached up and tried to grab my ankle, and I saw the long line of scratches on her arm. A set that was then joined by another set as Whiskers went for her again.

"Good kitty, now calm down." I picked my cat up and stood on the edge. By this time Nick and Buckey had joined me.

"You want to explain yourself before we call the cops, Rebecca?" I asked with my phone in my other hand.

"You'd never understand. You've always lived a life of privilege and you have no idea what it means to have someone not only rule your life but also ruin it. When I heard that he was considering changing his prenuptial agreement because Tracy had actually stuck around longer than he'd thought, I couldn't do it. And then he promised to put money toward an awful boat for her cousin. We Tisdales don't deal in glass-bottomed anything. We crash through the glass ceiling and make the world ours. I was not going to stand by and let her ruin everything I'd helped Jules build just because she knew enough not to walk away before she got everything she wanted."

"And Sheila? She was so grateful that you let her get a spa treatment. Why did you go after her?"

"That girl was going to inherit half of everything Jules owned. I asked the lawyer to wait to tell her until after she was married. As a professional courtesy he did. And then I realized that I could have it all. Jules was easy enough to kill and I was going to get away with it. The second murder was so much easier than the first."

"Should we get her off the ledge?" Nick asked me. His arms were crossed over his chest and a frown rested on his lips.

"Oh, I don't know, I think the ledge is pretty much where she's going to be for the next little while," Buckey said.

He too had a frown on his face. But, in contrast, Whiskers seemed to be smirking in her own feline way.

I decided that a smirk was really the way to go and made sure mine was one hundred percent visible when I placed the call to Captain Warrington.

Thankfully, I could now go back to my life as a gift shop owner and sometimes glass-bottom boat sailor. No more heroics from me for a while.

Felix came along the ridge behind the cops as I stood there with Rebecca on her ledge and my frowning bookends.

Was he really planning on staying?

The bigger question at the moment might be, was I going to let myself explore a real relationship with him? I waved to him as he approached.

That might be a mystery for another day.

Keep reading for a sneak peek at
SOMETHING FISHY THIS WAY COMES,
the next in the
Whit and Whiskers mystery series
coming soon from
Gabby Allan
and
Kensington Books.

"So I told Aaron Franklin that there was no way he'd seen an island loggerhead shrike because they just don't like to be seen, and you know what he said? That for a twitcher I was more of a twit. How do you like them clamshells, Whit?"

For the seventh time in five minutes (and yes I'd counted) I rolled my eyes as I stared down at my receipts for the day. The older man had said he was here for a gift for his granddaughter's sixteenth birthday, but he had yet to do anything more than lean on my counter and talk my ear off. He stopped in a few times a week to shoot the breeze, and normally it was okay, but not today.

Running a boutique gift shop on the small island of Catalina off the coast of California had been my dream and still was, but I hadn't necessarily considered the fact that I'd always have to be nice to the locals. Even the ones who irritated me. And I couldn't kick them out just because I had things to do. Well, not unless it was closing time, which was why I was watching the clock.

Ten more minutes and I could get rid of Manny Jackson and his bird stories of twitching rivalry with another resident on the island. The guy never seemed to run out of stories that constantly cast him in a great light while leaving others looking like underwater barnacles. Or at least that was his intention, but in truth that was rarely how it came across.

"We compared our notebooks of finds the other day, and he didn't even have a bald eagle on there. Calls himself a twitcher. Not hardly. Right? He's not a twitcher, right? I should tell him that again, shouldn't I?" He scoffed and thumbed the side of his nose when I didn't answer right away. I was not going to get in the middle of that argument.

The wrinkles on his forehead and the graying combover very clearly showed he was of an age where he thought he could do or say anything he wanted. And of course he could, but just maybe not in my store.

If I'd had customers in my little shop of baubles, I'd have shooed him out. But since few people had come in today, I didn't have an excuse.

"You have to have specific birds to be considered a twitcher?" Not that his conversation had any value to me, but with only seven minutes left, it might make good business sense to interact. He was an infrequent customer, but a customer nonetheless.

Although I had a feeling at this point that I was going to be ushering him out of the store without one of my gift bags.

"Oh, now, I don't know about specific, but there are some that are just common sense to have in there." He went on to list all the birds that were must-haves. Of course he did. I tuned back out until the front door opened and salvation came zooming into the store in the form of my best friend and roommate, Maribel Hernandez.

"Hey, Maribel, hey." There was definitely an edge of desperation to my voice, and I didn't even try to hide it. "Are you ready to go get something to eat?" I glanced at my clock. Three minutes left.

When I looked back up she had shock and dismay on her face and her hands clutched together. "We're not having dinner tonight,

Whit. Or are we? Did I forget? Oh man, I hope I didn't forget. I have a date tonight, but I can cancel it if you need me to."

And just like that she went from happy to worrywart in two point four seconds. I called it her spiral. Usually it wasn't that big of a deal and was easy to get her out of. But recently she'd had a lot on her mind with working the front desk at the Avalon Sheriff's Station and going to school for criminal justice, and I didn't want to add to it by making her think she'd forgotten me.

"Slow down, slow down. No need to get in a bunch," I said.

"But if I was supposed to do something with you . . ." She wrung her hands until her knuckles turned white.

"It's fine."

"But it's not."

"Maribel."

Poor Manny was turning his head at breakneck speed to keep the speaker in his line of vision. He looked like he was watching a ferocious tennis match instead of a conversation between friends that had gone awry. And how had it gone awry? Oh right, I'd tried to lie and that never went well for me.

"Yes?" she said and then both she and Manny looked expectantly at me.

Fortunately, I was saved from saying anything else because Manny's phone jingled in the breast pocket of his short-sleeved Hawaiian shirt.

When he opened his ages-old flip phone, he held up a finger as if to let us know it was time for silence. "What do you want, Aaron Franklin, you old sea dog? I don't have time for your shenanigans." He cocked his head to the side as the person on the phone answered his question. "You didn't!" Manny exclaimed. "You codger! You never did see an ashy storm-petrel. That's my bird, the one I've been looking for. You're lying to me. They're on the watch list and you darn well know it." Another pause where he wiped his brow and squinted his eyes as if he were in pain.

Was he going to have a heart attack? Should I call the emergency responders? I looked over at Maribel, but she looked as baffled as I was.

"I'll be right there!" Manny barked into the phone as several people strolled along the sidewalk out front and turned their heads to look in my quaint little shop.

"You'd better have pictures," Manny continued. "And don't you dare scare that thing off. If you are lying to me, I'm going to hang you by your binoculars from the nearest tree. Wait for me." With that he snapped his clamshell phone closed. There was no prying that thing away from him no matter how old it was. He didn't like new technology.

"Gotta go," he said, turning back to us. "Aaron, the rascal, says he saw a bird I've wanted in my book for ages, and he'd better be able to prove it before he puts it in that darn book of his."

"Aaron, who you were just complaining about thinking he was a twitcher? The one who called you a twit? Why would he even call you?"

"That one exactly. That whole family is a little squirrelly, if you don't mind me saying so. But that's not going to stop me from seeing what he's got out there at the golf course."

"But if you don't like him, why would you do that?" I asked. "Can't you go catch the view of the bird without interacting with him?"

"Girl, I said I didn't trust him and he was squirrelly, not that I didn't like him. Yeesh, us birders have to stay together. No one understands us like we do. We might not always see things the same way, but that doesn't mean I walk away from my brothers. Unlike those Aherns, our mayor being the worst of the lot."

Okay then, I thought as he took off out of my store like I'd browbeaten him and then tried to force him to eat raw seaweed by the mouthful.

He slammed the door closed behind him.

Maribel raised one dark eyebrow. "What on earth was that?"

"Your guess is as good as mine, but hopefully this Aaron really saw whatever bird he was taunting Manny with, or there's going to be a very steep price to pay. Death by binoculars. I don't think that would be a peaceful way to go."

Maribel snorted. "Yeah, I'd rather go quietly in my sleep, just not any time soon."

"Me too." I closed the receipts on the computer and then gave her my full attention. "So why did you come by? I thought you had things to do this afternoon."

"What about dinner? Did I really miss that or were you just trying to get rid of Manny?"

She knew me too well. I shrugged while flashing my teeth in my best smile, and she laughed at me.

"You had me there for a minute. I really thought I had forgotten. With going to school and trying to keep up with my work schedule, I'm forgetting all kinds of things, so it wouldn't have surprised me if I'd forgotten a dinner."

"Nah, it was just to get him to move along." I looked at the clock on the wall, decorated with the mountains on the island and the ocean spread out along the bottom like a carpet. "But I do have to get going. I have a treasure chest to deliver, and I want to get it out of the way so I can go rest. It's been a long day, even though I don't feel like I did much of anything."

My receipts said as much. I was going to have to give some serious thought to upping my game. My grandmother, Goldy, kept trying to get me to try different things, but I had had a specific dream when I'd opened this place and it didn't involve carrying a menagerie of scents and soaps. I tried to keep most of my stock handcrafted items from the locals, but they weren't selling as well as I'd like.

"Enough about me," I said, not wanting to think about selling and money right now or I'd go into my own spiral. "What did you need from me that had you bustling in here all smiles before I attempted to ruin it with my inept lies?"

"Oh!" She gripped her hands together in front of her chest and rocked back and forth. "I have a date."

"Yep, you mentioned that."

She snorted in laughter. "Fine then, I'm sure I didn't tell you who it was."

"Nope."

"Fabian Halston." She squealed and I barely held in a groan.

Ugh. I glanced at the clock again and realized I should have closed the store two minutes ago. I did not have the time to drag her through the hours of reasons he was not a candidate for actual dating. Regardless of the fact that he was hotter than an August afternoon, he was also as dangerous as not taking your trash with you after you visited with the bison on the other side of the island.

But this was my best friend. I couldn't let her walk into this one blind. I was in the process of coming up with the best way to tell her to stay the heck away from the guy when Goldy walked in.

"Fabian Halston," I began.

Goldy, in her usual way, cut me off with a flourish of her knee-length see-through swimsuit cover up. Always dressed for the beach, that was my grandmother. This one was royal purple and left little to the imagination. "Oh girl, you need to stay away from that one. He's trouble and never hesitates to let you know it with that cheeky smile and those reaching hands. Takes after his Uncle Milo as far as I'm concerned. He's an Ahern through and through, even if his mother tried to pass him off as a Halston."

"Manny was just in here complaining about Mayor Milo. He's related to Fabian?" How did I not know they were related? You'd think on an island with a little over three thousand permanent residents, I'd know who was who and who was related to whom, but that wasn't always necessarily true.

"I don't know what Manny was complaining about, and I really don't care. I just stopped in to let you know we have a delivery coming in tomorrow. And before you fight me, let me say that I paid for it with my own funds and am willing to let you take it on consignment. So be nice to the deliveryman, and I'll be in to unpack the shipment. Don't open it without me." Then with a flip of her purple cover-up, she was back out the door again, just like the small tornado I thought of her as.

"Now what was *that* all about?" Maribel asked.

"To be honest, I have no earthly idea. But I've been trying to hold in my groan about the guy you want to date, and I just can't do that, not if I really want to call myself your friend. He's not really a good guy."

She brushed her hand through the air as if whisking away my comment. "He doesn't have to be *the one*, Whitney Dagner. I can just have an interesting conversation and a good meal out of it. I'm not against exploring my options."

Putting a hand on my heart, I feigned hurt. "Don't I give you good conversation? And my spaghetti last night was absolutely divine."

With her hands on her hips, she laughed at me. "Yeah, and I had to share it with the adorable Felix, who I envy you for, but don't expect to get one of my own anytime soon. However, my choices are limited at the moment. I can't exactly go out with anyone from the sheriff's department right now if I want to be taken seriously. And while I like to take in the town by myself, or with you, I'd really like to hang with someone else who sees things from a different perspective."

"Hmm. Well, you'll definitely get that with Fabian. Just don't be angry if he's not worth the time for the conversation and make sure he at least pays his portion of the bill before he steps out to take a nonexistent phone call. It's his M.O."

She snorted. "I know all about guys like that, and I've been warned. Now I have to get going if I'm going to battle your cat for space in the bathroom and wrestle my curling iron away from her long enough to get ready for my date. Be careful with that treasure chest. I still can't forget what happened up at the sanctuary."

I couldn't either and worried about it sometimes. *It* being finding a dead body during a situation that had me looking for a killer while trying to clear my brother, Nick, from being a prime suspect. But there hadn't been another murder in months and Catalina Island was a relatively safe place.

"I've been properly warned also, then. I'm just hoping I don't run into Manny and Aaron in the middle of a fight over twitching."

Famous last words.